MAFIOSA PRINCESS: SACRIFICE

LIZA MALLOY

CHAPTER 1

Giada

"I know about Luca. I know what he did and who he is. I want to get away. And I'm sorry to drag you into this, but I need your help." As soon as the words left my mouth, a wave of nausea washed over me. I dashed to Adrian's bathroom, but there was nothing in my stomach to expel. So instead, I sobbed.

What had I done?

All of my mistakes settled over me like a dense fog. I'd had the perfect boyfriend—Adrian—but then we'd broken up because he had all these insane theories about my dad being a criminal. I fell for my high school boyfriend, Luca, again, only to learn that he was a criminal. And then I made out with my driver, Enzo, which prompted the evil boyfriend to beat him up and lie about it. Now it was too late for Adrian and me to get back together, but he was also the only person I trusted to help me get away from Luca.

Except now, I'd put Adrian in harm's way.

The whole way over, I told myself it was okay, that I had covered my tracks and that no one would ever know I was at Adrian's. But what if I was wrong? I hadn't realized anyone spotted me with Enzo, and he almost died for my carelessness. I couldn't risk that happening to Adrian.

I rushed out of the bathroom and slammed directly into Adrian's firm chest. Before I could move, his strong arms roped around me, holding me so tightly I couldn't catch my breath.

"You're okay now Gia. I won't let anyone hurt you. You are safe."

I relished the fleeting sensation of comfort, tried to let myself pretend he was right, but it was futile. I pushed back and shook my head. Even if I was safe, he wasn't. Not if I stayed much longer.

"Adrian, I'm so sorry. I should've never dragged you into this." I started towards his door, but he scrambled around and blocked my path.

Gazing into his piercing blue eyes framed by the most handsome and sincere face I could imagine, I remembered why I went to him in the first place. Adrian was someone I could trust. Perhaps he was the only trustworthy person in my life. I'd known the entire way over here that if I could just get to him, he'd help me. Adrian was that kind of guy, the kind who would help, even though he was seeing someone else now, and even though he had every reason to hate me.

But now that I was actually here, in the safety of his apartment, I understood how selfish my thinking was. He'd help me even if it endangered him, and that wasn't fair for me to ask.

"No, Gia. You're not leaving like this. I'm not scared of Luca right now. If he shows up, we'll call the cops. But you are not going anywhere. Not until you tell me what is going on."

"Adrian, really. I shouldn't tell you any of this, but Luca is... a monster. Do not trust him or any of the guys he brings around.

Don't go anywhere alone with them, don't let them near you. Do you understand?"

As he nodded, sadness filled his eyes.

"Do not tell anyone anything about him, okay? And stay away from me. Don't call, don't text, don't come to see me. Don't even wave if we pass on the street. Okay? Can you do that?"

The creases around his eyebrows deepened. "No."

"You have to promise, Adrian. He won't hurt me, but he…he nearly killed Enzo, and if he knows you're talking to me, you'll be next."

Adrian expelled a large breath as though this information provided some relief. "You know about Enzo," he said.

"Yes, it was Luca. Well, technically it probably was his asshole associates and not him, but it was Luca's way of punishing me for—"

"I saw him," Adrian interrupted. "I was early to pick you up for coffee. I would've told you the truth sooner, but Enzo made me swear I wouldn't."

I squeezed my eyes shut, wishing I could turn back time and not throw myself at Enzo. God, how that man had suffered all because of my shitty self-esteem and low alcohol tolerance. I'd known my boyfriend was a jealous, possessive man, but, I honestly hadn't realized he had someone spying on me *or* that he would hurt Enzo.

"Wait, why would Luca hurt Enzo to punish you?" Adrian asked, returning to my statement he'd interrupted.

I winced, embarrassed to have him know the truth. If Adrian didn't already despise me, he would after hearing what I'd done. I tried to minimize how horrific my behavior had been. "I kissed Enzo. It was after I learned Luca was cheating on me and lied about it. I was upset, and I'd been drinking. Enzo stopped it before anything of substance happened, and I didn't realize anyone saw, but apparently, one of Luca's stupid friends was spying on me and told him."

Adrian shook his head. "I watched Enzo go with them willingly. He had to know what they were going to do."

"Enzo told Luca he forced himself on me," I said, embarrassed to even hear the ridiculous notion out loud.

The transformation in Adrian's face was dramatic. "He forced himself on you?"

"No, no. *I* kissed *him*. Enzo only said that so Luca wouldn't be mad at both of us." I paused, flustered. "I'm sure Luca knew he was lying, but I guess it did help Luca save face in front of his guys or whatnot."

"Gia, between what I saw and what you know, we have more than enough for the police to charge Luca, even if Enzo doesn't come back to corroborate it all. You should get a restraining order against Luca."

I shook my head, trying to swallow the lump in my throat but finding my mouth too dry. "Adrian, I can't do that. You don't understand. Luca's father is…well, all those things you kept saying about my family, it's all true of Mr. Marino."

I paused a moment as Adrian's expression changed yet again while he processed this new information.

"Luca works for his father, and I don't know if his father is in the actual mafia or whatever, but it's definitely something like that. Luca carries huge wads of cash wherever he goes, he's always armed, and he doesn't go anywhere without a bodyguard. He has guys following me around too."

I glanced down at my cell phone. It was late. Sneaking away for a few minutes was one thing, but being gone for over an hour would raise questions. Apparently, my indirect route to Adrian's apartment took longer than I'd anticipated.

"I have to go. I snuck out the back entrance of the library, took a cab, and then walked the rest of the way so that no one would know I left, but if I don't get back there in a reasonable time for Alessio to drive me home, Luca will know something is up."

"Who is Alessio?"

"He's one of Luca's associates. I think you met him last summer. He's been driving me."

"Giada, you can't just go back to Luca!"

"I don't have a choice. If I disappear, there's no telling what Luca would do to you, or Gabriella, or my family…"

"Don't worry about your family, Giada. They can take care of themselves."

I wanted to strangle him. Yes, Adrian hated my family, but I didn't think he was insensitive enough to bring that up when I was so stressed out already. "I don't want to hear it, Adrian. I would never do anything to put them in harm's way."

"I know, Gia. I just mean I don't think your family is in danger. Your father and your brothers are tough guys." It was clear he wanted to say more, but he stopped and just shook his head. "You need to look out for yourself."

"I can handle Luca. I just have to do what he wants until he gets sick of me and breaks up with me. As long as I don't embarrass Luca again, I don't think anything will happen."

"You don't *think*? Gia, do you hear yourself? This is insane. You need to go to the police!"

"I can't." I squeezed my eyes shut, struggling to remember why I had come to Adrian in the first place. I felt safe around him, but what was the point? Had I really thought telling him what was going on would somehow bring up a solution? "I'm sorry I dragged you into this. I know you've moved on, and I promise I'm not trying to come between you and your new girlfriend. I just thought I needed to tell you."

Adrian still looked confused, but I started to the door.

"I don't have a new girlfriend," he said suddenly.

"Oh, well, new friend. Whoever she is," I said. It was apparent he still didn't know what I was talking about, and I didn't have the energy to pretend I hadn't seen him on a date. "I saw you at Marzetti's with some blonde girl. The night you said you were studying. Right after I found out Luca was cheating and right before I went and threw myself at Enzo. Anyway, it's totally fine. I don't want to mess that up for you."

"Hillary is her name. We aren't going out again, and it's not because of you, so don't worry."

"Oh. Well, I'll go now," I said, pulling my hood back up.

"Giada, call one of your brothers. Or your dad. Promise me you'll get someone you trust that Luca hasn't forbidden you to see and have them come up this weekend. Or better yet, head home for the weekend."

I considered that. I could never tell my family everything that was going on, but having Matteo around for a few hours would make me feel better. "Maybe. But they can't know any of the details."

"If you told them, they could help you. I'm sure of it. But even if you don't want to tell them the truth, just promise me you'll spend some time with them."

I nodded, then left.

When I returned home, Luca wasn't even there. Nervous energy flooded me, but I wasn't sure what to do with it all. He already knew I was upset with him, and he'd admitted hurting Enzo, so there was no point for me to act normal around him. But I didn't want him to see how scared I was either, in case that made him feel even more powerful.

I slumped onto the couch and rubbed my forehead. How had I ended up with the type of man who got a kick out of terrorizing me? Adrian had been the perfect boyfriend in every way, and I'd left him for a bully.

I was a fool. Even looking back, I couldn't figure out where exactly I'd gone wrong. I wanted to identify all the signs I'd missed and berate myself, but I couldn't. There had been no signs. Luca had been completely perfect.

Until he wasn't.

I waited up for a while, too anxious to sleep anyway. When I finally did go to bed, I propped a stack of books a few inches from the door. It wouldn't keep Luca out of the bedroom, but it would topple over and make enough noise to wake me when he returned. Even with the alarm system, I woke frequently throughout the night.

In the morning, my head pounded, my muscles ached and I was tense. But I was still alone. As I finished my second cup of coffee, Luca texted and told me he would be in Manhattan for business for a few days and that I should "behave" during his absence.

As infuriating and offensive as his terminology was, I felt nothing but relief.

I replayed my conversation with Adrian in my head and decided that of all of his suggestions, involving my brother did make sense. Luca couldn't possibly find fault with me seeing my own brother.

I called Matteo before I changed my mind. We chatted for a few minutes, and then I asked if he could meet me for lunch the next day.

"I'd love to see you Giada, but I'm swamped. Is everything okay?"

"Yeah," I said, trying to mask the disappointment in my voice. "I'm just feeling a bit homesick this week."

"Oh right, I forgot that Luca is down in the city too."

"Too? Who else is there?"

"Angelo. You know, your brother? Tall, dark-haired guy with receding hairline and bad attitude."

I had to laugh at Matteo's description of Angelo. Angelo was taller than Matteo, and while his hair was shorter, I didn't think his hairline was receding. Aside from those minor differences, my brothers were identical, and the general consensus of women seemed to be that they were both good-looking guys. I didn't disagree with the bad attitude comment, though. Angelo had been intense, grumpy, and at times intimidating, pretty much as long as I remembered.

"Things must be going well with you and Luca if you're missing him already," Matteo continued.

I cringed. "No, actually they're not. We had a fight before he left, and honestly, I don't think he's the person I thought he was."

"A fight? Like you hit him?"

Now I was exasperated. "Why would you assume *I* hit *him*?"

"Because you have a temper, and Luca would never in a million years lay a hand on you."

I rolled my eyes, annoyed that my favorite brother would take sides with the jackass micromanaging my every move.

"He didn't, did he?"

I sighed. "No. No one hit anyone. I guess 'fight' was the wrong word. We argued. The point is I don't think we should be together anymore, and I wanted some sympathy from my brother."

"Gi, you can't break up with Luca."

Okay, not the response I was looking for. "Why not?"

"Because you'll regret it. You and Luca belong together. You've got all that history together, and you're a perfect fit." He paused. "Besides, no one else would put up with your level of crazy like he does."

"Why do you keep implying I'm crazy?"

"I just know you that well."

"Look, Matteo, I know you're sort of friends with him, so I don't want to put you in a tough spot, but I really need some support here. I can't tell you all the details, but trust me when I say Luca is not a good person. He's bossy and jealous and controlling and…well, he's done some terrible things."

"Did he hurt you?"

"No, but…"

"Giada, listen to me," he interrupted. "I'm not saying Luca is perfect, and I see what you're saying about him being a little too possessive, but he acts that way because he cares about you. He doesn't want to lose you, and he doesn't want to see you get hurt. I've known him as long as you have, and he's not a bad guy."

"You don't know him the way I do," I snapped.

"I'd hope not." He paused. "Is this about Adrian? I wasn't going to say anything, but I heard that he's been hanging around your building some and waiting for you at church, and honestly, I think Luca's been pretty tolerant of that given your history with the guy. How would you feel if he was still flirting with his ex all the time? You just can't keep flitting back and forth from one to the other, Gi. I'm not saying you have to settle down and have kids yet, but you do have to act like a grown-up. You made your choice, now stick with it."

The firmness with which Matteo spoke brought tears to my eyes. He had always been the one I could talk to, my champion when everyone else in the house treated me like a child. Now, he was clearly siding with all of them. I didn't know what to say. I realized I needed to know if Adrian was right. If it came down to it, could I count on my family to protect me from Luca?

"Matteo, what if I told you I was afraid of Luca? What if I wanted to break up with him but was scared of what he might do or how he would react? Would you help me then?"

There was a lengthy silence. "I love you, Giada. I'd never let anyone hurt you."

"Okay, well—"

He cut me off before I could finish. "But if you said all that, I'd tell you that you were overreacting, that it would be a huge mistake to break up with him, and you should just appreciate what you have and everything he can give you."

I sucked in a breath, feeling my hands shaking already with the effort of trying not to cry. I had thought Matteo would be on my side. I'd assumed he'd be concerned for me, that he would comfort me. I hadn't expected a lecture. I gave him one more chance.

"Matteo, are you seriously telling me to stay with a man that I'm afraid of? That's how you want me to live?"

He took his time answering, which gave me hope.

"No, of course not. I'm telling you that you shouldn't be afraid of him. Luca won't hurt you."

I swallowed the lump growing in my throat.

"Look, I have to go. Just don't do anything stupid, okay?"

I was crying too hard to reply.

CHAPTER 2

Giada

When Luca returned from the city, he immediately barged into my apartment and told me to pack a bag for a two-week trip to Italy.

"I'm not going anywhere with you," I said, laughing at his arrogance.

"Why, because you're scared of me?" he taunted, a visible gleam in his eyes.

It only took me a moment to realize why he said that. "You spoke to Matteo," I said, crushed by the betrayal.

"I can't believe you thought he wouldn't tell me," Luca replied. "Now start packing, please. We are leaving for the airport in just over an hour."

"I can't go to Italy now. I have classes."

"Next week is fall break, and your father already arranged for you to miss this week. He told your teachers you had a family emergency. It seems everyone thinks it's important you and I spend some time together and get back on the right track."

My jaw dropped.

Luca turned on his heel and left the room. "We're going whether or not you pack, Princess."

Once alone, I quickly texted my dad to confirm he was aware of this Italy trip. When he replied that he did, I debated telling him I didn't want to go, that I was scared to be alone with Luca.

But I didn't.

If Matteo didn't take my side, my dad definitely wouldn't. Besides, the fact that others knew I was going with Luca at least offered me some reassurance that he couldn't kill me and expect to get away with it.

I'd managed to avoid talking to Luca the entire flight over, dividing my time equally between reading and sleeping. A black sedan picked us up at the Palermo airport and drove us to the beach villa. Luca and the driver spoke to each other the entire drive. I got the impression they were pretty close, but since they didn't bother to translate any of their conversation to English, I couldn't be sure what they were saying. The guy carried our bags into the villa for us before leaving, and that was when I remembered the villa had only one bed.

"I'm not sleeping with you," I said the moment the door closed.

"You're welcome to the couch, Princess," Luca replied, opening the windows to let in the breeze. Then he plopped onto the couch, kicked off his shoes, and turned on the television.

I ducked into the bathroom to freshen up and then changed into a casual sundress and sandals. Luca didn't even glance at me until I went to open the door.

"I'm going for a walk on the beach," I said.

"Alright. Paolo will accompany you."

"Is that the driver?"

He nodded.

"I am not stupid enough to get lost walking down the beach and back," I replied.

Luca chuckled. "Maybe he can teach you some Italian while you walk."

I slammed the door behind me and left. When I reached the beach path, Paolo met me, still wearing the suit pants and button-down shirt he'd had on earlier.

"You can stay here," I said.

He frowned. "Signore Marino was insistent I walk with you."

"Well, I'm insisting you don't."

"I'm afraid that Signore Marino…" he began.

"Signore Marino is going to be stabbed in his sleep if he doesn't back the fuck off," I replied. "You are not following me."

The guy's face turned ashen grey so quickly I nearly laughed. He swallowed loudly then pulled out his phone. I waited a moment, assuming he was talking to Luca, then gazed up. Luca stood on the balcony, smiling, cell phone against his ear. I gave him the finger, and he waved.

Paolo turned back to me. "Uh, he said just not to be gone more than one hour," he said, his accent thick.

I nodded and took off. As tempting as it was just to keep walking, to see how long I could go on before I ran out of shore-line or passed out from exhaustion, I was sleepy and hungry. We'd arrived early morning, local time, and even though I'd slept on the plane, the time change was getting to me.

I turned around and headed back, taking longer to reverse my route as my energy waned. When I reached the villa, Paolo was carrying the butcher block of knives.

I glared at Luca, and he simply smiled. "Oh wait, maybe I should give you the scissors," he said to Paolo. "Nah I'll just hide those."

I went into the apartment, stripped off my dress, and climbed into bed. Luca followed me.

"Oh, it's going to be like that, huh?" he asked.

"Touch me, and I guarantee I'll find something sharp in this villa," I said, lowering my sleep mask over my eyes.

The bed shifted as he crawled in beside me. "It always has been a huge turn on when you're feisty," he said.

I flipped over so my back was to him, and within minutes, I was asleep.

When I awoke, I felt groggier than before, but delicious smells filled the air.

I sat up to find Luca had left the bed. I slipped back into my dress and went into the kitchen. Luca stood there wearing cobalt blue jeans and nothing above the waist but a simple gold chain around his neck. I turned quickly to avoid my body's typical visceral reaction to how good he looked shirtless. Instead, I focused on the food. A caprese salad and a pan of baked mostaccioli sat on the counter, looking every bit as good as they smelled.

"Thought you might be hungry," Luca said, sliding a plate towards me. I filled my plate just as he handed me a cup. "You get one espresso. When this wears off, we'll go to bed, and you'll wake up on Italian time."

He was right, but I wanted to hate him right now, and that was harder when he was offering me my favorite foods and worrying about my jetlag.

I carried my plate onto the balcony, and a moment later, he joined me.

"Two weeks is a long time to ignore me," he said, sitting down.

I bit into a crisped tomato flanked with fresh basil and a chunk of mozzarella. As the flavors all blended together with the sweet balsamic dressing drizzled on top, I moaned, closed my eyes, and savored the taste. The first bite was always the sweetest.

Luca groaned. "Two weeks will feel even longer if you're going to make noises like that and prance around naked all day."

I continued to ignore him and concentrated instead on the delicious food and the gorgeous beach. I inhaled the salty sea air and exhaled to the sound of the waves gently lapping against the shore.

"I know you think I'm the villain here, but I'm actually not trying to ruin your life."

"Do you even remember the things you said to me?" I asked, still feeling the twinge of embarrassment and pain that hit me when he'd called me a slut.

"I was angry. You made a fool of me with Enzo and with Adrian."

"Well, you are a fool! You shouldn't have cheated on me if you wanted me to play nice."

"Duly noted."

We each ate a few bites in silence.

"Giada, you're not really frightened of me, right?"

I stared at my plate but sensed his eyes boring into me. I didn't know how to answer that. Right now, I wasn't afraid. I hadn't been too scared to fall asleep in his bed after my walk, either. I felt a distinct sense of shame over that fact, though. Any rational person would be terrified.

But it was hard to be afraid when he looked like the old Luca, so relaxed, so casual, so...shirtless. And he was feeding me my favorite foods. He seemed like himself, like the Luca I'd loved when we were teenagers. He looked just like my old best friend.

But that was the problem. Luca was the handsome, charming man that knew I loved southern Italy, fresh tomatoes, and sitting by the beach.

He was also the monster that beat up my friend in a fit of jealousy and threatened me when I didn't do what he wanted.

What I needed to figure out was how to survive both Lucas. I needed to protect myself against the scary one and avoid falling for the other one.

Luca gave up waiting on me to answer. "Look, we can both continue hating each other, or we can call a truce while we're here and actually enjoy this trip. We've got a gorgeous beach, time to relax, and nothing to distract us."

"I can't just forget that you nearly beat a man to death as punishment for my behavior."

He sighed. "I'm just as stuck here as you are, Giada. Do you think all of this was my choice?"

"Oh, would you be happier with your little model friend here?" I stood to carry my plate inside, but he moved to block my path.

"Giada, come on. This is ridiculous. We can make each other's lives miserable, but we don't have to."

I rolled my eyes. "It seems I don't know much about you, Luca, but even I can tell that I'm your absolute favorite person to hurt."

He stared back at me for a long time. "Just because I'm good at it doesn't mean I enjoy it," he said, finally moving to let me pass.

CHAPTER 3

Giada

The next morning, I wandered around the town, exploring and doing touristy things, with Paolo trailing me like a dog. That night, Luca dragged me out to dinner. I wanted to refuse, but I was hungry and bored. Besides, if he wanted to pretend we were a couple, I could play that game.

I hadn't packed dressy clothes, so I went with a cute sundress. Luca wore a suit and tie, but he didn't protest my attire.

As we sat at the table, I caught him checking me out.

I broke off a piece of the bread and drudged it in the oil, eying Luca seductively as I popped it into my mouth.

He rolled his eyes and reached for his phone.

The waiter returned with the wine before I opened my menu, but he and Luca seemed happy to chat. I didn't even realize what was going on until the waiter swiped my menu off the table and sauntered off.

"You ordered for me?"

"You don't speak Italian."

"I didn't even look at the menu yet."

"Again, you don't speak Italian. Or read Italian."

"I can read a menu," I said, certain it was true.

Luca motioned for the waiter, said something else in Italian, and then the waiter brought my menu back. I stared at the page, determined to ignore Luca's smirk. Aside from the various types of pasta, which for the most part were the same as in English, the only word I even recognized was parmigiano.

I slowly peered up from the menu.

"What'll it be, Princess?"

"A salad, and chicken parmesan with penne."

His expression didn't change as he returned my menu to the waiter and dismissed him with a polite "grazie," which meant 'thank you.'

"You didn't tell him what I wanted."

"That is what I'd already ordered for you."

"Seriously?" I tried to hide my surprise under a look of disbelief.

He shrugged calmly. "I ordered cavatappi instead of penne. I suppose I could change it if you like."

Crap. That did sound better. I hadn't even seen that on the menu. "No, that's fine."

He nodded, then sipped his wine.

I rapped my nails against the table, trying to think of a way to distract myself until the food arrived.

"How are your classes this semester?"

The question threw me off. Luca had never shown any interest in my studies before. "What do you care?" I retorted, realizing I sounded like an insolent tween.

My attitude didn't faze him in the slightest. "I would imagine now that you're nearing graduation, you're able to take more classes you enjoy."

That was true, but it meant nothing. "I bet you don't even know what I'm studying."

He licked his lips, then drew his wine glass to his mouth, sipping slowly and then replacing it on the table. "Interior design and fashion the last time I checked. Has that changed?"

It hadn't. Annoyed that he guessed correctly, I drained all but one sip of my wine, slamming the glass onto the table a little harder than I'd intended.

"What made you decide against Columbia?" he asked, cocking his head to the side as though truly interested in my response. "Too close to home?"

My stomach tightened. All through high school, I'd dreamed of moving to New York City after graduation and going to college there. NYU's curriculum was probably a better fit for me, but I'd set my sights on Columbia, reasoning that it was a little less in the middle of things and therefore possibly more likely to garner my father's approval. Luca had been the one to take me to the campus for the first time, during a weekend we'd spent together at his house while his parents had been out of town.

He'd been a perfect gentleman that entire weekend, and if he still remembered everything I'd told him about my college dreams, surely he remembered the rest of the details from that weekend.

"Yeah, maybe," I finally replied, not willing to admit that my father had refused to let me live anywhere near New York City. If I'd insisted on attending NYU or Columbia, he would've made me live at home, and probably would've forced poor Enzo to drive me to class every day.

"You're remembering our weekend together, aren't you?" he asked softly.

I glared in response, then downed the final sip of my wine.

Luca's mouth twitched as though he were trying not to smile, but his eyes betrayed his effort. He motioned for the waiter, who promptly refilled my glass.

"Thirsty tonight, are you?" Luca taunted.

I really wasn't. I already sensed the initial effects of the first glass, an unnerving combination of relaxation and indifference. But I needed something to keep myself busy. I supposed I could converse with my date, just not on his terms. I returned to the original question he'd posed to me.

"Classes are going well, although missing a full week now isn't ideal. How is work?"

He seemed taken aback by my question. "Work is good. Although missing a full two weeks now is not ideal for me either."

I rolled my eyes. "What exactly do you do for a living?"

"Business."

"Right. Could you be less specific?"

His eyes narrowed, reminding me how much of my sarcasm was often lost in translation with him.

"Shipping—you know, imports, exports. And of, course I help my papà with some properties he owns both here and in the U.S.," he finally answered.

"What sorts of things do you ship?"

He shrugged. "Whatever people want to ship. It isn't my stuff in the shipping crates."

"Give me an example. What is something someone would use your company to ship overseas?"

"Clothes, home furnishings, wine," he said, directing his eyes towards the waiter approaching with our salads.

The waiter said something to me then began grinding pepper onto my salad.

Luca watched my face for a moment, then spoke to the waiter. "Basta," he said. "Grazie."

I recalled that being a word for "enough," but I stopped myself before expressing gratitude to Luca for saving me from an excess of pepper.

"Do customers ever ship illegal things?" I asked, spearing a tomato with my fork.

"Shipping containers are inspected when they arrive on U.S. soil."

"By you?"

"Department of Homeland Security."

I supposed that made sense. "Every container?"

"No."

"What sorts of other properties does your father have?"

"He owns two dance clubs in Rome—Argento and Oro."

"Money and time?" I translated.

Luca laughed, shaking his head. "Silver and gold. How did you pass Italian class?"

"Gabriella helped me. So what about in the U.S.? Doesn't he own some clubs in New York?"

He nodded.

"Why haven't we ever been to them?"

"I've been to them many times. Too many to count."

"Well, I haven't. Maybe Gabby and I will go after fall break. We love dancing."

Luca's gaze intensified. "They're not your type of establishment. Besides, they aren't in good neighborhoods."

"Maybe you just don't know what my type of place is. There's a lot you don't know about me."

"Do you enjoy watching attractive women take off their clothes?" he asked, cocking his head to the side.

"Your father owns multiple strip clubs?"

He didn't answer.

"Strippers are cheap junkies with fake hair. They aren't attractive."

"They prefer to be called exotic dancers, and our clientele seem to find them very attractive. But I have eyes only for you."

"Right. And Mila, the model you cheated on me with."

It was Luca's turn to down the rest of his wine. "I regret that, but I can't change the past. I can only work to make you forgive me now."

He seemed sincere, but it didn't answer my questions.

"Why'd you do it then?" I asked.

Luca shrugged. "Because I could."

I couldn't hide my scowl at that response.

"I'm in the habit of doing what I want. I'm not used to having a girlfriend. I haven't been in a relationship like that since the last time we were together, in high school."

Our food arrived, and for several minutes, we managed to focus on our meals without speaking, aside from generic comments about our dishes. My cavatappi was amazing, of course, but I restrained myself from groaning at the delightful combination of flavors cooked to perfection. Between the bread and the wine, though, I could only eat a little more than half of my entrée.

Luca eyed me warily as I nudged my plate towards the center of the table. "Dessert? After dinner drink?"

I shook my head.

"Il conto per favore," Luca said to the waiter, whom I hadn't even realized was beside us. Even I knew that was his way of asking for the bill.

I excused myself to the restroom, and Luca stood politely as I left the table. I didn't actually have to use the bathroom, but I needed a moment alone before getting back into a car with him. The close proximity was…unnerving.

I didn't know what to make of our conversation tonight. He'd given seemingly honest answers to my questions, which made me more inclined to trust him. Granted, he hadn't told me much I didn't already know, but still, I hadn't expected such sincerity. I wished I could forget our history—forget that he cheated, forget that he hurt Enzo, and just focus on enjoying this idyllic place with a man to whom my body still reacted strongly.

I reminded myself that I should feel afraid of Luca, but I wasn't. None of it made sense, and my head swam as I struggled to reconcile the person I'd dated with the monster who'd committed some grave sins.

I thought back to our last trip to Italy and how different everything had been then. That time, we'd be completely in sync. I'd believed he was the other half of my soul, with how in tune our bodies and minds had been. Back then, he'd made me feel like a princess, and not in the helpless sort of way. Back then, he made me feel cherished and adored.

As I made my way back to the table, I slowed my pace, watching him chat with the waiter. Luca was charismatic, for sure. Everyone responded to him, not just me. But the way he interacted with me, well, that was different. I just wasn't sure if that was a good thing or not.

I slid back into my seat, and Luca fixed his eyes on me, his gaze reminding me of the way a wolf would eye its prey. "Is this your plan to make me forgive you? Time on the beach and fancy meals?"

He leaned back in his seat, frowning. He took his time answering, then simply said, "I don't know."

"When we were in Rome last time and met up with your father, you said he paid for your mom to have some sort of plastic surgery after he cheated. You said it wasn't the first time he'd been unfaithful." I watched his jaw tense as I spoke, but I remembered almost word for word what he'd told me. He couldn't deny that was how his parents operated. His father would cheat, and his mother didn't even seem to mind anymore, at least not according to Luca.

He didn't reply, so I pressed on. "Will I get used to it after a while? The humiliation? The betrayal? Or do I just wait for you to start using more than food to win me back?"

Luca's mouth pressed into a firm line as he rose to his feet. "Let's go home," he said, reaching for my hand and gripping it so tightly that I couldn't have resisted had I wanted to.

He didn't speak again until after we were seated in the back of the black sedan Paolo had driven. I'd turned towards the window, absentmindedly rubbing my finger where my ring had left an indentation mark from Luca squeezing.

His breath caressed my ear a second before he spoke, keeping his voice low.

"I'm not going to become like my papà, Giada. I won't," he said.

I turned to face him, gazed into his hooded brown eyes for a moment, then swiveled back to the window, watching the lights from passing cars blur together as tears filled my eyes.

Luca didn't say anything else to me that night, having taken a phone call in Italian as soon as we reached the villa.

I spent the day after that lounging on the beach, which I had to admit was relaxing.

I went back to the villa to shower, and when I stepped out, a new midnight blue sheath dress was draped over the side of the bed. I stroked the silky fabric, falling in love even before noting the Armani label. A pair of patent leather slingbacks with a contrasting toe was perched on top of the Prada box beside the dress. Next to it sat a black bikini with golden studs. The Versace label and five hundred dollar price tag were clearly visible. Finally, there was a pair of Aviator-style Fendi sunglasses.

I salivated at the sight of it all, but before I could even process what it would mean to accept such clearly expensive gifts, Luca appeared. He didn't say anything at first, simply watching me finger the various fabrics.

"Notice a theme?" he asked.

"They're all Italian designers," I said. As pro-Italian as Luca was, it still impressed me that he recognized the difference between an Italian designer and, say, a French one. But even back in high school, he'd been that way. In fact, back then, he may have known even more about fashion than I did. It was one of the things that had first endeared him to me. Other guys our age seemed to think it was an affront to their sexuality to even care about their attire, but Luca fully appreciated the difference between a designer suit and some off-the-rack knock-off. He'd also been fiercely loyal to Italian designers, even as a teen.

"If there's something you don't like or that isn't the right size, I'll take care of it," he said.

I didn't answer. I loved it all, and I suspected he knew that because it was all exactly my style. I'd have to try it all on, of course, but everything appeared to be my size. I thought about what he said, how he wasn't going to be the same as his father. "You can't buy my forgiveness, you know."

"Maybe not, but I can at least make you happy while I wait for you to forgive me," he said. "Besides, a beautiful woman should have beautiful things."

I sighed and picked up the dress. "Where are we going?"

Luca smiled. "Let's start with dinner," he said. He stepped out of the bedroom, giving me privacy to get dressed and tackle my hair and makeup.

When I finished, I came out to find Luca wearing a pristine midnight blue three-piece suit. He looked good enough to eat.

"Wow," he said, stepping close. "You are breathtaking."

My cheeks flushed but I didn't answer. If my appearance was breathtaking, well, his left me speechless. I certainly wasn't about to tell him that, though.

"Who dressed you?" I asked him as we walked to the car.

"Valentino, of course," he said with a wink. He led me to the Maserati and then paused, "I can trust you not to injure my baby, right?"

I tilted my head side to side as though undecided. "I suppose I can behave for one night."

"So where are we really going?" I asked, certain we hadn't dressed up this much for a random old dinner date.

"Some charity ball. My papà asked us to attend in his stead. There will be plenty of food, some dancing, and hopefully enough alcohol to help you pretend to like me for the photographers."

The event did sound fun, so I decided to put aside my anger for the night and let myself enjoy it. In public, Luca was always the perfect gentleman anyway. We posed for a few photos upon entering, and then he quickly found me a drink. He introduced me to people he spoke with, and even when they spoke in Italian, he translated to English for me so I could follow along. The food was fantastic, and by the time we finished eating, I'd downed three delicious cocktails.

"Care to dance?" Luca asked, holding his hand out to me.

"Love to," I said, following him to the dance floor.

"You must be drunker than I thought," he teased.

I resisted the urge to stick out my tongue and instead focused on the music. Luca was a suave dancer, and I could easily disassociate myself from the mess we were in and focus on him as a dance partner.

I must have played the part of the happy couple a little too well though, because after a few songs, Luca gazed down at me. Before I figured out his intentions, he kissed me.

I didn't yank away, but when the kiss naturally ended and our eyes met, I shook my head. "I'm not there yet," I said.

Luca seemed disappointed but nodded.

I rested my head against his shoulder for the remainder of the song and tried to figure out why I'd added "yet."

That night, I fell asleep quickly, likely thanks to the cocktails, but then awoke insanely early. Luca was still sound asleep on his side of the bed, and even though we'd been sharing the bed since our arrival, something about his proximity now was particularly unsettling.

Luca looked so calm, so…unsuspecting when he slept. It was almost as though he'd forgotten my earlier threat to stab him in his sleep. Or maybe he assumed I'd never actually do it.

I gazed across the room, where he'd neatly draped his jacket, vest, and pants over a chair and thought back on the evening. I'd honestly had fun. The food was yummy, the music was perfect, and the company was… pleasant. Charming, even.

I mean, obviously, I'd been drunk.

Luca was hot but soul-less. There was no point for me to pretend he wasn't ridiculously good looking, especially in a suit. The sooner I accepted that fact, the less startling it would be every time I saw him and felt nauseatingly attracted to him.

But to think he'd been good company last night, well, that was disturbing. Surely, it had been the alcohol. Well, and he'd been pretending. Not just pretending to be a real couple, but pretending to be a decent human. That was the troubling part.

When he acted that way, I started to consider him a friend. I started to forgive him. I started to forget everything else.

And really, I so desperately wanted to forget, to let myself be swept off my feet yet again by Luca's charms. I finally understood the expression, 'ignorance is bliss.' Except in my case, ignorance could also be dangerous.

I rolled out of bed, grabbing a hooded sweatshirt before walking over to the balcony. I unlatched the door and slipped out quietly, peering back through the door to confirm I hadn't woken Luca opening and shutting the door. It was cooler out, but not freezing…probably in the 60s.

The sky was still dark, but the sounds of the ocean soothed me nonetheless. As my eyes adjusted to the sliver of light from the moon, I could make out the shape of the waves in the distance. I wasn't sure how long I sat there, but I grew so sleepy that I nearly fell back asleep. I probably could've slept there till morning, except that I dreaded waking to find bug bites all over my bare legs.

I stood, causing the chair to creak as it slid backwards. Then I opened the door and crept back inside. I faced the balcony as I shut the door, moving slowly so as not to wake Luca.

Just when I was about to turn, I heard a click and felt something hard press firmly against my back.

I screamed and turned, coming face to face with Luca.

He swore loudly in Italian, dropped his arms, and backed up. "Jesus Christ, Giada. What were you doing? What are you wearing?"

I was so startled that I didn't have any answers for him immediately. I gazed at him, my pulse still racing, and realized he must have just rolled out of bed. He was barefoot and shirtless, wearing only his thin pajama pants. His right arm was bent suspiciously behind his back.

"I couldn't sleep, so I went to sit on the balcony for a bit. I borrowed your sweatshirt. Sorry to wake you," I said.

He mumbled something that I assumed was another Italian swear word. "I thought you were an intruder."

"Well, I'm not. And I was coming in to go back to sleep, but you scared me half to death, so now I'm wide awake."

Judging from Luca's rapid breathing and the look on his face, he faced the same conundrum. As I stepped closer to Luca, he backed up.

"What is behind your back?" I asked.

He hesitated, then dropped his arm back to his side briefly before turning and tugging open the drawer of his nightstand. I didn't get a long look, but even I grasped that the object he was now stashing was a gun.

"Seriously? You pulled a fucking gun on me?"

He looked sheepish but didn't answer.

"Is it loaded?" I asked.

"Of course it's loaded. What is the point of an unloaded gun?"

I flung my hands in the air, beyond exasperated with myself. Not so long ago, I'd been struggling to remember all the reasons I hated him so much, and now he'd nearly killed me. I brushed past him and out of the bedroom.

"I guess you aren't too concerned I'll shoot you," I mumbled, aware that he had followed me.

He snorted. "I keep it on me when you're awake."

"Right. So that you can pull it on me whenever I get a bout of insomnia. Super."

"I didn't know it was you. You didn't tell me you were sneaking out."

"I didn't want to wake you!" I shouted.

Silence surrounded us, and I found myself wondering if we'd woken whatever neighbors lived in the building.

I stomped over to the coffee maker, staring at it for a good full minute trying to decipher what went where. When I sensed Luca's arms on me, I jumped.

He squeezed my arms and rested his chin on the top of my head. "Go back to bed, Giada. Please. I'm so sorry. I'm not usually a deep sleeper, so I don't know how you got out without waking me, but when I heard you come in…" He sighed. "I was trying to protect you. I wouldn't have shot you."

I believed him, but that really didn't make it any better.

"Go back to bed," he said. I'll stay out here on the couch. I'll make you coffee later, when the sun's up."

Adrian

After the clandestine discussion with Giada at my apartment, I was on edge for the next few days. Whenever I left my apartment, I was hyperaware of my surroundings, half expecting some crazed mafioso to jump out of the bushes. I barely slept that night but felt jittery and alert all day as though I'd had a surplus of caffeine. In reality, it was adrenaline. I'd hoped to see Giada, or at least to hear from her, but I didn't start to truly worry until a full four days passed after we spoke.

Remembering her instructions, I didn't dare call or text, but I was desperate for information, so I tried to hunt down her best friend.

I finally tracked down Gabriella outside the liberal arts building. The way she calmly waved when she spotted me reassured me that most likely, Giada wasn't dead. Surely Gabriella wouldn't seem so peaceful if her best friend were in some sort of serious trouble. I rushed closer.

"Hey Adrian, how are you?"

"Good, listen. Is everything okay with Giada? I haven't seen her around lately, and I'm worried."

"Yeah, she's in Italy."

"Italy?" That made no sense whatsoever. She certainly hadn't mentioned an upcoming vacation when we spoke.

"Last minute trip, I guess. They left a couple days ago and are staying through fall break, so she's missing a whole week of classes, but I guess when your dad owns half the university you can do that," she said, without any bitterness in her voice.

I sighed with relief. That was so brilliant that I chastised myself for not thinking of it. A last-minute family vacation to Italy gave her the space she needed to figure stuff out.

"So is her whole family there, or just Giada and her brother, or…?"

Gabriella's mouth twisted to the side like she'd tasted a bad apple. "She's not with her family."

I guessed the answer to my next question before I spoke the words aloud, but I had to ask. "Is she alone?"

"She's with Luca," Gabriella replied apologetically.

Shit shit shit. I focused on keeping my breathing level. "Have you spoken to her since she left? Is she okay?"

"Yes, she's fine. What is going on, Adrian?"

"Nothing. When did you last talk to her?"

She pulled out her phone and clicked on her texts from Giada. "She texted yesterday."

"And you're sure it's her? Like it sounds like she's writing it?"

"Yes. Who else would text me from her phone?" She began to read the messages, but I was impatient. I tugged the phone out of her hand and quickly scrolled along. Nothing sounded out of the ordinary, and nothing seemed to suggest it was Luca pretending to be her.

I handed Gabriella her phone. "Sorry."

"Are you alright?"

"Not really. I'm a little…" I shook my head and sighed. "How well do you know Luca?"

"Not well. He travels a lot and works nonstop. We've never hung out or anything. Are you… well, does Giada know you want her back?"

"I don't. I mean, that's not why I'm asking. I just had a bad feeling something had happened to her."

Gabriella was looking at her phone again. She had clicked on Instagram and held it up. "Here, didn't you see these? I think this one is from last night. She looks like she's doing great to me."

I didn't want to tell her that Giada had blocked me on all social media, but I did look closely at the photos. Most pictures were of various places in Sicily, but there was one selfie of her on a boat, and another of her with Luca. They were both dressed to the nines, and his arm was around her waist as she curved towards him and placed her hand on his chest. I chewed the inside of my lip. The couple in that picture looked like they belonged together. They appeared happy, comfortable with one another, and, as much as I hated to say it, in love.

Still, pictures could be deceiving. Giada was not faking the terror in her eyes when she showed up at my apartment Sunday night.

"I have a weird request. Could you check in with Giada every day that she's gone and make sure she's okay, and if you don't hear back or something seems off, can you call me?"

She nodded and took my number, but seemed perplexed.

"When Giada gets back, you can tell her I asked you to do this, but only if you're alone, and please don't say anything to her about me in a text or when Luca's around. Okay?"

She made a sour face and, for a moment, looked like she would ask a question, but then she just nodded.

Now she clearly thought I was insane.

CHAPTER 4

Giada

I fell into a nice routine over the next few days, sleeping in late then heading to the beach. Luca gave me space the whole time, so I spent my days reading books and listening to music.

One evening, just before I went inside to change for dinner, I called Gabriella. She was heading out for a movie but seemed so excited to hear from me.

We didn't talk for long since the international call would be pricey, but I desperately needed to hear her voice. We kept the call light and cheery until the end, when she asked if I was okay. She spoke in that special best friend tone that told me she knew the answer wasn't yes but needed to hear me say it.

"I'll be fine. Luca and I had an argument before we left, and so it's just been weird."

"Did the argument have anything to do with Adrian?"

"Why?"

She hesitated. "Well, I ran into him yesterday, and he was worried about you. He didn't know you were in Italy, and he seemed convinced something was wrong or that you were in some sort of trouble."

"Shit."

"Giada?"

"Sorry. Umm, could you do me a favor? Can you call him and tell him I'm fine and that he should forget everything I told him because I was completely wrong about it all?"

Gabriella was slow to answer. "Well, I could, but…"

"Please? I know it's a lot to ask, but I sort of said some things I shouldn't have to Adrian when I was upset with Luca, and I need to just move on. If Luca heard I'd even talked to Adrian he'd be jealous."

"Okay. I'll call him," she promised. "But when you get back, you and I are going to talk for real, okay?"

I agreed, and then we hung up. When I went inside, Luca was on the phone as well. He didn't even glance up as I walked through the room, a clear sign he was stressed. He spoke Italian, and his gestures were almost as indecipherable as his words. I walked past him into the bedroom, shutting the door behind me. I stood in the closet, staring at the items I'd brought—plus amassed since arriving—and tried to decide what to wear. Then, I got a better idea.

I could still hear Luca on his call, so why was I wasting time getting dressed when I didn't even know what our evening plans would be? I circled back to the bed, inching open the drawer on his nightstand. Even though he told me he didn't leave the gun there during the day, I was surprised to see the drawer mostly empty. There were a few receipts in the drawer and one folded letter. It was in Italian, and I didn't have time to translate, so I wedged it back in place. In the back of the drawer, I found two long strips of condoms. I gagged and shut the drawer, trying not to envision when—and with whom— he'd been using those.

Next, I checked out the bathroom drawers, but those were equally uninteresting. I moved on to the closet, convinced I wouldn't find anything there, either, but as I pulled out a shoebox and cracked it open, I was thrilled to find it didn't contain shoes.

Instead, it held pictures and notes and other memorabilia. There was a cufflink that I recognized as one I'd bought for Luca back in high school. A faded strip of photo booth pictures of Luca and me making silly faces. A program from a charity holiday party he'd helped me organize for a children's hospital. And from the looks of it, every single note I'd ever written him.

There was also a framed picture I remembered giving to him. It was a selfie of the two of us, taken it on the beach one carefree day when we were just out having fun. My arm was around Luca, and I was gazing at him like a lovesick puppy, but he had the purest smile on his face I'd ever seen.

As the bedroom door clicked open, I shoved the box back onto the shelf and jumped to my feet. "In here!" I called, unnecessarily since there weren't exactly many hiding spots.

He poked his head around the corner. "Whatcha doing?"

"Trying to decide what to wear. Are we going anyplace for dinner?"

"No, I thought you could cook."

We both laughed at that notion.

Something caught Luca's eye, and he glanced down.

Crap. I'd forgotten to put the framed photo back in the box.

Luca bent down and picked it up, eying me warily.

"Oh, I just bumped into that while I was looking for a dress," I explained.

"In a shoe box on a shelf behind my jeans?" His smirk let me know he wasn't too mad.

"I still love this picture," I admitted.

Luca snatched it out of my hands and stared at it for a moment before reaching for the box. "Of course you like it. You look gorgeous. I look ridiculous in it."

"You look happy," I corrected.

He opened the box, but instead of putting the photo back, he sifted through other items in the box. We reminisced together, laughing and talking about each item. Conversation flowed easily for the next twenty minutes, almost as though we were still friends. As though the last three years hadn't happened.

"I'm surprised you saved all of this," I told him. Luca wasn't the sentimental type, and he didn't have piles of stuff laying around his apartment.

"It's a good reminder."

"Of?"

"You, obviously." He shrugged. "And me, a little. The old me, the guy I was before..." He stood and placed the box back in its spot on the shelf.

"Before what?" I asked.

Luca's stare was pointed, but he didn't answer, so I moved on.

"You don't have to keep me hidden in a box, you know."

From the way he eyed me, I expected him to disagree. "I don't," he said, but then he nodded for me to follow him.

He made his way into the living room, stopping at the small grey desk in the corner. He tugged open the desk drawer and rifled under some papers. There was a photo of me. It was more recent, and I appeared to be sleeping.

"Am I asleep?"

Luca chuckled. "Yep. I happen to prefer you that way. You never argue with me when you're asleep."

I rolled my eyes but secretly loved that he kept a picture of me in his desk drawer.

Then he walked into the kitchen. He opened a cabinet in the corner. Stuck on the inside of the cabinet drawer was another photo, also of me. This photo was from high school, and I was smiling and gazing just off center from the camera. I suspected he'd told me to smile but then said something to make me blush right before he snapped the picture. I wished I could remember that day.

"Don't you see? You're everywhere, Giada."

I didn't have a response for that.

The next morning, I felt different than I had before. I no longer feared or hated Luca, and that fact plagued me with guilt. I told myself it was the location. Being back in the town where I'd fallen for him before was dangerous, stirring up a slew of memories I couldn't trust.

The last time I'd been in Palermo with Luca, he'd been flirty and cocky, but he'd also been sensitive about my feelings for Adrian. He'd been sweet and romantic and genuine, or so I'd thought. Now, I wasn't sure if he ever really loved me or if it was all part of his plan. Luca was with me because it pleased his father. He didn't want *me* so much as he wanted parental approval. Making me think otherwise had been cruel and manipulative. And what he'd done to Enzo was unforgivable.

I should've hated Luca with a vengeance.

And part of me did, for sure, especially when I thought about everything he'd done. But I didn't trust my own emotions anymore. When I caught Luca staring at me on the beach when he thought I was reading, I could've sworn I saw love in his eyes. When he brought me breakfast in bed, I sensed remorse. And when he watched me styling my hair or putting on jewelry, there was definitely lust.

But it didn't make sense for him to feel conflicted. He chose to behave the way he had. I was the victim, not him.

Instead of attempting to decipher his familiar looks, I should've been focusing on my self-destructive behavior. I tried to stay busy, listening to music on my headphones instead of conversing with Luca or eavesdropping on his many phone calls (which were all in Italian anyway, rendering it pointless to eavesdrop). Even though I never understood his words, something about Luca's accent always made my knees feel weak.

I tried to eat alone. If I did end up at the table at the same time as Luca, I'd focus on my phone so as not to get drawn into his lips. It was distracting, the way he licked them between bites or how his jaw shifted forcefully, reminding me of the endurance he had when using his mouth for other activities. He didn't flaunt his body in front of me, but he made no effort to conceal it either, rarely wearing a shirt unless out in public.

I couldn't deny the attraction was still there. My body reacted to his deep voice, the fresh masculine scent of his aftershave, even the confident, smooth way he walked. It was maddening.

By the second week in Italy, I couldn't take it anymore. I'd tossed and turned all night, in the bed I shared with the cause of all my confusion. Once Luca got up, I made a decision. I needed to talk to my brother. Or maybe Lorenzo. Or even just Gabby. I sat up in bed, rubbed my eyes, and reached for my phone to check what time it was back on the east coast.

Crap. They'd all be asleep still.

I sighed. Matteo had told me Enzo was doing well, but he didn't know what had actually happened. I wondered again if Matteo still would've pushed me to give Luca another chance if he knew what he'd done.

I gritted my teeth and punched my pillow right as the door opened. Luca sauntered in, looking nothing like the sociopath I recognized him to be. He was shirtless—jerk—and wore thin grey sweatpants that concealed none of his physical perfections but made it even more impossible to see him for the devil he was.

Ugh. I needed clarification.

"What is the point of all of this?" I asked as Luca placed a cappuccino and a croissant on the nightstand beside me.

He startled at my tone, splashing a bit of the coffee onto the saucer. Then he turned to me and laughed. "La colazione," he replied.

I rolled my eyes. "Yes, I see that it's breakfast. Why are you bringing it to me in bed every day?"

"To be nice?"

"There!" I pounded my fist into the pillow beside me. "That's what I'm wondering. Are you really doing it to be nice? And if so, why?"

Luca's smug, contented expression was exasperating. I wanted to smack that stupid grin right off his face.

"What are you smiling about?" I demanded.

"I can't help it. You're cute when you're feisty."

"Answer the question," I said between gritted teeth.

"Okay, yes, I'm being nice."

"Why?"

He shrugged. "Maybe I'm just a nice guy."

"You are *not* a nice guy."

"Ouch."

"I'm serious. I need to know your motivation here. Do you want me to forgive you? Or do you just feel bad?"

"Why should I feel any worse than you? You certainly weren't chastely awaiting my return home."

I clenched my fist, struggling against the urge to punch him. "I have not slept with anyone else since you and I started dating over the summer. But even if we're ignoring the fact that you're a man-whore incapable of monogamy, you couldn't possibly have already forgotten that you nearly beat Enzo to death."

"*I* didn't lay a finger on Lorenzo," Luca replied.

I lunged at him, ready to strangle him, but the second my hands reached his neck, Luca jumped back.

We both stared at each other for a minute, and then he spoke.

"If you want me to answer your little questions, you can't keep attacking me."

I shook my head. "I have all the answers I need. You're a sociopath, and you feel no remorse, so you're certainly not seeking my forgiveness. And you've already made it clear you don't want to try to repair our relationship, so the only possible explanation for these little nice things you keep doing for me is that you're trying to fuck with my head."

His eyebrows furrow. "What makes you think I don't want to repair our relationship?"

"Our first day here. You told me we were both pawns. You basically admitted you were only dating me to impress your father."

I watched Luca's face as a variety of expressions crossed his eyes. I waited, patiently, for him to deny it. Instead, he just sighed and plopped down on the foot of the bed. After another lengthy silence, he spoke.

"My entire life, my papà has been disappointed in me. He wants so badly for me to follow in his footsteps, but everything I do is wrong. I'm not as good as him, I never will be, and I don't even think I want to be."

He paused and gazed out the window. The ocean was visible in the distance, beyond the gauzy white curtains. "You wouldn't understand that because your father worships the ground you walk on. When he calls you his princess, it's because he treasures you. You're more valuable to him than anything else in the world."

"Bullshit," I interrupted. "My dad loves the idea of having a daughter but can't stand being around me. He banished me to boarding school because he couldn't even look at me without thinking about how I caused his father's death. So don't talk to me about shitty father-child relationships as if that's an excuse to be an asshole."

Luca's expression changed yet again, but this time, I saw pity in his eyes. Disgusted that I'd made myself even more pathetic to him, I turned away, focusing instead on my coffee. I blew the foam to the side and sipped the frothy beige liquid.

"Giada, your nonno was murdered. That wasn't your fault. Your father sent you to boarding school because he wanted you to be safe. And that's the exact same reason why he likes seeing you with me. He knows I'd never let anyone hurt you."

"Except you," I said, ignoring the brunt of his statement.

He sighed again. "I'm not perfect, Giada, and you're not either. But we had a good run there for a while. Yes, our families were both ecstatic when we were together, but so were you and I." He reached for my free hand and squeezed it.

I sipped the rest of my cappuccino without pause, thankful the foam had cooled it enough to avoid scalding myself. When I finally finished and had no choice but to look up, Luca was still staring at me.

"I don't know what you expect me to say. You aren't the person I thought you were. I can't just overlook the fact that you told your…associates…to beat up my driver just because I kissed him. It's not even a matter of forgiveness because nothing you ever do will change the fact that you're the type of man that can intentionally hurt someone."

Luca leaned away. "So you're choosing Lorenzo over me?"

I rolled my eyes dramatically. "I'm not dating Enzo, nor will I ever. I was just drunk and mad at you, and…" Fortunately, I stopped myself before I added in that I'd had a huge, yet mostly harmless, crush on Enzo for the last five or six years of my life. Sure, he was a good-looking man, but Luca sure didn't need to hear that.

"I'd rather be single than date someone like your father," I finally said.

Judging from his face, my words had their intended effect. Any pity or compassion I'd sensed in his expression earlier was now gone, replaced with clear anger.

"I want to go to church," I said.

"It isn't Sunday."

"There is mass every day," I told him, perturbed that he'd been Catholic his whole life and still didn't know that.

"You don't speak Italian."

"No, but you do. And I'm not the one who needs to work on my morality."

He rolled his eyes.

Rather than sit around and discuss further, I crawled out from under the covers and headed out onto the balcony. I half expected Luca to drag me back inside, knowing full well he wouldn't want anyone on the beach seeing me in my flimsy white slip, but he left me alone for a few minutes.

Just as I was starting to calm down enough to realize we hadn't settled anything, I heard Luca step up behind me. He held out my robe, which I only accepted because I was too tired to fight about that, too.

"I'd like to fly home today and spend the rest of my fall break with my family," I said.

"There's no available flight today."

"Tomorrow then," I said.

"We'll fly home Saturday as planned," he said calmly.

"I don't want to stay here with you until then. I'm not going to get back together with you, Luca."

"Technically, we never broke up."

Honestly, I rolled my eyes more when Luca and I discussed our relationship status than as a teen talking with my mom. "I disagree, but just to clear up any confusion, this is me, officially breaking up with you. For good."

"I don't accept."

"There's nothing to accept, Luca. It's not like a divorce where you have to sign off on it. If I say I'm out, I'm out."

"I don't think you mean that, and if you do, you're just not thinking through the consequences."

I shivered at the word "consequences."

"We are supposed to have dinner with my papà on Wednesday. He's expecting both of us to attend as a couple."

"That's not my problem."

"It will be if you don't attend." His eyes narrowed, and he reached for my arm. "Call your brother or your father if you need a second opinion on that."

I opened my mouth to protest then shut it. Then I started to say something else, but also stopped myself. Between the look in his eyes and his grip on my wrist, Luca's meaning was clear. And if I had to tolerate a few more days with Luca to ensure nothing bad would happen to my family, so be it.

I yanked free of his grip. "You do not get to touch me, not if it has to be this way."

"It doesn't have to be this way at all, Giada. I flew you to Italy and put you up in a swanky beachfront villa. I spent a fortune buying you high-end Italian clothes and accessories, and I bring you breakfast in bed every day. You act like I'm some monster, but at least I'm making an effort. You aren't even trying to make this work."

I swung back to face him, but grossly miscalculated the distance between us and landed with my lips mere inches from his. "That's because I don't want this to work. You just didn't give me a choice in the matter."

I stormed back into the villa, grabbed the croissant still on the plate by the bed, and locked myself in the bathroom, running a hot bath.

~

I successfully avoided most interactions with Luca until it was time for dinner with his father. I wasn't surprised to see that he'd bought me a new dress and jewelry to wear, and I also made no pretense of refusing his gifts. I should feel guilty about it all, but I deserved it. As long as I was stuck with Luca in my life, I might as well accept the benefits.

As we drove to the restaurant, Luca reached for my hand over the console. I was so flustered that it took me a moment to yank it away and realize I didn't have to pretend to like him quite yet. I tried to focus on the scenery blurring past as we drove, but I couldn't help but notice he was eying me warily.

"What?" I growled.

"You seem tense."

"No shit I'm tense. I'm headed to dinner with my evil fake boyfriend and his equally evil father. Not exactly a recipe for relaxation."

"You don't need to worry, Giada. My papà loves *you*."

I winced at the way his intonation made it abundantly clear that Luca didn't believe his father felt the same about him. The last time we'd gone to dinner with his father, we'd been a couple for real, and I was the one who'd told Mr. Marino we were dating because I wanted to deflect pressure off of Luca. Even when Luca topped my list of enemies, I wouldn't wish the wrath of his father on him.

"Your father is terrifying. What if I mess up and say something I shouldn't?"

"Like what?" Luca paused only for a moment. "Giada, there is nothing you could say that would matter. I'd prefer you not scowl at me the whole night, but even if you do, he'll just assume we're quarreling. The fact that you're with me is enough."

"Enough for you, maybe, but is it enough to keep me safe?"

"Safe? What do you mean?"

I shrugged, not sure how such a basic concept could be clarified.

"My papà would never hurt you, Giada. Never."

He sounded serious, and yet, there was no way he could know for sure, and certainly nothing he could do to prevent it. "You're more afraid of him than I am, so why would I believe that you'd stand up to him for me?"

"I would," he insisted. "But even if I couldn't, someone else would."

"Who?"

Luca blew out a sigh, clearly irritated with me. "It doesn't matter, Giada. All you need to know is that my papà would never hurt you because he knows there are other people who would protect you."

I opened my mouth to protest, but he shushed me.

"Would you just trust me for once?"

"Trust is earned," I said, throwing one of his favorite expressions back in his face.

He swerved the car to the side of the road, nearly giving me whiplash as he shifted into park and thumped his hands against the steering wheel in frustration.

I waited for him to calm down.

"Fine, then you won't go with me. I'll call for a ride for you. I'll make up an excuse for why you aren't with me."

"I already said I'd go. I'm wearing the dress you bought me. What more do you want?"

"I don't *want* any of this, Giada! And I'm not taking you if you're scared."

I cringed. "I'm more scared of what your father will do if I don't go."

Luca appeared to consider that. After a too-long pause, he spoke again. "Nothing. There's nothing he can do to you. I am telling you now that no matter what you do or don't do, you are untouchable. I promise."

As Luca stared straight ahead, his face uncannily still in contrast to what I suspected was a flurry of thoughts in his mind, I took the opportunity to look at him closely. I wished I could simply believe him because he'd never lied to me before, but that wasn't the case. But that didn't mean I could never trust him with anything.

Gazing at him, I thought he was sincere. I believed he didn't want me to be scared, and I believed he was willing to let me sit out this dinner even though it was so important to his father. For now, that would have to be enough.

"Fine. If you say I don't need to be afraid of your father, I won't be. Just don't leave me alone with him."

"I wouldn't dream of it."

Luca stared at me for a long moment, then checked the side

mirrors and navigated back onto the road. When we arrived at the restaurant, he left the car with some shady-looking guy by the front. Since Luca treated his car like his baby, it seemed odd.

"Was that the valet?" I asked.

"No," he replied, gripping my hand and leading me towards the restaurant.

I swiveled to see the guy climb into the front seat of the car.

"Umm why did you give him your keys then?"

He blew out a sigh. "It's a friend of my father. I don't trust valets, and he's going to watch it for us."

I had so many more questions, but it was obvious Luca wasn't in the mood to answer them. So I kept my mouth shut during the dinner, speaking only when spoken to, and spending the rest of the time focusing on my food or wine.

If Salvatore noticed something different about my behavior, he didn't say anything to me at least.

CHAPTER 5

Adrian

I returned to campus the day before classes resumed following fall break. As I made my way to the law building to study for a few hours, my feet slowed to a stop before I even consciously realized what I was seeing. It was Enzo, walking out of Gia's apartment. Against my better judgment, I turned abruptly towards him.

He watched me approach but didn't smile or greet me with any familiarity.

"Is Giada back?" I asked.

"Their flight lands soon. I was just dropping off some groceries for her."

"What if Luca sees you?"

Enzo frowned. "Luca was the one who told me to do this."

My mouth ran dry. It was one thing for Enzo to tell me to pretend I hadn't seen what I saw, but it was another matter altogether for him to pretend he hadn't gone through what he had. "You aren't concerned that he'll..." I didn't even know how to finish that sentence.

"All of that is resolved. I did something I shouldn't have, and there were consequences. Unless I mess up again, which I won't, there's no problem."

Nausea washed over me. It wasn't normal for someone to accept this series of events as a normal occurrence. "Giada told me what you did."

"She shouldn't have," he interrupted.

"Well, she did. And even if you're not scared of Luca, she is. She needs someone to help her get away from him for good."

Enzo glanced left then right before shaking his head. "Luca will always be in her life, and she has no reason to be afraid of him."

I stepped closer. "He's a dangerous sociopath. How can you act like you care about her and then let him get close to her? You know what he is!"

Enzo countered my step with one of his own. Suddenly, the kind, handsome Italian man seemed much more antagonistic. "I do know what he is, and if you do, as well, then you would be wise to back off and stay away from both of them. Luca's father does business with Giada's father. Luca knows that. So when I say he will never hurt Giada, I mean it."

I stumbled back several inches and considered his words. He was telling me Giada was safe, so that should be reassuring. But he had also, perhaps inadvertently, confirmed what I'd suspected about Marco. Before I could even formulate another question, though, Enzo had transformed back into his typical easygoing self and began speaking again.

"You don't need to worry about Giada, but if I were you, I'd stay away from her and her apartment. Luca doesn't appreciate other men hanging around his girlfriend."

"I'm not afraid of him," I said.

Enzo chuckled. "You should be," he said. Then he walked back to his car, driving off with me still wondering what the fuck just transpired.

Giada

"**I** need an adjective," Luca said suddenly, jolting me from my boredom.

We were still somewhere over the Atlantic, and I'd already finished a movie on my iPad and grown bored of my book. I'd had too much caffeine earlier in the day to sleep, but my eyes were tired from having stared at a screen too long.

"What?"

"An adjective," Luca repeated.

I opened my eyes and turned towards him. He held up a small book labeled "Road Trip Mad Libs."

I snorted.

"Hey, don't knock it. My mother used to do these with me on all our international flights. This is how I learned English."

"Scruffy," I said.

He frowned.

"That's my adjective," I explained.

He nodded, wrote it down, then asked for a verb. After I supplied all the necessary parts of speech, he read me the silly story, then we swapped. It took less than fifteen minutes total but was a welcomed distraction nonetheless. As Luca turned back to the stack of papers his father had sent over to him that morning, I settled back into my seat.

Since the dinner with his father, Luca had been nothing but nice to me. He'd continued spoiling me with presents and delicious treats, and he'd given me space to relax on the beach. He even sent me to an Italian spa the day before we left. In the apartment, he didn't touch me. He even slept on the couch the last few nights. But out in public, he'd still hold my hand or place his hand on the small of my back.

I suspected I should recoil at his touch, but I didn't. I found it easy to play the public role of his girlfriend. Too easy. But that would all change when we were back home. The presents would stop, the vacation would end, and Luca wouldn't even be in town with me most of the time. His family's home was in Staten Island, so he could commute anywhere in NYC but also theoretically visit me at school in upstate New York or even at my family home in Bridgeport.

If I'd failed at presenting myself as a loyal girlfriend in Luca's absence when I was actually in love with him, I didn't stand a chance at the charade now that my feelings were, at best, ambivalent.

"What's going to happen once we get home?" I asked.

Luca turned to me and squinted as though trying to read my mind. "I guess that's up to you," he finally said.

"I mean with us."

He shrugged.

"I assume we're not breaking up," I continued.

"That's still what you want?" He actually looked disappointed, which was ridiculous. We hadn't kissed since the charity event, and that was obviously a drunken slipup on my part. We alternated between arguing, ignoring each other, and quietly tolerating each other's presence. I didn't see how any of those interactions made him think I'd possibly changed my mind on dating him.

I didn't dare say that out loud, so instead, I offered a slight nod of my head.

Luca frowned. "It wasn't too long ago that you said you loved me."

I started to remind him of the many, many things that had changed since then, but he continued.

"But as soon as you see I'm not perfect, that all changes, and nothing I do can earn your forgiveness," he said. "I wouldn't have thought I'd already be past the point of redemption before I even hit twenty-five."

"I don't think you're past the point of redemption," I said, starting to feel guilty.

"I believe the term 'unforgivable' is how you phrased it."

"I just don't see things with us going back to the way they were anytime soon."

He sighed. "Well, I've got work to do, so I'll stay out of your way. But whether or not we're in the same apartment doesn't change the fact that both of our families are counting on us to remain a couple, if you know what I mean."

"For how long?"

Luca shrugged. "I don't know. But I assume you understand that as long as everyone believes we are a couple, you need to behave as expected. That means no binge drinking with your driver, no coincidental church meetups with your ex-boyfriend…" He paused and shook his head. "Actually, no meetings of any sort with any men."

"Oh, is that all?" I snapped.

"Don't act like you're surprised. If you make me look like a fool again, I won't have any choice but to punish the poor guy you're using to make me jealous. I have a reputation to protect, and you know it."

I swiveled towards the window. Maybe Luca was past the point of redemption.

"Do you understand?"

"Yes, I think I do."

He hadn't left much to the imagination, so there wasn't any room for confusion. Although, I did have to wonder if there would be a double standard. "What about my reputation? I don't think it's appropriate for you to be gallivanting with Swiss models whenever I'm not around."

"Giada, I won't do anything your papà wouldn't like," he promised.

I wasn't sure how comforting that was supposed to be, but luckily the flight attendant came on and announced the preparations for landing.

When we finally reached the baggage claim, I spotted Alessio in the corner. I prepared to stay out of the way and let the guys collect my bags, when I noticed Lorenzo standing several feet away.

"Enzo!" I shrieked happily. I had never in my whole life been so relieved to see someone. I started towards him, ready to hug him, when Luca grabbed my hand.

I turned back to him and immediately stiffened at the look in his eyes. He tugged me closer.

"I promised you I'd bring him back, and I did. Don't make me regret it."

"I won't," I said, nearly adding 'thank you' before remembering how ridiculous that would be in light of Luca's past treatment of Enzo.

"I'm going straight home tonight so I can get some work done, and Enzo will take you directly to your apartment. I asked him to pick up groceries for you earlier, so you should be well stocked."

"Thanks."

"I'll see you in a couple of weeks," he said. Then, before I could reply, he placed his free hand on my cheek and leaned in to kiss me softly. I realized it was part of the game, that Alessio would have questions if Luca didn't kiss his girlfriend goodbye, but it was confusing nonetheless. Luca's familiar aftershave wafted into my nostrils, assaulting them with the same pleasant flurry of emotions that flooded my mouth when his soft lips made contact.

Hating him would be much easier if everything about him weren't so attractive to me.

Adrian

I asked Gabriella to have Giada call me when she was back in town, but I was still surprised when Gabriella's name popped up on my caller ID the next day. I probably sounded confused when I answered, since I assumed it had to be bad news for Gabby to call me. Instead of her bubbly voice on the other line, it was Giada.

"Hi," she said timidly. "Gabby said you wanted me to call."

"Uh, yeah," I said, fumbling for the remote to mute my television. "I wasn't expecting you to use her phone though."

"Oh, well, I couldn't…" Giada didn't finish the sentence, but then she didn't have to. Obviously, she couldn't use her own phone. That bastard probably scoured over her phone records.

"How was your trip? Gabriella showed me some of your photos. Looks like you two had a nice time."

There was a long pause. "Palermo is beautiful," she finally said.

Her voice sounded so quiet, so uncertain. It just wasn't like her. "Are you alone now, Giada?"

"Yes. I'm at Gabby's apartment, but she's in a different room."

"Is Luca in your apartment?"

"No. He's in New York City. I don't know when he'll be in town again."

"So you're not back together with him?"

"I…it's complicated."

"Giada, please. Can you just tell me what's going on? I've been worried about you."

"I know, and I'm sorry. I was panicking that night, and I needed someone to talk to. I should've left you out of it. It wasn't fair to drag you into my mess. You don't need to worry about me, though. I'm not in any danger."

"Enzo said the same thing. He said Luca wouldn't hurt you."

"He won't."

"Then why are you calling me from your friend's phone in your friend's apartment?"

"I'm still technically with Luca. I don't think it would look right if people found out you and I were still talking. I don't want to give him any reason to be jealous."

"Why are you still with him? Giada, that's insane. He nearly killed Enzo."

"He didn't personally lay a hand on Enzo," she replied.

My body temperature dropped ten degrees. "Really, Giada? That's a distinction you're going to make now? Jesus, maybe you do belong with him."

She mumbled a swear word under her breath. "No, it's not. Adrian, hang on. I don't want to defend him. It was horrible and awful, and none of this is okay, but…" she exhaled loudly.

I could hear the tension in her breath as she continued. "I don't want to be with Luca now, but I can't break up with him. Not just yet. I mean, he's not even in town. We aren't together still, not in any meaningful sort of way. The situation is complicated, so I don't even know how to explain it all, but I can handle it myself."

I tried to understand what she was saying, but it didn't make sense. She was still with him, but she didn't want to be? I had so many questions, but she kept right on rambling.

"You are such a nice guy to want to help me get out of this mess when you're not even interested in me anymore, but you shouldn't be involved. It's my mess, and I can handle it alone."

"Who said I'm not interested in you anymore?" I asked, regretting my words the second they left my mouth.

"You've been dating other people."

"One person, and only because you left for Italy with your ex-boyfriend when you and I were on a break. You moved on, so I didn't realize I was supposed to wait around pining for you."

"You're not! I don't expect you to want anything to do with me. I screwed up when I went back to Luca, and I never should've gotten involved with him. I see that now. I'm sorry I didn't just go to Chicago with you when you asked. I just…well you kept saying all that stuff about my family, and I felt like they were always under attack with you. But Luca knows my family, and he's always been on good terms with them."

I snorted.

"I'm just trying to apologize, Adrian. I know it's too late for us, but I wanted to say I'm sorry. And I wanted to tell you not to worry about me."

"Until you're able to live your life like a normal person, seeing and calling whomever you want whenever you want, I'm going to worry about you. The fact that you can admit you messed up when you chose Luca but that you're still with him tells me I need to be worried."

"I told you it's complicated. We aren't together, not really. When we're alone, we don't even talk. It's all just for show. We need his father to believe we're still a couple."

"Or what?"

"I don't know, just it won't be good."

"For Luca? Or for you? Did his father threaten you?"

"Mostly for Luca."

"Well, fuck him. He's made his bed. Let him lie in it."

"It'll be bad for my family also if Mr. Marino is upset."

I shut my eyes and rubbed my forehead. "Giada, you have to talk to your father about this, or at least your brother. I promise you they can help you."

"They won't," she said quickly. "I spoke with Matteo, and he told me not to break up with Luca. He was abundantly clear. And my father encouraged the trip to Italy with Luca."

Shit. That didn't make sense at all.

"I don't want you to worry, Adrian. I'm fine. Enzo is back driving me again, so that's nice, and Gabby and I are spending a bunch of time together, so…"

Her voice trailed off, but I still didn't know what to say. Eventually, she continued. "How are your classes going? Is law school as bad as they say it is?"

"Worse," I said with a laugh. I told her about my professors, and before I knew it, we'd spend a full half hour discussing totally normal topics. Before hanging up, though, I had to make one more suggestion, even if it wasn't one she'd like.

"You and Gabriella still go to the gym a lot, right?" I began.

"I wouldn't say a lot," she replied.

I suppressed a laugh. Giada had been blessed with a body that suggested she exercised much harder than she did. I didn't think she was out of shape by any means, but her trips to the gym were more about socializing and justifying her collection of workout gear than building muscle. She'd never been a huge fan of sweating.

"There's a self-defense class at the gym," I continued. "I'd worry less if you'd sign up. Plenty of women take it just as a precaution, so no one would think anything suspicious about it if they found out."

She was quiet for a moment. "Maybe," she finally agreed.

I suspected that was as good as I'd get for now, so I dropped it.

CHAPTER 6

Giada

With Luca out of town, our arrangement didn't bother me. I could go about my life the same as I had for years when I'd been single. I didn't have to see Luca, and for the most part, we didn't even talk.

The hardest part was lying to Gabriella. She'd support me whatever I did, but I felt like such a fake telling her that Luca and I were still working on things. She knew about the pictures, how I'd assumed he was cheating on me, and she didn't give me a hard time when I claimed the photos were old. Gabriella was also aware that it was Adrian that I was talking with so often, and she didn't lecture me about that, either. All she did was offer a gentle encouragement that I choose between the two men.

Over the next two weeks, I fell into the habit of calling Adrian every couple of nights, always from Gabby's apartment and always on her phone. Having never been friends before we'd started dating, it was new territory for us, but I liked it. Nothing could change the past or erase the fact that I'd ruined a perfectly good relationship with him, but I wasn't about to miss out on a chance to be friends with him, as long as I could do it without endangering him.

We'd been talking for about a half hour on Thursday when my own cellphone rang. I was about to ignore it until I noticed that it was Luca.

"Oh shit," I blurted out in the middle of Adrian's story.

"You alright?"

"Yeah, but I have to go. Sorry," I said, disconnecting and tossing the phone to the side as though Luca could somehow see through my cell phone.

I took a cleansing breath then answered.

"Hey babe," Luca said casually.

"Uh hi," I replied, much less certain.

"What are you up to?"

My stomach clenched. What if he was at my apartment looking for me? "Nothing, just hanging out at Gabby's apartment."

"Oh, okay. Tell her I said hi," he said.

He'd never asked me to say anything to my best friend, so that alone was weird.

"Do you have plans tomorrow night?" he continued.

I was so thrown that it took me a minute to think of whether I did have anything on my calendar. Before I could answer, he kept speaking.

"Let me rephrase. I'm going to be in town tomorrow night, and I'd love to take my favorite girl out to dinner. Will that work for you?"

I frowned. Was he actually asking? Did I have any real say in the matter? "Um, sure?"

He paused. "Okay. So I'll just text when I'm close to campus."

I started to agree, but he hung up. I stared at my phone for a minute before redialing Adrian, just in case he was worried about the weird way I'd hung up. Then I said goodnight to Gabby and returned to my own apartment to stress about what to wear.

When Gabby and I returned from the gym Friday afternoon, we headed to my apartment to mix up some protein smoothies that probably negated any calorie burn from our exercise. She walked two steps into the entry before stopping abruptly.

Luca stood, flipped off the television, and smiled.

"I wasn't expecting you till later," I said, confused.

"I missed you too," he replied, pulling me in for a kiss. Then he turned to Gabby. "Good to see you, Gabriella."

"You too. I'm going home to shower," she said, flashing me an obvious look of discomfort.

"I should shower too," I said, once she left. "I thought you were texting first."

"I decided to surprise you."

I started into my bedroom, aware that he was following me, but stopped when I spotted the dress hanging on the closet door. It was a sleeveless, floor-length silky red gown with vivid gold beading around the high neckline and a slight slit over the breasts. Damn him and his impeccable taste.

"Fresh from Italy," Luca said, startling me by how close he'd come while I was dazed by the dress. "You like?" His cocky grin told me that he already knew exactly how I felt about the dress, but I didn't want to be impolite in the face of such a gift.

"Of course I do. It's gorgeous." I stroked the fabric gently. "For tonight?"

"No, save it for the holidays. Send me a picture when you wear it, though."

"You won't be here?"

He shook his head. "I'm in the middle of some things in Italy. I'll probably move back here full time in the spring."

"I should shower," I repeated, still absorbing what he'd just told me.

"Yeah, I could go for a shower," Luca agreed, pretending he was about to slip off his shirt.

I ducked into the bathroom and pulled the door behind me, so it was only a crack open. I let the water warm up while I undressed, wincing at my sweaty reflection. "Where are we going tonight?"

"Isn't Marzetti's your favorite? I figured we'd go there."

I salivated at the thought.

"And maybe tomorrow we can try Capri's for breakfast," he continued, naming my favorite local café. "Then I have a meeting."

"Where do you plan to stay the night?" I asked, sudsing up my hair.

"In your bed, of course, ideally with you all sweaty and naked and wrapped around me."

"You can have the couch." I rinsed my hair, wrung out the excess water, then reached for my conditioner.

"Wow, you are not a forgiving person. Has anyone ever told you that?"

"No one else has done so much that needs forgiveness."

"Sounds like everyone else you know is boring. Speaking of, what have you been up to lately? Whenever I ask Lorenzo what you're up to, he tells me you're just hanging around Gabriella's apartment."

I paused halfway up the leg I was shaving and considered his words. Luca had to realize Enzo would give me the benefit of the doubt on any shady activities, so for Luca to reply on his report was definite progress. But the fact he knew I was in Gabby's apartment instead of my own…, well, that was creepy.

"So you're still spying on me?"

"I prefer to call it checking in. But why don't you two ever spend time here? And who are you talking with on the phone all evening?"

I bit down on my lip hard. Enzo probably glimpsed me

through the window and figured there was no harm reporting that I was on the phone since we both figured nosy Luca would check my phone records if he cared. But I wasn't talking on my own phone, so that would definitely raise some flags. I was grateful to be in the shower, where Luca couldn't see my face, and I could buy myself some time to lie.

Before I could craft up a decent explanation, though, Luca continued.

"Would it be possible for you to be nice to me tonight?" he asked.

"How nice?" I asked, suddenly suspicious.

He laughed. "I would prefer really nice, but I'll settle for publicly nice. You know, maybe hold my hand or even initiate a kiss or two."

"Who are we meeting for dinner?"

"No one. I just want twenty-four hours where you pretend the last ten weeks didn't happen, and then I'll go back to Italy."

I considered what he was asking, and especially since he hadn't pestered me more about the secret phone calls, it seemed doable. "Yeah, okay." I agreed.

When I finished showering, I heard the TV back on again. *Wow.* Luca had actually given me privacy to get ready for our "date." I dried off and massaged lotion onto my legs while planning out my makeup. Honestly, it would be nice to forget about the recent past with Luca and just have a nice night. Before we hated each other, we had fun together. Surely we could recreate that for one night.

In the end, we did. We put on a great show, and if I were one to write in my diary, I'd divulge that I had a good time. Being with Luca—without all the baggage—was fun and easy. And the way he gazed at only me even in a crowded room made me feel like royalty, even as I reminded myself he was only acting.

After dinner, Luca insisted we head out for a walk, even

though it was cold out. As we looped around the law school, I realized his plan.

"You want Adrian to see us, don't you?"

Luca tightened his arm around my waist and kissed my cheek. "You didn't think I'd guess who you're talking to all the time? If it's not him, it's someone else who needs to see you're not available."

"He knows, and it's just talking. I've done absolutely nothing to tarnish your precious reputation, and besides, he's not interested in me romantically anyway."

Luca turned and eyed me warily. "Your naivety used to be one of my favorite things about you," he said. "I found it endearing. Now I wonder if you're willfully oblivious just to make your life simpler."

"If I have to be nice for twenty-four hours, so do you," I reminded him. "And if you ever do anything to Adrian…"

He pressed another kiss to my forehead. "I wouldn't dream of it."

Luca slept in my bed that night, but in a purely platonic way, and only because he refused to take the couch. When I woke the next morning, he was already up and making coffee. I scrolled through some emails on my phone, not ready to leave the comfort of my bed quite yet, and then he returned.

I watched as he crossed the room, comfortably clothed in a pair of grey joggers and a white undershirt, and I thought for the millionth time how my life would be so much easier if Luca weren't ridiculously attractive in everything he wore.

"Buongiorno amore," he cooed, kissing my cheek and handing me a mug of coffee.

"Do you love me?" I blurted out, deciding it was time to call him out on his terms of endearment.

Luca laughed and backed away. "If my memory serves me correctly, it was you who said I was incapable of loving another human being, no?"

He started out of the room, leaving me to assume his answer was a no.

"Get dressed, and we'll go get breakfast. I'm meeting with your brother at one, so I don't have all day," he said.

"Your meeting is with my brother?" I said, sitting so abruptly that my coffee splashed on the sheets. "Wait, which one?"

"Don't worry about it," he replied dismissively.

I rolled my eyes, certain that meant he'd offer me no other details.

~

Adrian

I rarely answered phone calls from unfamiliar numbers, but I did that afternoon. Still, I wasn't expecting what awaited me on the other line.

"Adrian? It's Angelo Conti," the deep voice said.

My pulse instantly skyrocketed. "Is Giada okay?" There could be no other reason why he'd call me.

There was a painful pause. "I assume so. She's with Luca, so..." his voice trailed off, and I heard someone else speaking in the background. "Sorry. Look, I'm near campus today, and my father wanted me to discuss something with you. Is there a time you're free to meet?"

My relief over the confirmation that Giada was unharmed had now been replaced with concern for my own safety. "Unfortunately, I have a pretty busy day lined up, what with finals coming up and everything," I began. "Can we just discuss whatever this is over the phone?"

"No. I could swing by your apartment if that helps."

I cringed. Being alone with Angelo would be much worse.

"Well, I was going to be at the law school later today, and there's a coffee shop right across from the school, so I could meet you briefly there."

"Can you be there in an hour?"

I glanced at my watch. It was 1:15. "Yeah, that should work," I started, trying to decide how to ask exactly what we'd be discussing. But before I could, he said he'd see me then and hung up.

Shit.

I'd never been more conscious of my surroundings than I was on my walk to the coffee shop that day. I kept my hands free and out of my pockets, ready to fight off anyone coming to jump me for talking with Giada lately. The adrenaline was practically beading off me by the time I reached the coffee shop. I ducked inside quickly, then exhaled with relief. I glanced around, noting one suspicious Italian-looking guy in the corner, but no Angelo.

As I placed my order, Angelo approached from the back hall-way. He nodded and offered a half-smile, then gestured to a table by the corner where a coffee and a manila envelope were sitting, unattended.

"Sorry, had to make a phone call," he said when I joined him with my coffee. "Thanks for meeting me. I won't take up much of your time. My father asked me to give this to you," he said, sliding the envelope across the table to me.

I frowned and started to open it.

Angelo's hand darted out to stop me. "Actually, he specified for you not to look at the contents. But I can tell you that it's simply information. Confidential information."

I sighed. "Why does he want me to have it if I can't read it?"

Angelo glanced at his phone, frowning at an incoming text. He tapped out a quick response then turned back to me. "You still have contacts at the prosecutor's office, right?"

I shrugged. I hadn't spoken with anyone since they fired me, but presumably they still remembered who I was.

"My father needs this to make its way onto Jeremy Newman's desk."

"Well, you live right by there, so it seems like you'd be a more logical choice to deliver it. Or there's always the postal service…"

"This needs to arrive on his desk without Mr. Newman knowing who provided the information."

"The office accepts anonymous tips all the time."

Angelo's expression hardened. "That won't work. And the office is locked, so only someone with access to the office could get back there and make sure this ends up where it needs to be without anyone seeing it."

I didn't need to be a mind-reader to see that Angelo wasn't asking me to do this so much as telling me, but I wasn't about to get sucked back in. "I have final exams, and even if I didn't, I have no plans to return to your town any time soon. Besides, the prosecutor's office fired me. I don't have access to the office anymore."

He cocked his head to the side. "You're a likable guy. Invite one of your old friends out for lunch, go back to the office with him after to say hi to some of your old coworkers, slip away to use the bathroom and drop this on the desk. You can handle it."

I started to reiterate my plethora of legit excuses, but Angelo was focused back on his phone again. He clicked on something and then held his phone out towards me, showing me a picture of the Jaguar I'd taken for a test drive with Marco Conti back in June. "My father says your car is ready."

Angelo stared pointedly, one eyebrow raised.

"Absolutely not," I said, in my firmest voice possible. I shook my head, now too flustered to even think straight. "What kind of shit does he want me to deliver that merits a car?"

"He's a generous man if you stay on his good side."

"I need to go," I said, hoping my wobbly knees would still support me.

"Sit. Stay," Angelo ordered.

I was a grown man, with free will, in a public place, for Christ's sake. But nothing in me could will my legs to move after that scary man commanded me to stay.

"So you don't care about cars, what about my sister? Luca says you two have been rather chatty lately."

My breath caught in my throat. Giada had told me she'd be with Luca the night before. If Luca was aware we'd been talking, there was no telling what he could have done to her. "Are you threatening your own sister? Do you have any idea what he's like with her?"

Angelo bristled visibly. "No one will ever hurt my sister. Certainly not Luca. But I recall you being quite fond of her. Wouldn't you like to see Luca out of her life?"

Every rational fiber in my being told me to reiterate my refusal to help him and leave before I agreed to something stupid. But instead, I stayed.

"What do you mean?" I asked.

"You pick the day next week, make the lunch plans. I'll arrange for a car to pick you up so you can study while you ride there. Get the envelope delivered without Mr. Newman knowing where it came from, and my sister will be a single woman again, free to date whomever she chooses."

"Why should I believe you?"

"I'm a man of my word," he replied, looking offended that I'd questioned his integrity. "Without honor, a man has nothing."

I stared out the window and sipped my coffee for several minutes, acutely aware that my heart rate had probably surpassed the healthy max. I considered my options and the possibility that my instincts were leading me astray. After all, it wasn't like he was asking me to shoot someone. I was literally just delivering a packet of papers. Information couldn't hurt anyone, and besides, Jeremy Newman was a smart guy. If the documents were full of lies, he'd know.

I swallowed the lump in my throat and reached for the packet.

"I have a class until ten fifteen on Wednesday, and I need to be back on campus by three thirty. I'll set the lunch up for half past twelve."

Angelo nodded. "Not a word of any of this to Giada. I'll speak with Luca and make sure he breaks it off with her before he leaves town today."

I stood to go, leaving my coffee on the table.

Giada

I'd left my evening plans up in the air, uncertain when Luca might return or what he had in mind for the rest of his visit. Eager to hear what he discussed with my brother, I found myself in an unusual position for a Saturday afternoon—studying. Luckily, I didn't have to wait for long.

Luca knocked once before using his key to let himself in. His entitlement at simply barging annoyed me, but not enough to distract me from the fact that he was meeting with my brother.

I popped out of my seat to see if Angelo was with him, but Luca entered alone. I sunk back down onto the couch.

"Angelo couldn't even spare five minutes to say hi?"

"He had another meeting in town right after me. He said to tell you hello," Luca said, draping his jacket over the couch. "How'd you know I was with him?"

"I texted Matteo. You should know by now I don't like being kept in the dark."

Luca chuckled. "He wasn't very helpful, was he?"

"Nope. So tell me, how's my big brother?"

"He's good, I guess. Seems stressed and not as confident as I remember him."

I scrunched my forehead trying to think why that would be. "That's odd."

Luca shrugged and swung my feet out of the way so he could sit beside me on the couch. "To be fair, I'd initially asked to meet with your father when I was in town, but I wasn't too surprised when he sent Angelo instead. He's a busy man."

I stifled a yawn. A meeting with my father meant it was business-related, and as much as I hated being left out of the loop, nothing bored me more than shop talk.

"So, are you headed back to Italy soon?"

"You don't even want to know what we discussed?"

"I'm sure if it was anything remotely interesting, you'd tell me."

"I told Angelo you were still interested in Adrian."

I swiveled my head so quickly that my neck hurt. "Why would you say that?"

"It's the truth, isn't it?"

"Luca, please. We've just been talking. That's it."

Luca looked indifferent. "It doesn't matter. I already told my papà about a girl in Rome I'd like to date. Those Italian women are something else, you know," he said with a wink.

I resisted the urge to gag and punched him in the gut instead. "What is wrong with you?"

He raised his hands defensively. "Seriously? I thought you'd thank me. If you want to be my girlfriend for real, by all means then, go for it. I'll give up all other women. But if that's the case, I'll expect a little more when I visit than a kiss after dinner and thirty percent of your bed at night."

"You're an asshole."

"So which will it be? You want to be with me, or you don't?"

I swallowed, trying to decide if it was a trick. "I don't."

"Okay, then we finally agree on something."

I waited for him to say something else, but he didn't. "Really?

That's it? We just broke up? You won't stalk me anymore, won't threaten guys I go out with?"

Luca shook his head. "I assume you'll wait an appropriate amount of time before seeing someone new, but aside from that, you're a free woman. Angelo ran it by your papà and got the official stamp of approval."

"Why would my dad care?"

Luca rolled his eyes as though I were some sort of idiot, and then he startled me by kissing me roughly on the lips. "Sorry, needed one last one for the road." He stood and slipped back into his jacket. "If you change your mind, shoot me a text in the next forty-eight hours or so. Once I'm back in Italy, well, you might be too late."

I stood and followed him to the door, struggling to comprehend what had just happened.

"I'd appreciate it if you'd wait to tell Adrian till tomorrow, just so I can get out of town before you humiliate me." he said. "And if you see pictures of me with some other girl, don't go crying to papà. Remember, you're the one who wanted this break up."

My lips parted to speak, but all words left me.

"Goodbye, tesoro."

He pulled the door shut behind him, leaving me totally flummoxed.

I should've been relieved, but instead, I felt rejected. I didn't want to be chained to Luca Marino, metaphorically or otherwise, but being so easily shoved to the side, well, that was almost offensive. At least when he was still possessively preventing me from seeing anyone else, I could pretend it was because he truly wanted to be with me.

Now I had no choice but to accept the obvious. Luca Marino was a bastard who'd simply wanted to control my life just because he could. What other kind of man would call a girl his "treasure" while dumping her?

"Fuck him," I said aloud, feeling more confident already.

Then, remembering it was Saturday night, I called Gabriella. She answered on the first ring.

"Luca just broke up with me," I said.

"Oh my God!" She paused only for a moment. "Should I come over now? Are we gorging ourselves on comfort food and coconut rum, or…"

"We're going clubbing," I declared.

There was a lengthy silence before she answered this time. "Okay, I'll be down at nine."

I hung up and smiled. Oh, how I'd missed the single life.

⌇

Adrian

The day after my clandestine meeting with Angelo, Giada called me. The second her name popped up on the caller ID instead of Gabriella's, I knew Angelo had kept his end of the bargain. A large part of me had hoped he wouldn't have, and that I'd then have an excuse not to perform my end of the bargain. But hearing Giada was happy and relaxed gave me the confidence I needed to be able to follow through with it all.

I'd followed the plan precisely as Angelo outlined it with one major change. Certain I'd be too nervous to eat lunch let alone make casual conversation knowing I would have to drop off the envelope after lunch, I arrived at the office a little early. I told the receptionist who I was meeting for lunch and then went on back to say hello to some other coworkers, casually depositing the envelope on Jeremy's desk without being noticed.

As I relaxed in the car on the way back to campus, I quickly texted Angelo. Within seconds, my phone rang.

"Never text that sort of information," he barked.

"What? All I said was 'done.' One word, no information." I scowled alone in the backseat, having thought the prick was calling me to express gratitude.

"What is done, exactly?" he asked.

"What do you mean? I did what you said. You know what is done."

"Exactly. I do know, and anyone who read that text would know that I know." He sighed loudly into the phone. "Just don't fucking text anymore, okay? If you're going to work for me, then—"

"I am never going to work for you. Our business is concluded. And by the way, you're welcome!"

Angelo laughed now. "My sister must drive you insane. I'll never understand what you two have in common."

Before I could respond to what I assumed was yet another insult, he continued.

"Delete that text. And thanks."

I gave my phone the finger as I hung up, but then relaxed against the leather seat and gazed out the window. The sky was grey, its dreariness seemingly extending for miles. While I should have felt celebratory, my mood matched my environment. Sure, I'd achieved my goal. I'd gotten Giada away from Luca. She was now happy and safe, and theoretically, I could now ask her out again.

Not a day had gone by since we broke up that I hadn't thought about Giada. I missed her laugh, missed her kisses, even missed the sassy way she'd refuse to go along with anything I ever suggested. I strongly suspected that whatever happened, I'd never date another woman as beautiful, fun, or willfully oblivious to reality as Giada.

The problem was that last part. As much as I believed her family would never hurt *her, I* would always be fair game. Unless Giada suddenly woke up and acknowledged the true nature of her family business, I'd have to be a fool to become romantically involved with her again.

Unfortunately, where Giada was concerned, I always acted the part of the fool. All she had to do was bat those ridiculously long black lashes of hers, and I'd jump before she ever even asked. That left me with one option—avoiding face-to-face interactions with her at all costs. Luckily, my next two weeks would be consumed with writing an appellate brief for my legal writing class, and then I was returning to Chicago for the holidays.

CHAPTER 7

Adrian

The next two weeks passed uneventfully, but I'd still been nearly as tense about Angelo's "favor" as my appellate brief. As I stepped off the plane in Chicago, relief flooded me. Being back home for Thanksgiving conjured all kinds of warm fuzzy feelings but mostly the promise of a simple, stress-free holiday. I didn't have to think about contracts or cases. I didn't have to think about Giada, or dating, or anything remotely romantic. I could also safely push any thoughts or concerns about the mafia out of my mind.

All I needed to do the next few days was catch up with my family and eat turkey. It would be divine.

On Wednesday night, after a pizza dinner at home, my sister April and I went to a local bar to catch up with some of our old high school friends. After the year I'd had, such a normal social outing felt so simple and easy, and that was exactly what I needed.

As we headed home, April teased me about the wishy washy response I'd given to everyone who asked if I was dating anyone.

My go-to response had been "not exactly," which was completely true. I'd elaborated to one person that it had been an on-again, off-again relationship but that it was probably off for good.

"What's wrong with my answer? It was accurate."

"You're either dating her, or you're not."

"Well, I'm not."

"But you want to be," my sister insisted.

"No."

"Then why not just tell people you're single?"

I frowned.

April laughed. "Look, it sounds like you still have feelings for Giada, and from everything you've said, it seems like she's still interested in you. So, I guess what I'm trying to understand is why you don't just give it another try."

"Giada is complicated," I said, glad there was such a perfect word to describe everything she brought into my life.

"So?"

"I'm just not sure I can handle another round with her. Every time she goes back to her old boyfriend, she leaves me more tangled up in her web than before. And her family is…" I shook my head, unable to find a word to describe them. Telling my sister my would-be girlfriend came from a family of mafia masterminds didn't seem wise.

"Well, I'm just saying. You only live once, and if you want something, you have to go for it."

"Gee, thanks." I said, laughing at the sisterly advice.

We played a friendly game of football with the extended family the next morning while the food cooked, and then we all made friendly banter throughout the meal. It all felt so normal that I didn't even notice anything was strange until after dinner, when my mother meekly announced she was too tired to join us all at the movies as was our usual tradition. My father assured us it was simply exhaustion from all the cooking, so we left without her. We should have known better.

The next morning, we'd just sat down to breakfast, with the news playing in the background so we could mock the people frantically attempting Black Friday shopping. Everything about the moment was so ordinary, and yet I knew it would stand out in my mind for years to come.

My mother made small talk, asking my sister and me both how we slept, and then my father calmly said they had some news to share. The way he placed his hand on my mother's shoulder instantly signaled it wasn't good news.

"I've had a recurrence," my mother said calmly. "During my last mammogram, they identified a suspicious spot in the tissue lining the chest wall, and it was cancer. I had surgery to remove the new growth at the start of the month, and it was enormously successful, with clear margins and everything. They started weekly radiation treatments this Monday, but it's just a precaution. Everything looks good."

The bite I'd been chewing grew heavy against my tongue, but I was sure I'd forgotten how to swallow. My sister burst into tears and flew out of her chair to hug my mother while I just sat there, stunned. After so many years of clean scans, I'd grown complacent, accustomed to the good reports. I assumed the scary C word was entirely in our past.

Somehow, we finished breakfast, and then my father dragged my sister and me out to help him get a Christmas tree while my mom rested. We spent the afternoon gorging ourselves on leftovers and decorating the tree, with festive Christmas playing in the background. It was all so normal that I wanted to pretend the conversation from earlier was just a bad dream.

Of course, it wasn't.

My mind was still spinning that evening when Giada's personal ring tone blared from my phone. I wasn't sure if I needed a distraction or comfort, but either way, Giada was the only person who could make me feel better. I tried to mask my anxiety when I answered, still undecided if I'd tell her the bad news or just let her ramble on in her usual way and distract me. Apparently, I failed.

"What's wrong?"

I hesitated but then realized it was stupid to keep this from her. "My mom's cancer is back."

"Oh my God. Adrian, I'm so sorry!"

"Thanks."

"What have the doctors said so far?"

I caught her up, reiterating that the prognosis was excellent, more for my own reassurance than hers. But it was the truth. The recurrence was local, which was good. Apparently the fact that it took this long to grow enough for detection meant it was slow growing, but obviously, any recurrence was a bad thing.

Giada listened to everything I said, then promised to add my mom to her prayers. I figured that counted for something, since the prayers of someone who attended mass every single week ought to be worth more than the prayers of the rest of us sinners.

"I'm sorry there's nothing else I can do to help," she continued. "You don't…well, I'm assuming you don't want me to fly out there to keep you company, but I will if there's even a chance that would make you feel better."

I sighed, certain she spoke the truth. If a friend or relative needed Giada, no matter how busy she was, she'd drop everything and rush to their side. That's just the type of girl she was. And what kind of man did that make me, essentially punishing her for her loyalty to her family?

I needed to come clean.

"I really appreciate the offer, Gia. It means a lot to me."

"But you're not going to accept because you're avoiding me like the plague," she finished for me.

I had to laugh at her astute observation.

"It's alright. I didn't mean to make you feel guilty. If I were you, I wouldn't come near me either. I'm T-R-O-U-B-L-E."

I was laughing harder at the way she spelled the adjective that certainly did describe her well. "Gia, I'm sorry."

"You don't have to explain, Adrian. I had a chance to be with you, and I blew it. And then you offered to help me get out of that mess with Luca because you're a nice guy, but you have zero interest in subjecting yourself to torture all over again by dating me."

"I've enjoyed talking with you lately," I said lamely.

"You are an amazing friend, Adrian. So if that's the only capacity in which I can have you in my life, I am more than happy to take it. I love our phone calls. But you can be my friend in person, too. I promise not to seduce you."

"Everything you do seduces me," I admitted. "You can't help it. You could just sit there with a bag on your head, and I'd still want you."

"Hmm. I'm not sure what that says about me," she teased.

"I'm serious, Gia. I never got over you, and I don't want to be just friends with you. But nothing has changed. We never resolved anything, and I don't want to get back together with you just to start fighting again."

She was quiet for a minute. "I guess what I should say then is that you were right."

I held my breath. For her to finally accept the truth about her father would be huge. Once she found out about Luca, I'd hoped it would only be a matter of time, but I wasn't sure. This could change everything. I felt myself grinning widely as she continued.

"You warned me that Luca was trouble, and I didn't listen. And while I don't know how aware my dad was about the details of the Marino's business, the fact that he even does business with people like them is a bad reflection on his ability to judge a person's character."

She paused. "Family has always been important to me, and I think they always will be. Maybe we could agree that I'll accept that they aren't perfect, and you'll try not to insinuate that my family members are criminals just because they associate with them."

I couldn't pretend I wasn't disappointed at her speech, but I supposed it was better than nothing. "I could live with that, assuming you don't expect me to hang around your hometown ever again."

"Deal," she quickly agreed. "Honestly, it bothered me how close my brothers were with Luca. I hate how they all talk down to me and keep me in the dark about everything. I'm not sure if I ever told you this, but I appreciated how honest you were with me. Even if I didn't like what you were saying, I always liked that I could trust you to tell me everything. It's like every other man in my life is constantly working deals behind my back. It's offensive, even if it's only because they assume I don't care."

I smiled. Sometimes, Giada's naivety bordered on obtuse, but no one would ever think she was stupid. Her observation was spot on about the other men in her life hiding the truth from her at all costs. They acted that way out of a misguided desire to protect her. They didn't necessarily think she couldn't handle the truth, only that she shouldn't have to worry about it at all.

Giada and I stayed on the phone until my sister called me downstairs for dinner. I had to admit. It was good talking to her.

My first day back on campus, I took Gia out for sushi. She sashayed out of her apartment wearing a short dress that resembled a suit jacket and glossy black boots that came up past her knees. I felt my jaw drop and other parts of my body reacted as well.

She beamed, then winked. I wasn't sure if proper protocol for a first-date-with-the-ex demanded I greet her with a hug or a kiss, so I played it safe, leaning in for an awkward side hug.

"You look phenomenal, as always," I said. "But won't you get cold?" There was a several-inch gap between her boots and hemline where bare skin peeked out.

Gia pursed her bold red lips and shook her head. "Not unless we're eating dinner outside."

I cringed. "That wasn't the right thing to say, was it? God, and I'm completely underdressed."

"You look dapper," she said, eying my dark denim and deep grey Henley. She looped her arm around mine and started towards my car.

"I'm sorry. I didn't expect to be nervous. This shouldn't feel like a first date."

Her warm smile calmed me. "If this is a date, you definitely don't need to be nervous. You already know I like you."

I tried not to dwell too much on the "if" and instead just focused on the company. There was no denying that Gia and I had great chemistry. She made me laugh, and there were no awkward lulls in the conversation. She smiled at me the entire meal, touching my leg or stroking my arm often.

With how much we'd talked over break, I trusted that things were over with Luca, that this wouldn't be just some rebound fling for her. But I still wasn't sure where we stood.

"I really like spending time with you," I admitted after paying the bill. I wrapped my arm around her as we walked to the car, under the guise of needing to keep her warm.

"I love being with you, too," she said, tweaking my words just enough to make me stop in my tracks.

"Gia, I…" I paused, having no idea how to finish my sentiment. I wanted to know what we were doing and if it was the right move. I wanted a guarantee that this was for real, that we could work together like real partners this time without her leaving me for a sociopath when her family butted in between us.

Her dark eyes peered up at me, seemingly understanding everything I was saying. "What are we doing?" she asked.

I nodded, and she laughed shyly.

"I don't know, but it feels right, doesn't it? I know why you're hesitating, and I wouldn't trust me again yet either," she continued. "I let you down, and we never really worked everything out before, but…I feel like I'm older now. Wiser, maybe even."

She giggled again, but I smiled. She was wiser now. Or at least, less naïve.

"What do you want?" I asked.

"Right now? You," she replied with a mischievous look in her eyes. "But I think we should take it slow this time."

I exhaled the breath I'd been holding. Yes, we could do that.

I drove back to her apartment and walked her to the exterior door before releasing her hand.

"Thank you for a lovely evening, Adrian Patras."

"The pleasure was all mine, Giada Francesca," I replied. I hesitated, then leaned in slowly. I watched the corners of her mouth curl up before she bent forward to meet me.

Our lips came together lightly, but we both lingered there. After a moment, I deepened the kiss, raising my hand to the side of her hair, feeling her silky smooth hair beneath my fingers as the warmth of her mouth welcomed me in the most dizzying of ways.

Giada was the one to end the kiss, but I didn't blame her. Another minute and we'd both be tempted to renege on our plan to take it slow.

"Good night," she whispered with a wink, disappearing into her building.

Giada

*B*ack at school, life was good. Adrian was swamped with studying, so I didn't see him as often as I'd like, but the mere awareness that I was back in his good graces was enough to satiate me until we could spend more time together. And when we were together, it was nice. Better than nice, really.

Despite pledging to take it slowly, we didn't so much start dating again as launch into an actual relationship. We weren't quite back to how we used to be before the breakup, but I suspected the hesitation I sensed from Adrian was more related to his stress about his mom than hang-ups about our relationship.

The next weekend, he was particularly tense. I'd convinced him to enjoy a brief Saturday night study break to eat dinner with his favorite Italian and then burn off the calories in bed. As we snuggled together after, he was so quiet that I wondered if he'd fallen asleep. But when I slowly inched away to gaze up at his face, he was tensely staring at the ceiling.

"You okay? You look…stressed," I said, wishing there was a stronger word to capture what I saw on his face.

"Yes."

His one-word response didn't strike me as a good sign. "Can I help you study?"

Adrian frowned, as though he'd forgotten he still had two finals. Then he shook his head. "No, I should try to get some sleep. Are you staying?"

I rolled on top of him, relieved when his arms wrapped around me to hold me in place. "I could stay, but I won't be offended if you think you'll get more rest without me here."

The crease at the bridge of his nose deepened. "I think I sleep better when you are here."

I couldn't help but smile at that. "Okay then. Any specific services I can offer to lull you to sleep?" I teased, wiggling my hips against his groin.

He didn't even crack a smile. I scooted off of him and sat up, tugging a tee shirt over my head.

"What's wrong? Is it final exams?"

A look of confusion washed over his face, and then he shook his head. "No. I was thinking about my mother."

"I'm sorry Adrian. How is she doing?"

"Good. She's responding well to the radiation. I mean, it's making her tired, but that's it so far, and she just has a couple more weeks of treatment."

"That's wonderful." I said. I was relieved until I realized he still looked tenser than the first time I left him alone with my dad. "So what's bothering you?"

"When my dad called earlier to give me the update, he just mentioned that finances are tight. Apparently, there was some lifetime cap on their health insurance benefits, and the first round of cancer treatments maxed that out, so they switched to this new policy with an insanely high deductible."

Adrian pinched the top of his nose then rubbed his eyes before continuing.

"I guess between helping my sister and me with school and paying out of pocket for all the bills for the monitoring over the years, they have nothing left in savings. He said I shouldn't worry, that he'll find a way to help with tuition. I don't want them taking out another loan on the house or digging themselves further into debt. But I also can't imagine working many hours myself while also taking classes. Law school is too intense for that, at least this year."

"You can take out student loans."

"Yeah, and I have. But I guess I need more."

"Maybe there is some temporary job you could do over spring break?"

He shrugged. "Maybe."

I hesitated before saying the last part. "I could loan you some money."

"No."

There was no wiggle room in his terse response, so I let it drop.

Long after he fell asleep, though, I was awake, pondering his dilemma. Never having lacked for money, I probably should've taken it for granted, but instead, I'd always felt quite the opposite. To me, money represented security, opportunity, and choice. I couldn't fathom having to base all of my major decisions in life on what I could afford rather than what I preferred. Adrian was such a hard worker and had sacrificed so much to get into law school. It wasn't fair for him to have to forfeit his potential good grades by spending all his time working instead of studying.

I'd been waiting for an opportunity to show him how much I loved him and how sorry I was for the way things had ended between us over the summer. Maybe this was my chance.

CHAPTER 8

Giada

The following week, as Enzo steered the car up past the gate, I could barely contain my excitement. It hadn't been long since my last visit to my childhood home, but so much had changed in my life. I no longer had the anxiety of final exams hanging over me, for starters. Not that I'd really pushed myself too hard with the studying, but now I had absolutely no obligations until school resumed in January. And even then, I'd be in my last semester of college ever.

Even better, the last time I'd been home, I was single, and now, I had Adrian. Well, I didn't have him with me, per se, but he was officially mine again. Hopefully, that fact would quell the jokes and comments from my extended family about my ruined relationship with Luca.

When I pushed my way through the thick front door, silence greeted me. I struggled to hide my disappointment over the absence of an enthusiastic welcome. I dropped my purse on the table in the foyer then walked towards the left staircase, but stopped when I heard a distant noise. The door to my dad's office was closed, so I knocked tentatively. Suddenly, there was an enormous commotion within the room, and after a moment, my uncle Vinny opened the door just wide enough to peek out.

Vinny's tense expression relaxed when he spotted me. "Giada!" he greeted me, squeezing out the door and pulling it shut behind him.

He tugged me to him in a hug. "How are you, bellissima? You are early, no?"

I shrugged, then startled at a thunk behind me. I turned to see Enzo appearing with my bags. He mouthed an apology to Vinny.

"Is my dad in there?" I asked.

Vinny hesitated, glancing at the door uncertainly. I was about to ask what was going on, when the door opened, and my dad stepped out, leaving the door open to reveal a dozen other men in the office with him.

"Giada Francesca, how are you my darling?" my dad asked, kissing both of my cheeks then hugging me tightly.

As each of the other men filed out of his office, greeted me similarly, then stepped back, I had to laugh. "Your office is like a clown car! How many guys do you have hidden in there?"

My dad smiled and gazed at the other men. They were all uncles or cousins of mine, or guys we referred to as uncles or cousins because they were such good friends, but technically weren't related to me at all.

"We were just discussing the family business," he said. "Your mother is out with the other ladies, and we will have dinner together later. Now, I have just another small matter to finish up, so why don't you catch up with Angelo for a bit?"

My brother made no attempt to hide his annoyance at having been delegated to entertain me.

"It's alright. I can go unpack, and we can talk later," I assured him, starting up the stairs. Still, Angelo followed.

We made small talk for a few minutes, covering my final exams, his dating life or lack thereof, and Matteo's whereabouts.

Then Angelo brought up the family trip to Italy. They were leaving the day after Christmas, but I'd already said I was not going.

"I've spent loads of time in Italy this past year," I reminded him. "I don't want to go back yet."

"Because of Luca?"

I nodded. I could pretend it was the long flight, but no one would believe me anyway. Italy was gorgeous, and Palermo was significantly warmer than Connecticut, so were it not for the fact that everything there reminded me of Luca, I would definitely go.

"He's still there," Angelo said.

I wrinkled my nose, certain that didn't make me more likely to go. "Is his new girlfriend with him?"

Angelo frowned but didn't answer.

It didn't matter anyway. "Well, I'm back with Adrian now. I'm going to visit him in Chicago for the new year."

Angelo's eyes widened, so clearly it was news to him. Not wanting to allow him time to protest my plans, I kept talking.

"His mom had breast cancer a while ago, and then she was in remission, but now she's had a recurrence. Everything is going well, but apparently their insurance sucks. So, Adrian has been super stressed about how to help his parents with their medical bills and how to pay for his law school."

"Has he tried working?"

I rolled my eyes. "Law school is more than a full-time job. It's not like undergrad. And even if he wanted to work, they have all these rules restricting your ability to work the first year. The only jobs they allow are for academic-related things like office assistant or tutoring, and it's not like he'd make enough money tutoring to cover tuition."

Angelo's expression changed sharply. "Is he familiar with Judge Roberts? I just read that he was going to be teaching a trial procedure class at the law school next semester."

I shrugged. I didn't even know the names of Adrian's current professors, let alone ones at the school he didn't even have.

"Ask him for me, okay?"

I nodded, then we went downstairs to join the crowd as the ladies returned home from their shopping mission.

~

Adrian

The one benefit to a cancer diagnosis is the newfound appreciation of the little things, like time with your family. So even though jetting to Florida with Giada would've been a great way to ring in the new year, spending the entire Christmas break with my family was a no-brainer. Giada was flying in for a visit, and I was determined to make it a fun, romantic week with her…while still clocking quality time with my family.

I was getting ready to leave for the airport to pick up Giada when a call came in from an unknown number. Not sure if it was something related to her flight, I answered immediately. To my surprise, it was Giada's father.

Marco Conti launched into the conversation politely enough, asking about my Christmas, the weather, and my finals. But all of my past experiences with Mr. Conti convinced me he wasn't calling to shoot the breeze. He wanted something. Still, when he inquired about my mom's health, even going so far as to ask which hospital was providing her treatments, I felt a little less wary of his meddling.

As it turned out, he was only worried about Giada. Despite her being a perfectly capable twenty-one-year-old woman, Mr. Conti treated her like a child. He paid his workers to drive her around campus, monitor her behavior, and serve as bodyguards when necessary. So I supposed it shouldn't come as a shock to me that he was wary about her flying alone to spend time with me in an unfamiliar city. I assured him I would personally collect her from the airport and that I wouldn't be leaving her alone at any point. Thankfully, that seemed to reassure him.

"The situation at the docks has gotten almost untenable as of late," he confessed. "We've seen an influx of illegal shipments, and I'm making more than my fair share of enemies. My greatest fear has always been Giada suffering because of my business," he said.

I said nothing.

I was certain Mr. Conti was in the mafia, but equally certain that wasn't something I should tell him I knew. Still, he had to realize that choosing a life of crime would jeopardize his daughter's safety. It wasn't like he couldn't have seen these risks coming.

"Well, she certainly won't be in danger because of anything *I* do," I said, hoping to reassure him while also reminding him that my lifestyle wasn't the one he should worry about.

"I'm glad to hear it," he said. "Hey, Giada mentioned you might be looking for a part-time job with a flexible schedule. There's a judge that we know who I hear is teaching some trial prep course next semester. I checked in with him, and he said he hasn't found a teaching assistant yet, but planned to accept applications once the semester began. From the sound of things, he's just looking for someone to do some research and do some basic office work for a few hours a week. I can't imagine that'll cover much of your expenses, but every little bit counts, eh?"

"Uh, yeah," I agreed. I had considered looking for similar positions, but most of the open ones went to upperclassmen. "I doubt I'm the most qualified candidate, though."

"Maybe. But since he hasn't officially advertised the position yet, you'd be well suited to slip in as the only candidate if you sent a résumé on over to him."

As amazing as the position sounded, I couldn't forget the fact that less than a year ago, Mr. Conti had secured what seemed to be an ideal internship for me, only to get me fired when I refused to weasel my way into confidential records.

"Well, give Giada my best, and I'll send you the Judge's university email address in case you're interested. I wouldn't mention I recommended you apply or anything if you do contact him. Better to just wow him with your own skills."

He hung up before I could reply. I had a good half hour before I needed to leave for the airport, so I did some online research on the guy. He was Jewish, not Catholic, and didn't look Italian. Based on his resume, I had a hard time believing he was affiliated with the mob in any way. He seemed like a hardworking, smart, and good guy. He was listed as teaching the trial prep classes for third-year law students, and since his actual students wouldn't be eligible to assist him for ethical reasons, my only competition would be second-year students. It would be an ideal position, giving me some good experience and a boost for my resume when I began hunting for summer jobs.

Before I had a chance to second guess myself, I typed out a quick, professional sounding email to him. I mentioned that as a first-year student, I had more availability than upperclassmen. I also threw in a line about how my mother's cancer had helped me mature and focus on my work. I figured it never hurt to play the sympathy card. I ended the email by volunteering my services as his assistant for the semester and an offer to send over my resume and transcript.

Then all that was left to do was wait.

Fortunately, with Giada in town, waiting was a breeze. Showing her around Chicago was a blast, and she still got along beautifully with my family. We knocked out all the major touristy activities the first four days, then hung around my house the fifth day, exhausted from walking too many museums over a short period of time.

Giada excused herself around lunch to talk with her parents, whom I knew were visiting Italy at the time. So, I took the opportunity to check my email.

"Yes!" I exclaimed, stomping my foot with glee as I read the first email.

My parents both came into the room, both of them grinning before I even spoke.

"Fantastic news," I said. "I emailed a new professor about maybe serving as his teaching assistant next semester, and he seems interested. He asked for my transcript and résumé."

"That's great," my mom agreed. "But I didn't know you were looking for a job. I thought you were too busy."

"This will be flexible," I assured her.

"Is this the one you said was a longshot because you're a first year?" my dad wanted to know.

"Yep. Just goes to show that it never hurts to try." I sighed happily. It wasn't a sure thing yet, but I had a solid transcript and thanks to my previous internships, a great résumé. The biggest obstacle for me getting this job would've been my lack of experience in law school, but if that were a dealbreaker, he wouldn't have asked for more information.

"We have some good news too," my mom said.

"Oh yeah?"

She nodded. "Some anonymous donor paid off our balance with the hospital."

"What? People actually do that sort of thing?"

"Apparently so," my dad said. "We tried to find out a name or at least an address to send a thank you, but the hospital was firm about their confidentiality policy."

"Huh." I swiveled back and forth in my chair, grinning so widely that it hurt. Sometimes, life really did go in our favor.

Or did it?

I paused mid-spin of my chair. All of it sounded a little too good to be true. "Did they say how many patient balances were paid off?"

"No," my dad said. "I was curious too. The lady I spoke with in the billing department did divulge that the person hadn't paid all of the outstanding balances, which makes sense. That would've been a steep debt to repay."

I frowned. "How did they choose which accounts to pay off? Surely it wasn't random."

My dad shrugged. "My guess is the donor has some personal experience with breast cancer and wanted to help a patient with that specific disease. Because you're right, how else would they choose who to help?" He shook his head. "Either way, what a load off my chest!"

I nodded and smiled, but once my parents left the room again, I replayed my discussion with Marco in my mind. I had definitely told him which hospital was treating my mother. So it couldn't all be coincidental. The only true mystery was what Marco Conti expected in return.

Giada

Gabby and I met for a boozy brunch at the end of the first week back at school. For Senior year, we'd meticulously planned our schedules to avoid Friday classes, so mimosas and muffins were definitely going to be a regular occurrence.

"It's too bad Adrian couldn't join us," Gabby mused as we waited for the check. "He always is fun to hang out with."

"Apparently, law school is an everyday sort of thing," I replied, wrinkling my nose. I admired Adrian's dedication and work ethic, but nothing about law school appealed to me. It sounded tedious, boring, and stressful. "He'll have even less time for me now because he got that job he wanted working for one of the professors."

"That's cool. Isn't he busy enough, though?" Gabby slipped her credit card to the waiter before I could even offer. "Is he trying to work himself to death?"

"I hear some people have to work to earn money," I said cheekily.

My friend grinned. "What's next on our grueling agenda? Manicures or shopping?"

I gazed at my nails, quickly confirming they could use some love. But my phone rang before I could answer her. It was my brother.

I answered quickly, confused as to why he'd be calling me. "Angelo?"

"Giada," he said, relief evident in his voice.

"What's wrong?"

"Nothing. I just checked for you at your apartment and you weren't here."

"Gabby and I went to brunch."

"Lorenzo should be with you."

I sighed. "I don't need a driver on campus."

"Giada, this is not a good week to assert your independence. There has been some difficulty at the shipyard this week, and our father is more worried than usual about keeping all of us safe. It would mean a lot to me if you could just take some extra precautions for a while and keep Lorenzo around when you're out of the apartment. Please?"

I was so accustomed to Angelo barking orders at me that his polite request was unsettling. Still, if he was going to show me the respect to ask, I wasn't going to discourage him by refusing, even if the concept of needing security on campus was utterly ridiculous.

"Sure. I'll talk to Enzo."

"Thank you. I'll talk with you later."

"Wait! Didn't you just say you're here in town?" I couldn't imagine my brother would drive all this way and not want to at least briefly see me.

"Yes, but unfortunately, I have a packed day, so I can't stick around. Enjoy your brunch."

He disconnected before I could question him further.

～

Adrian

I met Angelo at the same coffee shop as before, ignoring the sickly feeling that it was starting to become a routine. Luckily, now I wasn't scared. Maybe that was foolish, but I was confident he wanted something from me and didn't simply plan to beat me.

I arrived at the shop early, reading cases from my Constitutional Law hornbook while I waited. I sensed Angelo's presence the moment he swept in the door.

He ordered a drink, then greeted me with a thin, forced smile before sitting down.

"Giada says you study incessantly," he said, nodding at the textbook.

I shrugged. "That's pretty much the essence of law school."

He grimaced. "Well, congratulations on the new job. My sister mentioned you were hired."

I nodded. "I'm sure your father had nothing to do with that?"

"He didn't. He has some connections to most of the other judges in the district, but Judge Roberts is a wildcard. That's not to say we weren't hoping you'd get the job."

I sighed. "There's no opportunity for me to access his grade-book or frame a student for cheating or any other shenanigans like that you might have in mind, so I'm sorry if you've wasted a trip here for nothing."

"Shenanigans are not my style," he said, shaking his head distastefully. "But we would love a little more information on the man. Who is Judge Roberts? What are his passions? Where did he come from? What makes him tick?"

I raised an eyebrow.

"He's been assigned to a case of interest to our family. As you get to know him, we'd appreciate if you let us know what you've learned."

I swallowed. What he was asking didn't sound illegal or even harmful, so I was probably misunderstanding. "Like, you want to know his favorite food?"

Angelo rolled his eyes. "Anything you learn might be helpful."

"I'm not snooping or spying on him."

"No one is asking you to."

I blew out a sigh then sipped my coffee. "I wondered what you'd ask in exchange for paying off that hospital bill."

He cocked his head to the side. "I'm not sure I know what you're talking about." His voice was level and so void of emotion that I shuddered.

"And let me guess. You'd rather I not mention this meeting to Giada, right?"

"I wouldn't, but if you want to pick a fight with her, then sure. By all means, let her know you've been meeting with her brother in secret." He paused, casually sipping his drink. "That reminds me, though. While we were in Italy, there were some problems at the shipyard, and everything came to a head a few days ago. My father is concerned that some bad people might want to come after our family. We don't have any specific threats, so nothing to warrant pulling Giada out of school, but I spoke with her and asked her to stay near Lorenzo. I would appreciate if you could look out for her as well."

"I always do."

"You're a good man." He nodded and reached across the table to shake my hand. My inner politeness won out over my rational thinking, and I accepted his hand. Luckily, he then promptly left.

I didn't hear anything more from Angelo for another week. I settled into my new schedule, helping Judge Roberts for an hour or two most days. As I worked, I made a few notes about him. I recorded the type of tea he liked, the hours he typically kept, and the titles of a few of the books he kept in his small office in the law school. We didn't spend much time chatting, but when he did mention his own law school days, favorite sports teams, or his aging labradoodle's skin condition, I recorded that as well.

The following Thursday, Marco Conti phoned me in the afternoon, leaving a cryptic message on my voice mail. When I returned the call, he asked me about the various things I'd learned about the judge, and I shared my notes. Though Marco praised my efforts, I wasn't surprised when he said he wanted more.

"I'm not sure there is much more I can tell you. We don't spend much time together, and he doesn't share much about his personal life."

"Well, he's married, right? With two daughters?"

"I think so," I said, gritting my teeth and telling myself Marco would never hurt someone's children.

"What about his mistress?"

"I doubt he has one. He seems like a good guy."

"No one is without secrets, Adrian. I need you to find his, and soon. He's been assigned to a case involving some bad men, and if the case goes to trial with him as the judge, he could be in grave danger. Like you said, he's a good man. I don't want to see him get hurt. I also don't want to see his career fall apart when he has so much potential. If you could find just one tidbit of information that might be used to encourage him to recuse himself from the case, well, that would be better for everyone involved."

"You want to blackmail Judge Roberts?" I said, unable to hide the incredulity in my voice.

Mr. Conti sighed loudly. "I'm offended that you don't know me better by now, Adrian. Of course, I don't want to blackmail anyone. And I'm also not asking you to trick a man into having an affair. I'm only asking you to find some information out about the one we all know he's having."

He paused. "Giada tells me your mother has her last couple of rounds of radiation coming up. Does your new job pay well enough to cover those treatments?"

Nausea washed over me. "Giada is coming over soon. I should go," I lied, hanging up.

What had I gotten myself into?

CHAPTER 9

Giada

My excitement about Adrian's new job faded fast. Between classes, studying, and his indentured servitude for Professor Roberts, Adrian never had time for me. He worked Friday night, then studied all day Saturday. He promised to make it up to me by taking me to dinner Saturday night before a party we'd agreed to attend.

When the time came for him to meet me at my apartment for dinner though, Adrian was a no show.

My phone rang seconds after I disconnected the call right as it went to voice mail.

"Adrian!" I answered the phone already in full drama mode. "I don't like being stood up. Are you dead?"

"Shit, no. I'm so sorry Giada. I'm just leaving the law school. I was with Judge Roberts, and then I got started on a project for him, and I lost track of time."

"It's Saturday night."

"I know. Babe, I'm sorry. I'll be at your place in ten minutes."

"We've already missed our dinner reservations, so you might

as well go home to change first. Enzo can drive me to your place so we can ride to the party together."

I hung up and sighed. When I was with Luca, he'd stand me up for work "emergencies" all the time. But it was definitely the first time Adrian had blown me off. And for what? A part-time job that barely paid more than working as a barista? *Ouch.*

I turned to face myself in the jeweled floor-length mirror. It was gaudy and gauche but reminded me of my childhood trips to Italy, when I was obsessed with Venetian glass. My hair was still pristine, glossy, and smoothly styled into long loose waves. My makeup, however, was a mess. Apparently, I'd broken out in a sweat on account of all the pacing I'd done, and my lipstick was all but gone thanks to my nervous lip-licking. Since my dinner plans were now off, though, I might as well eat a bite before remedying that issue.

I alternated bites of granola bar with apple slices and then remembered I needed to call Enzo. Right as I dialed, there was a knock at the door. I opened without checking, certain it was either Enzo or Adrian. Instead, I was face-to-face with Luca.

He grinned widely and brushed past me into the apartment. Alessio lingered in the hall behind him.

"Hello?" Enzo's voice on the phone startled me.

"Sorry, I need to call you back," I said, turning to my unwelcomed guests. "Er, actually, can you come pick me up and take me to Adrian's?"

He paused a little too long. "Isn't Luca there?"

I sighed and hung up.

"No, no, no." I said to Luca.

He chuckled, making no attempt to hide his eyes' roaming my body. "Really? Because that dress screams yes, yes, yes."

"I'm meeting Adrian in a few minutes. I can uber, or you can drive me."

Luca frowned. "Change of plans. Your papà is concerned

about your safety. It seems he pissed off the wrong people with some shipping mishap at the docks."

That must've been what Angelo had mentioned.

"He wants you to come home for a week or two till it blows over."

I rolled my eyes, but it occurred to me Luca would never leave me alone. So I texted Adrian instead, begging him to come get me right away.

"I have classes, so that isn't happening. You guys will all just need to back off for a few more months until I graduate, and then I can move far, far away from all this craziness."

"Like to Chicago?" he asked. "Kinda cold there, wasn't it?"

I ignored him and went into my bathroom to reapply my makeup. A few minutes later, the commotion outside my bedroom alerted me that Adrian had arrived.

I scurried out, suddenly concerned Alessio would mess with Adrian, but literally slammed into his chest. He held on to me for a moment, then walked us both into my bedroom, shutting and locking the door behind him.

"What the fuck?"

I sighed and plopped onto the bed. "They just showed up."

"They? I just saw Luca."

Alessio must have left. Or maybe he was sitting in the car so it didn't get towed. "Luca said my dad was worried about my safety."

"Yeah, your dad mentioned something to me as well."

"When did you talk to my dad?"

A flicker of panic crossed his face. "Last week. Sorry I forgot to mention it. He was calling to check in on my mom, which seemed nice."

"Well, he's a nice guy," I said pointedly.

Adrian nodded meekly. "So about Luca?"

"Yeah, I don't know. I say we just go to the party as planned."

"And leave him here?"

"Sure. Let me grab some stuff, assuming it's okay if I stay over at your place?"

"Of course," he said, grinning.

Luca was lounged on my couch watching TV when we returned. He barely glanced up at me until I cleared my throat impatiently.

"I'm leaving now and won't be back tonight, so you can go." I didn't specify where I was going, but the way Adrian stood mere centimeters away from me, Luca could probably guess.

Luca switched off the TV and stood, turning directly to Adrian. "Don't leave her alone, even for a moment. Understood?"

Adrian nodded, and Luca continued to glare for a moment before turning and walking out.

Adrian

When Giada left the next day, it was nearly noon, and my first call was to Marco. If he was sending Luca to campus as some sort of warning sign, well, I wasn't going to sit back and take it like a chump. Marco answered immediately, sounding surprisingly happy to hear from me.

"Luca was in Giada's apartment last night," I said, jumping right into it.

"Yes. I asked him to come get her from school. I think she'd be better off home for a couple weeks."

"What specifically is the danger to her? Is there some reason Enzo couldn't just have driven her home?"

"I did not think she would willingly go with him, and I cannot divulge the details of the confidential business transaction that has led me to harbor these concerns."

Figured. Blowing out a sigh, I decided to just get to my point. "Look, I might have found some useful information about Judge Roberts. I'm assuming you can get Luca to back off, right?"

Marco chuckled. "I don't see the connection."

I gritted my teeth. Did he really think I didn't see what he was doing, showing me he'd push Giada back into Luca's arms if I didn't help with his stupid spy mission?

"I can keep Giada safe," I insisted.

"What is the information you found?"

I hesitated, knowing I was about to cross a line. I'd gone over the information in my head since I'd seen it, trying to come up with any possible explanation for what I'd seen other than my first assumption, but there was nothing. Still, all signs indicated Judge Roberts was a good man. Maybe he made a mistake, but that shouldn't justify me ruining his life.

"I caught a glimpse of Judge Roberts's banking records. Every month, he sends money to some woman in Florida."

"It's probably alimony or child support."

"That's what I thought, but the amounts vary each month. There's no record of him having any previous marriages or children outside his marriage. And he's never lived in Florida, but he takes a couple of solo trips there each year."

"This is great, Adrian," he said.

I could tell he was smiling by his tone, and that sickened me. "He's a good man, Mr. Conti. He doesn't deserve to have his life ruined."

"Agreed. And he won't. Getting him off this case will potentially save his life. Although," he began, pausing. "If he's as good as you say, he wouldn't be supporting his mistress."

"There could be another explanation."

"Such as?"

He had me there.

"Luca has some business in New York he can tend to for a

couple weeks. In the meantime, I'm counting on you to keep my daughter safe," he said.

"Sure. Bye."

I hung up, feeling sleazy and worthless.

Giada

*L*uca left town, but my father and Angelo kept harassing me about coming home the next weekend. I would've, except Gabriella got tickets for the two of us to attend a fashion show in NYC. Obviously, that won out. I invited Adrian along, but he declined, and Enzo offered up his chauffeur services to get us there. Surprisingly, my dad wasn't too worried about our safety in New York. Apparently, he was just trying to control my life on campus.

We were all packed and ready to leave town when my brother Matteo showed up unexpectedly at my apartment. I groaned and contemplated not letting him in but finally relented.

"I'm not coming home with you. You'll have to carry me to the car kicking and screaming," I said.

He laughed. "Actually, I'm here to see Adrian. Dad sent me all the way out here with a little thank you for Adrian, but I couldn't find him at his apartment."

"He's probably at the law school. Whenever he isn't in class, he's following around this judge like a trained puppy."

"Judge Roberts?"

I squinted at my brother. "How do you know about him?"

"Dad told me. I guess Adrian has been helping him out with something. Judging by the present Dad sent, your boy did good."

My mouth went dry. "Adrian said he got that job on his own."

Matteo shrugged, clearly unaware that he'd just revealed way too much. "Then he probably did. Anyway, I'm sure Dad also wasn't so keen on you riding around in that old jalopy of Adrian's."

I started to remind him that a Honda Accord wasn't exactly a junker, but then the reality of what he was saying set in. "Wait, you don't mean that dad bought Adrian a car?"

Matteo grinned and nodded. "Grab a coat, and let's go down to see. Call your man, and tell him to get over here, too."

I did as he asked, more than eager to hear Adrian's explanation.

~

Adrian

Giada called me at the worst possible moment, but I knew her well enough to realize when she asked me to come over immediately, she wouldn't accept anything but a yes.

My day hadn't started out half bad, but as soon as I'd arrived at work, Marco had called to tell me that Judge Roberts had recused himself the previous afternoon. Marco was thrilled and thanked me for my "instrumental" role as if I would be proud of my actions. He assured me my help hadn't gone unnoticed, then hung up.

I was nervous when Judge Roberts arrived, fully expecting the bad mood that encapsulated him upon arrival. What I hadn't anticipated, though, was that he'd be in no mood to work. Instead, he invited me to lunch, where he'd drank his body weight in gin and tonics and started to ramble on about his life.

As soon as he moved on to his family life, I'd braced myself for a horrific confession about the affair. He lamented the public nature of his job and said no matter how much you try to protect someone, the public could find out. After trying to decipher his comments for several minutes, I just asked him point blank what he meant and who he was trying to protect. And that's when my day took a sharp turn for the worse.

He told me about his sister. She lived in a mental institution in the Florida panhandle. Apparently, she was schizophrenic, and some time ago, she'd tried to push someone off a bridge during an episode while she was off her meds. The judge had supported her ever since, but his greatest hope was that she could put the past fully behind her.

Now, thanks to me, that was a little bit harder.

The guilt hit me with such a sudden intensity that I felt sick. I excused myself to the restroom but managed to pull myself together without losing my lunch. How had I been such a fool? Why couldn't I ever trust my instincts? Everything I'd known about Judge Roberts told me he was a good man, and yet when I'd seen those stupid payments, I'd been so ready to dismiss him as a creep that I hadn't even considered other possibilities.

I certainly couldn't face the man any longer, knowing I'd ruined all his efforts to help his poor sister. So, I excused myself quickly and made my way over to Giada's. I comforted myself with the thought that my day couldn't get any worse. But once I spotted her brother Matteo, standing next to the metallic gray Jaguar that I'd taken for a test drive, I realized how wrong I'd been.

Giada approached me, her expression cold. "My brother came to deliver a gift from my dad. Apparently, he was pleased with some work you did for him. I hope you enjoy driving around in it alone," she said. She turned on her heals and stormed off, climbing into the back of Enzo's car where Gabriella was waiting.

Fuck.

I tried calling Giada to explain, but after she rejected my first two calls, I just texted and told her to enjoy her weekend with Gabby. I promised to explain when she got home and said I'd leave her alone until then.

After that, I was shocked when she called me the next evening. I answered the call, already spouting my apologies, but she cut me off.

"I don't have that much time, Adrian. I just…well, I'm here in New York trying to enjoy a fashion show, and I can't even focus. I feel betrayed, and I don't want to hear excuses or that I shouldn't feel that way. I just want to know what happened. Why did my brother deliver a car to you?"

"Honestly, I don't know how I…" I cut myself off before saying I'd gotten sucked in again. "I think your dad paid off my mom's medical bill. He did it anonymously, so I'm not positive, and he didn't ask for anything in return. He also told me that Judge Roberts would need an assistant and encouraged me to apply. As far as I know, I was hired based on my own qualifications. But then your dad told me he wanted Judge Roberts removed from a case. He asked me to look for information on him basically that could be used as blackmail."

"My dad did not tell you to blackmail someone," Gia interrupted.

"No, you're right. He never used that word, and he made it seem like the judge might be in danger if he stayed on the case. I found out Judge Roberts gave money to this woman in Florida each month, and I told your dad, because I assumed the woman was his mistress. Right around the time the judge recused himself from the case, I learned it was his sister that he was supporting."

"Why would the judge agree to leave the case if he didn't have a dirty secret to hide?"

"His sister has some mental illness issues. I think he's just a good guy and wanted to ensure her privacy. Anyway, I didn't know your father would get me a car. It was completely unexpected, and I told him I don't want it, but your brother left it anyway."

"Is that all?"

"No, it isn't all. Giada, I love you. I didn't mean to keep secrets from you. I am so sorry. I want you, not the money, not the car, not even the job."

She snorted. "Oh please, you love that job."

"It's been neat seeing the fun side of the law is all. I think I'd enjoy lecturing and writing and maybe even serving on the judiciary someday. It's a better fit for me than prosecutor or corporate lawyer."

Giada sighed, then took her time talking. "I appreciate you telling me the truth about all of this, Adrian. But…"

I braced myself as she continued.

"I was devastated when we broke up, and then Luca was there and he was being nice. So instead of fully mourning the loss of what you and I had, I think I just shifted all of that to him. And then when he turned out not to be the person I thought, I went straight back to you without considering whether I should."

"Of course you should, Giada. We're good together. You love me."

"I do," she agreed. "But what if I'm in love with the idea of you, and you're not really the person I think you are, either?"

"Giada, it was one mistake. I'm not a different person…"

"Adrian, hang on. I don't want to break up and I don't want to see anyone else, but I can't be with you right now. I just need some time."

My stomach muscles tightened uncomfortably. "How much time?"

"A week or two?"

I clenched my free hand into a fist and cast my eyes to the ceiling. It was the worst kind of déjà vu. "I don't want to take a break from you. I can tell you now that I'm sorry. I know I messed up, and it won't happen again."

She didn't speak, which told me her mind was already made up. I didn't have a choice in the matter, so I might as well be dignified about it.

"Fine. Take a week or two, and then we will talk again. If you're ready sooner, I'm here."

"Thank you, Adrian."

"Enjoy the City," I said, disconnecting before I said something I'd regret.

~

Giada

After one week apart from Adrian, I had no more clarity on our relationship than before. I didn't doubt Adrian's sincerity. Despite multiple lies over the past couple of weeks, I still trusted him, but I was also deeply disappointed. What had pulled me back to Adrian was my need for someone pure and good in my life. His openness with me was the only thing that made me feel like his equal. None of the other men in my life ever even pretended to communicate openly with me.

Adrian and I had broken up before because he didn't understand my family. He'd also kept secrets from me. Clearly, neither of those things had changed. So why had I gone back to Adrian? Was it just because he was the polar opposite of Luca?

Sure, I loved Adrian. He was brilliant and hardworking, sweet and romantic. He was a phenomenal chef, a giving lover, and oh so hot. We could talk for hours without boring of each other—and honestly, that was what I missed the most right now. Aside from Gabriella, Adrian was my best friend. He was someone I could always count on. Even though my design classes were a joke compared to his property law, tax law, and whatever other legalese he was studying, Adrian never teased when I vented about my own class projects. He was always supportive.

But if Adrian was indeed the perfect man, why was I still thinking about Luca?

If I were writing my life story, Luca would surely be the villain. He lied, he manipulated, and he pushed every one of my buttons. My struggles amused him, and I seriously doubted whether my best interests were ever his concern. Despite all that, just thinking about him made my heart thud erratically in a way it rarely did with Adrian. Even when he infuriated me, I couldn't ignore his delicious smell or the warmth in the pit of my belly from the tenor of his voice.

Clearly, my brain wanted Adrian and my body leaned towards Luca. But now that Adrian was keeping secrets of his own from me, was he really that much better than Luca? If Adrian's honesty was what I valued in him, what did it mean when he faltered in that respect?

Maybe I couldn't trust my brain or my body to lead me in the right direction.

Unfortunately, what I needed to figure it all out was time away from both men. But before my two-week break from Adrian was up, my dad called.

Never a man for small talk, he jumped right into it. "There's been some trouble at the docks, Giada. There were some men transporting illegal goods through our shipyard, and they're not happy that we stopped them. I'm worried they might try to retaliate."

"Oh my God!" I exclaimed, my mind instantly flitting to my grandfather. "Are you okay? Can the police—"

"You don't need to worry about me, Giada. I've got security around the clock here, and so do your brothers. It's you I'm concerned about. I know you think school is so far away that nothing can get to you, but you're just a couple of hours away. I can't keep you safe there. I need you to come home."

"I can't just—"

"It'll only be for a few days, Giada. Hopefully, this will all blow over in a week or two."

"A week or two? Dad, I have midterms. I can't just come home."

"I need Lorenzo here, Giada. I don't have anyone else who can come babysit you." He paused, but just as I was about to protest his implication that I needed a babysitter, he continued. "Unless…let me check with Salvatore. He owes me a favor. Maybe Luca can help us out."

"No!"

"Giada, if you don't want me to see if Luca can come stay with you, then you'll need to come home. I'm not taking chances with your safety, and frankly, I don't have time to worry about all of this."

I considered my options. It was Senior year, and I couldn't afford to miss midterms. I groaned.

"Fine, you can see if Luca can help out until the weekend, and then I'll come home. But I have to be back at school Monday, and I'm not bringing a babysitter."

My dad sighed, then told me to get some sleep, even though I'd just finished dinner.

I waited until morning to call Adrian, certain he wasn't going to respond well when I told him my ex-boyfriend was coming to crash on my couch for a few days.

I blurted out the whole sordid thing before Adrian had a chance to even say hello, but then he surprised me with his acceptance of it all. In light of his extreme hatred of Luca, that seemed fishy.

"Why are you okay with this?" I asked, frowning into my phone.

"It's not like you were asking my permission," he said. "I'd rather you come stay here, with me, but I'm guessing that violates the rules of this whole break we're taking."

"There's nothing going on between me and Luca. He's got an Italian girlfriend now, if that makes you feel any better."

"It doesn't, but I trust you. And if your family is this concerned about your safety, I don't think you should ignore them. But why not just head home now?"

"I have classes."

"Your brother and your dad both asked me to watch out for you. I thought you should know," he said.

"Thank you for telling me," I said, cringing at how awkward and overly formal our conversation had become. "Okay, well, Luca should be here any minute, so I'll talk with you later."

I hung up, turned around, and screamed.

Luca was standing in my bedroom.

"God, can you not knock like a normal human?"

He laughed. "What's the point of a key if I have to knock?"

I resisted the urge to strangle him. "I need to study, so feel free to go set up your little couch bed."

His face contorted like he'd eaten a rotten fruit. "We aren't really sleeping that way are we?"

"Yes. Besides, I don't think your Italian girlfriend would appreciate you sleeping in my bed."

"I have no girlfriend."

"What?"

He nodded. "We broke up pretty much as soon as we started dating. Turns out I like someone else. So, good news is that I am all yours."

"I'm still with Adrian."

"That's not what it sounded like to me."

"Well, I am. We are just taking a little break."

"Because he lied to you about working for your papà?"

I opened and shut my mouth without saying a word. Nothing was more infuriating than Luca being right about something.

"It must be hard to accept that Golden Boy is no better than the rest of us," he said, showing himself out of my room.

CHAPTER 10

Giada

After my classes Thursday, I took my time packing. Then, just because I hated being bossed around, I pushed back, insisting Enzo drive me to Luca's new apartment in Stamford. Unfortunately, that totally backfired. Not only did Luca not mind, but Alessio, Thomas, and Giovanni also showed up at my apartment. If the five Italian men escorting me off campus didn't raise eyebrows, the two-car caravan might.

"This is a little ridiculous," I told Luca as he passed off my last bag to Enzo.

"Actually, I think your papà is being too lax this time," he replied, his face tense. "I don't want to scare you with the details, but he got on the wrong side of some bad people. They're known for targeting the family of men who anger them, and we have reason to think they might have some guys in town."

His words frightened me, but I reminded myself that Luca was a master manipulator. He wanted to scare me, and he would say whatever it took to achieve that goal. Besides, if I was truly in such dire danger, my dad wouldn't have given me the option of staying at Luca's. He would've kidnapped me as soon as they learned of the threat and locked me in my fortress-style childhood home.

"That doesn't make any sense. Who exactly did he piss off, and what did he do?" I asked.

"Don't concern yourself with the details, Giada. What you need to know is that you aren't safe here and that you're going to stay with me until your papà is sure there is no more threat."

I let Luca walk me out towards the car, again reminded of the contrast between Luca—forcing me to stay with him without even telling me the exact risk—and Adrian, who trusted me enough to let me go with Luca.

We reached the car, and I froze. "Hang on. I need to run back in real quick for one more thing."

Luca glanced at his watch again and sighed, making me feel like a petulant child. I wasn't intentionally trying to stall; I was certain I had forgotten something.

"One minute, Luca," I said. "If you're in that big of a hurry, you can go on ahead since Enzo is taking me anyway."

I darted back towards the building before he could protest. Once inside, I surveyed the room and quickly located what I needed. It was the pendant Adrian had given me back for my birthday. It wasn't my priciest or fanciest piece of jewelry, but it was possibly the most valuable. The fact that he'd given me such a meaningful gift had touched me. Even now that I was annoyed with him, I wanted the pendant with me.

I crammed the necklace into my pocket and then grabbed a small spiral notepad with some of my old design doodles in it, just to have something to show Luca if he asked what was so important.

When I got back outside, Luca flung his hands in the air like I'd been gone for hours instead of under five minutes. The gesture, likely intended to speed up my pace, caused my steps to slow noticeably.

I had nearly reached Luca's Audi when I noticed a dark blue sedan driving slowly. The window rolled down, so I peered closer, half expecting an old friend to wave. But before I could see who it was, a loud popping sound filled the air. I screamed, not expecting Fourth of July-style fireworks in the middle of March.

After that, everything else was a blur.

Luca screamed my name and then slammed into me like a freight train, knocking me to the pavement. My hip hit the ground hard, but my head bounced off his arm instead of smashing into the concrete. Pain radiated through the entire right side of my body.

Instead of helping me up, Luca rolled over me, smashing me into the ground. His weight was crushing to the point that I couldn't have breathed even if he hadn't had his arm fully covering my face. The explosive booms stopped, and I wondered if I was just deaf now from the impact.

Luca dragged me to my feet and practically threw me at Enzo and Thomas. I wanted to yell at him for nearly killing me, but they were already shoving me into the back of the Escalade.

"Take her to my place!" Luca shouted, slamming the door.

The Audi in front of us started to pull away from the curb as Luca was still climbing into the passenger seat. Once he was in, the car peeled off, hitting its max speed within seconds. I wanted to watch where it went, but Enzo had steered the Escalade in the opposite direction, and Thomas was forcing my head down at an awkward angle so I couldn't see anything above window-level.

"Let go of me!" I shrieked, trying to hit his arm.

"Stay down!"

I was about to protest again when the phone rang. Enzo must have clicked to answer because a moment later, Luca's voice boomed through the vehicle's sound system. "Is she hurt?" he asked.

"Yes!" I shouted, pissed as hell. Everything hurt.

"Hang on," Enzo said. He turned, shooting Thomas a look.

Thomas shifted me slightly, still forcing my head down towards the seat cushion, then ran his hands inappropriately over my entire body.

"Hey!" I protested the violation.

"She wasn't hit," he said.

"Go inside when you get there, and stay with her till I'm back," Luca said. Then the line went dead.

"What the fuck is going on?" I asked.

No one answered, and my neck was throbbing from the angle. I tried to remember some of the moves they'd taught in my self-defense class that might work in this position. As soon as it came to me, I shifted and bit into Thomas's hand.

"Ow, fuck! Giada!" he shouted, shifting his hand but tightening his grip on me. "Stop fighting me. I'm trying to keep you from getting shot."

"What?" A billion thoughts raced through my head all at once, and suddenly, I couldn't breathe. "I need to sit up. I can't breathe."

"Giada, calm down," Enzo said softly. "You're fine. You're safe. I'm right here. We are driving you to Luca's."

"I don't want to go to Luca's. Did you not see him just tackle me? He could've killed me."

Thomas snorted. "Those men were shooting at you, Giada. You would've been killed if not for Luca. Now keep your head down in case they come back."

I tried to process his words, but they didn't make sense. Who was shooting at me? And why? A crushing sensation settled over my chest. "Let me up. I need to get out of the car. I can't breathe," I said, shoving at Thomas. I reached my hand around and touched what I suspected was a gun by his hip. Just as I wrapped my fist around it, Thomas swatted my hand away.

He and Enzo both began shouting in Italian, and my head swung towards the seat in front of me as the car swerved. Enzo retrieved something from the glove box and handed it to Thomas.

"Giada, you have to calm down. I can't stop here. It isn't safe. I need you to focus on your breathing," Enzo said.

"Let go of me!" I repeated, kicking at Thomas.

Thomas swore under his breath, which only encouraged me to fight harder.

"I'm trying not to hurt you," he grumbled as if that was somehow supposed to comfort me.

"Giada!" Enzo shouted before saying something else in Italian to Thomas.

"Giada, this pill will help you relax. Just take this, and I'll let you sit up when you calm down," Thomas said, his voice sickly sweet.

I swatted at his hand, determined to knock the small pill out of his grasp.

Now it was Enzo who swore, then said, "It's too long of a drive. Just do it, Thomas."

Before I could figure out what they were talking about, Thomas's grip on me tightened. He roughly forced his finger into my mouth, but before I could bite down, he removed it, instead pressing it over my lips like he was smothering me. I tried to scream but could barely breathe let alone make a noise. So instead, I decided to spit the pill out the second he moved his hand. Unfortunately, when he finally moved his hand, my mouth felt empty and dry. I couldn't even muster enough spit, and the pill seemed to have completely dissolved.

"Luca is not going to be happy that you're drugging me," I told him. It was true. Luca didn't even seem to like when I drank too much.

Thomas said something in Italian, and Enzo replied quickly. Just as I was about to ask for a translation, Thomas loosened my grip on me. I suspected I should seize the opportunity to fight him, but I no longer cared. I was tired and dizzy.

"Everything is spinning," I mumbled, shifting in my seat.

I started to sit up, but Thomas stopped me. "Your head needs to stay below window level still," he said.

I rolled my eyes, but that made me even dizzier and confused. Why was someone shooting at me? Had that been a joke?

"How many did you give her?" Enzo asked.

I heard Thomas answer, but his voice sounded distant, and before I could protest further, the car went dark.

My eyes flew open as the car jerked to a stop. I felt like only a few minutes had passed, yet somehow I was confused as to where I was. Peering around, I quickly ascertained I was in a car, and I recognized Enzo in the driver's seat. But as I peeked directly above me, my eyes landed on Thomas.

I shrieked and tried to sit up. Thomas shushed me, but nudged my shoulder to help me lift my head off his lap.

"I think you're good," Enzo said after a moment. He climbed out of the car and walked around and opened my door.

I tried to stand, but my feet didn't fully work, so Enzo lifted me out, and he and Thomas both held on to me as they scurried into the building. Once inside, Enzo locked the door and then turned to me.

"Are you okay?" he asked.

I was as far from okay as I'd ever been. I was breathing hard and fast but still couldn't catch my breath. My head was pounding, and I was dizzy. I was sweaty but cold. My hip and my arm burned as if half the road was embedded inside them. I was scared. And I was so confused.

"I want to talk to Luca," I said, surprised at how calm my voice sounded.

Enzo stared at me for a moment, then glanced down at his phone right as it rang. He clicked to accept the call. "Marco,

Thomas and I are with her at Luca's. He went after them with Alessio and Giovanni. She's safe. We'll keep you posted."

He hung up, and I realized I was all done. I couldn't handle a single other thing. "Is there a guestroom?" I asked. I'd never been in this apartment, wasn't even sure when Luca had moved in.

Thomas shook his head, then pointed to the room closest to me. "That's Luca's room. Make yourself at home."

I turned and went into Luca's bedroom, shutting and locking the door behind me. I went into the bathroom, shocked at how wrecked I looked in the mirror. I let the shower heat up, then undressed slowly, taking in the cuts and bruises along the side of my body.

As I stepped into the warm spray, I cringed, the water stinging my fresh wounds. I stood there for a long time without actually washing anything, trying to figure out what had happened. By the time I shut off the water and grabbed one of Luca's fluffy white towels to dry off, I felt calmer but still completely confused about what had transpired.

Surely Enzo wasn't serious that people were shooting at us. That sort of thing didn't just happen to people, did it?

I rubbed the towel through my hair again and made my way to Luca's closet. I didn't expect to find any of my clothes, but Luca was organized, so I quickly located a pair of soft boxer shorts and a tee shirt. Once I dressed, there was a knock at the door.

It was Enzo. Again. "You okay?"

"No. Go away," I replied. I pulled the blinds shut and crawled under the covers.

I was drowsy but not asleep when the next knock came. Blinking, I realized there was no longer light peeking between the curtains. I wondered if I'd drifted off for a few hours or just laid there in shock.

The knock repeated, followed by a clicking sound of a key in the lock. I heard the door open and shut, and I suspected I should scream, but I was too terrified to even breathe. I reminded myself that Enzo was there, that he wouldn't have left me, but still I was uneasy. Footsteps approached the bed, and I squeezed my eyes shut like a child scared of a monster.

A hand touched my back, and I stiffened.

"Giada, it's Luca," he said, softly. I relaxed, then suddenly realized I'd been scared for him. I turned to confirm it was him, then squeezed my eyes shut once more.

"Oh, baby, you're shaking," he said. I heard a thunk as his shoes hit the ground, and then he stretched out behind me. "Are you cold? Your hair is wet."

I shook my head in response to the first question, but then my teeth started chattering.

Luca pulled me closer and wrapped his arm all the way over my body, holding me tightly. The sensation was so eerily similar to what I'd experienced earlier, when he apparently shielded me from flying bullets, that I couldn't control the tears any longer. I convulsed into full-blown heaving sobs against the pillow.

"Shh, Giada, baby, you're okay," Luca whispered in my ear and cuddled me tighter and tighter until finally he rolled me to face him.

At first, I kept my face pressed against the pillow, embarrassed by how terrible I must look, but as Luca pulled me closer and closer, I finally relented and pressed my face against his chest.

When I fully calmed down, Luca pressed a kiss against the top of my head.

"I need a shower," he said.

"Don't leave me," I begged.

He didn't move. "Those guys won't come after you again. You're safe."

I lifted my head to look at him. "You protected me," I said.

Luca simply stared at me.

"You knocked me out of the way and then sheltered me with

your own body," I said, suddenly seeing the events of the day with greater clarity. "I didn't even realize what was going on, and you saved me without even hesitating."

"Of course, I did. That's my job, Giada. If I can't keep you safe, I'm nothing."

"But then you left me," I reminded him.

He sighed. "Tesoro, we had to go after them."

"You could've been killed."

"We can take care of ourselves," he said, as though any part of me was concerned about his stupid associates. "Enzo hit one of their tires, and their gas tank while you were still on the ground, so we knew they wouldn't get far."

"Enzo shot at them?"

Luca nodded and grinned. "Yeah, he's got great aim. Why do you think your dad likes him so much?"

I wasn't sure what to say about that. "So you found them?"

"Yeah. They won't bother you ever again."

"They're in jail?"

He pressed his lips against my forehead, lingering this time. I interpreted that as a yes.

"I'm sorry I made you wait. If I hadn't gone back in…"

"You didn't know, Giada," he said.

I felt even more pathetic, realizing he was forsaking the perfect opportunity to lecture me on my stupidity and recklessness.

"I've been such a jerk to you, and you still saved me."

"Amore, I'll always save you. Tu sei il sole della mia vita. Per te farei di tutto. You're…everything to me. I'd do anything for you."

Even though I suspected his translation was more of an approximation, my heart fluttered a little, as it always did when he spoke Italian. Now a new sensation was replacing the anxiety and fear coursing through my veins. I licked my lips then kissed Luca on the mouth, tentatively at first. I was fairly certain he'd reject me, but I had to try. He hesitated, clearly not having expected the kiss, but then he reciprocated.

His lips responded to mine slowly at first, then more aggressively as I parted my lips, letting his tongue slip into my mouth and swirl around my own. Luca thrust his hand into my damp hair, holding my head close to him, and my hand wandered over to his back and slid down to grip his taut butt.

We went on like that for a while, devouring each other's mouths like we'd been apart for years, and then Luca slipped his hand between us. He paused as he reached my waistband.

"You're wearing my clothes," he whispered with a breathy laugh. "I like it."

Before I could reply, his hand went up the tee shirt, reaching straight to my breast. The contact sent an immediate jolt of pleasure straight down my core, where the tension was building like a tightly coiled spring. I moaned loudly into his mouth.

Luca pulled back, shushed me, then replaced his hand with his lips, making it impossible for me to obey. He slid one hand down my abdomen, not stopping until he reached my damp slit. The pressure of his fingers against my aching clit provided instant relief, and I arched my hips against his hand, needing more contact, more friction, more everything. I moaned again, and Luca responded by pressing his other hand gently over my mouth. I nipped at his finger, but he simply chuckled, his breath falling hot and heavy against my hardened nipple.

I wanted more of Luca, wanted all of him, but before I could even tell him that, my orgasm swept through me with a fast and ferocious intensity that made me cry out even louder. As we waited for my body to still, Luca laughed again.

"So much for staying quiet," he mumbled. He lifted his head to face me so I could see he wasn't really mad, and then he licked his fingers, in possibly the most erotic move I'd ever witnessed. All the pressure he'd just released ratcheted back up again, and I reached for his belt.

Luca pulled away and stood, and my body ached from the separation almost immediately. But I watched as he undressed, so I smiled and followed suit. As he rejoined me under the sheets, covering my body with his, he paused and caught my eye. I stared into his deep brown, mysterious eyes and tried to figure out what I was doing with this beautiful, troubled man. We hurt each other over and over, yet every time we ended up right back where we started, tangled up in a slick, panting mess of pleasure.

I lifted my head and kissed his neck, parting my legs to make room for him. He was thick and hard, and already pressing against the apex of my sex, but he made no move to enter. I slid my hands up his back, relishing the smoothness of his skin and the sensation of his weight pressing against my sensitive nipples. He rolled his hips against me, hitting right where I craved the pressure the most. I was eager to move on, but Luca still simply stared at me.

"Fuck, what will I do with you Giada?" he mused.

"I have some ideas if you'd cooperate," I replied, arching my back to lift my pelvis against him.

He moaned softly then kissed me with renewed vigor. Finally, after an eternity, he thrust into me, the sudden fullness granting me the closeness I'd so needed.

"Oh, Luca," I whispered, raising my hips to meet him again.

Suddenly, there was a loud knock on the door.

We both froze.

"Marco's on the phone," Enzo's voice called through the door. I winced at the uncertainty and discomfort in his tone, almost positive he had heard us and appreciated what he was interrupting.

Luca groaned.

"I'll call him later," I hollered.

"He asked to speak with Luca," Enzo said timidly.

Luca plopped his head against my chest and sighed.

"He can leave a message," I said in a voice only Luca could hear.

Luca kissed me in response, so I thought we were in agreement, but then he climbed off of me. My body ached at the sudden emptiness. He tugged his shirt over his head then stepped back into his suit pants without bothering with the boxers.

"I'm sorry, baby," he said, planting a kiss on my forehead as I pouted dramatically. He opened the door only a crack to sneak out, and then I was alone.

Nearly twenty minutes went by before he returned, and as soon as I saw him, I knew our moment had passed.

"Everything okay?" I asked.

He exhaled, clearly exhausted. "It will be."

I stared expectantly.

"Look, Giada, you know I want you, but I'm just not sure we should…"

I waited for him to finish the sentiment, but he didn't.

"I need a shower," he said instead, turning and heading into the bathroom.

CHAPTER 11

Giada

Instead of letting me stay with Luca until midterms were over as planned, my dad summoned me home the next day. I wasn't the slightest bit surprised. What did surprise me, though, was that he sent Angelo to bring me home instead of just letting Luca drive me. Although it wasn't a long drive, it felt that way with my brother beside me in the car. Angelo had never been overly chatty, and I ran out of random musings to share with him by the time we hit the interstate. I asked Enzo to turn up the radio, but Angelo's judgmental expressions were enough to discourage me from dancing or singing along like I normally would.

"So what's the boss want to chat about?" I asked, certain Angelo knew our dad's agenda.

Angelo abruptly turned to me. "Why did you call him that?"

"Boss?" I laughed at his wacky overreaction. "Because you

work for him, don't you? I thought you were in training to take over the family business."

"Oh."

"I assume he's concerned about what happened yesterday and wants to talk me into skipping the last several weeks of my collegiate career?"

"No. Well, maybe. What he really wants to know is what you are doing with Luca."

"What?"

Angelo waved a hand dismissively. "We'll be there soon enough, and you can talk with him yourself."

I rolled my eyes and pulled out a book to do some studying. Despite being targeted in a drive-by, I still had one more midterm exam to prepare for.

When we got home, our dad greeted us outside and pulled me in for the longest, firmest hug we'd ever shared. When he finally released me, he held me at arm's distance and scrutinized me as though confirming I wasn't broken. Once he finished, my uncles did the same, and then I went inside to greet my mother, who was bawling.

"Alright, so clearly you all heard what happened, and I'm okay and as you may know, I am graduating in a few weeks, so I need some time to study." I said.

Then I turned to my dad. "You wanted to talk?"

He nodded, but instead of leading me to his study, we went out back, to the patio. Mom brought us tall glasses of iced tea, and we got comfortable on the cushioned outdoor couch.

"Luca came to see me before the holidays. He said you weren't interested in him romantically, and he didn't want to pressure you to be with him in those circumstances," he began.

My jaw dropped. I hadn't realized that Luca asked for my dad's blessing to break up with me, and honestly, I wasn't sure how I felt about it.

"After that, I thought you were seeing Adrian again. He's

never been my first choice for you, but I was trying to be supportive and help him out. I gave him a job as a courtesy to you. Now it has come to my attention that you broke up with him because you didn't like him working for me. I don't know what to make of any of this, Giada."

My face heated up. If there was anything more mortifying to discuss with my father than my dating choices, I sure didn't know what it was.

"Adrian didn't tell me he was working for you. I don't need to be with someone who lies to me."

My father frowned. "A man is entitled to live his own life and not tell you every detail of what goes on during the business day. Not everything has to do with you, and the sooner you accept that and stop asking so many questions of all the men in your life, the easier your transition into adulthood will be."

I stifled an eye roll, not ready to show *that* much disrespect. "You've treated me differently from my brothers for years, and I always told myself if was because I was younger. But it isn't, is it? You're always going to treat me like a child, aren't you?"

"Only if you continue to act like a child."

"How am I acting like a child?"

He leaned forward and slammed his fist into the table. "If you had listened the first time yesterday, you wouldn't have almost been killed."

"If you were honest with me from the get-go about why random people want me dead, I would've listened!" I shouted back.

My dad leaned back and shut his eyes for a minute. He looked as though he were meditating. I assumed he sensed his blood pressure enter the danger zone and decided to back off before he gave himself a stroke.

"Not everyone who wants to import and export goods at our shipyards is a good, law-abiding citizen. Fortunately, I have the financial resources to enable us to say no when I don't want to work with those criminals, but sometimes, they don't like that answer. You are my only daughter, Giada. You are my princess. I couldn't live with myself if I let anything happen to you." He paused, but I didn't jump in just yet.

"I can keep you safe when you're at the house, but you've made it clear you want your own life away from us. So I send Enzo to try to keep you safe at school. And I try to make sure that whoever you're romantically involved with shares my same concerns about your safety. I can't do that when you're thwarting your security detail like it's a game and bouncing from one man to another like they're tissues to use and throw away."

I squeezed my hands into fists. He had officially erased any goodwill he'd earned by saying how important I was to him.

"It's now come to my attention that you may be romantically interested in Luca again, so I felt compelled to have a chat with you and let you know I strongly advise you not screw it up this time. Luca will not always be there waiting for you to grow up and settle down."

"What? The only reason I was even with Luca yesterday is because he told me you wanted him to babysit me."

"That's correct, and thank God for that. Enzo told me Luca was the one who shielded you." He shook his head as though still traumatized by the events. "But I'm talking about afterwards. When I called you dozens of times and was told you wouldn't answer my calls because you were alone with Luca in his bedroom."

Okay, maybe there was something more mortifying. I made a mental note to murder whoever told my dad, and then I said a quick prayer that they didn't also tell him any moans or other crazy sex noises they may have overheard.

"It isn't your business whether I'm involved with Luca or not."

"It absolutely is. His father and I partner on many business deals, and if you destroy his son again, I'm not sure he'll be willing to work with me."

"Luca is a big boy. He can handle a breakup without ruining his dad's business prospects."

"I'm not so sure about that. But there's more. Those people who came after you yesterday won't be a problem again, but they may have other associates who are still a threat. Mr. Marino is well known and powerful in the business world. If you're associated with him, you'll automatically be safer. And as long as you're with Luca, he'll keep you safe. You won't just have Luca looking after you but all his father's people and all his people."

I sighed and tried to focus on what he was saying. "So you do want me to date Luca?"

"I would love that, but only if you're serious about it and not if you plan to return to Adrian in a week or two. You need to make a commitment."

"I'm not going to make a commitment to someone just because you think it would be good for business."

"It's not just business. There's your safety to consider as well."

"If Luca is this upstanding guy you think he is, shouldn't he keep me safe regardless of who I'm dating?" I posited.

"I thought he was doing that now. He wasted his Saturday night driving over to keep an eye on you, and you ditched him for Adrian."

"So, what's the problem?"

Frustration filled my father's face. "The problem is that I got the impression you were starting another romantic relationship with Luca."

I flung my hands up. The conversation was exasperating. "You just finished saying you'd love for me to date Luca!"

"What I don't want is for you to ruin what you have now. If you don't want to stay with him, don't give him the wrong idea and don't start dating him now. He will continue watching out for your safety as a friend and as a favor to me. But if you do start a relationship with him, you could very well ruin all of that if you break his heart again."

My mother sat beside my father, and I startled, not having even realized she'd joined us outside. "We raised you to be a good Catholic girl, Giada. If your father won't say it, I will. You can't get intimately involved with these grown men if you aren't ready to marry them."

I could no longer suppress the eye roll. "I'm fairly sure the bible doesn't say a thing about me having to marry the first grown-up I date," I said, mimicking her dumb terminology.

"For God's sake, Giada. You can't just sleep around and not expect consequences. You are a representative of this family, whether you like it or not, and I'm sick of watching you act like a floozy flitting from Adrian to Luca and back again!"

All the air rushed out of me. So much for being daddy's little girl. Once he basically called me a slut, that whole innocent image was off the table. I stood to walk inside.

"Giada, sit down," my father commanded.

I was poised to spew out some sassy quip, but instead, I just obeyed for once. "If you and Luca could publicly appear to be a couple, just until the trouble brews over, that would keep you the safest. The criminals won't touch you if they know you're engaged to Luca Marino. Once it's safe, you can do whatever you want."

"Engaged? Geez, you just told me you didn't want me to toy with his heart, and now you're asking me to fake an engagement so your crazy business associates don't shoot me?"

"That's the distinction I'm trying to make you understand. If you are continuing a relationship with Luca for purposes of ensuring your safety, make sure he knows that. Don't cross that line. Don't mix business with pleasure."

I winced, half expecting him to tell me to close my legs.

"But if you're ready to settle down, and you've got that Adrian out of your system, by all means, have a real relationship with Luca. Either way, he did some shopping in New York back in the fall so I know he has a ring just waiting to go on your finger."

I shook my head, flabbergasted. But before I could attempt to storm off a second time, my father dismissed me with a quick wave of his hand.

"You may go to your room to study," he said.

I flung my hands in the air but high-tailed it out of his way.

~

Adrian

When Giada called me and told me she'd been involved in a drive-by shooting, I'd laughed, certain it was a joke. But as she explained, a heavy pang of unease settled over me. She assured me no one was hurt and that Enzo and Luca saved her life. I should've been grateful she was uninjured—and I was—but I was also deeply resentful that Luca was there to help her. I could tell she was filled with gratitude for them, which bothered me. In reality, she was only in danger because of them and the other men like them in her life.

What came next shouldn't have surprised me, but it did.

"I can't focus on a real relationship now," she said. "I know I said I just needed a quick break to think things over, but I can't even think about what's going on between you and me when I also have all this drama in my life. I should be focused on finals and graduation and having fun now, not boyfriends who lie to me or strangers who may shoot at me."

"Come stay with me until school is out. You're stressed out, and scared, and you shouldn't be alone."

"Adrian, I can't be with you now. That's what I'm saying. I thought if we took a short break, I'd have some clarity and I'd know what I wanted, but it's been almost two weeks and—"

"And you don't miss me," I supplied. My heart ached just saying it out loud. I missed her so much that it hurt, but I wasn't so naïve as to think she felt the same way after she'd asked for more time apart.

"I do miss you, Adrian. Aside from Gabriella, you're my best friend. There's no one else I can talk to like I do you. I just don't know if I can be with you romantically. I don't know how to rebuild the trust, and I can't focus on all of that now."

"So you need more time?"

The ensuing silence was telling.

"Oh, I see," I said.

"Adrian, I'd love to tell you I just need another week to straighten things out, but I don't know. I want to get us back to where we were last year, but we've been trying, and it still doesn't feel right. It's not fair for me to ask you to put your life on hold while I figure stuff out. I think a clean break is better for you."

I nearly snorted out loud at that notion.

"You should be free to date other people," she said. Then she paused. "And after graduation, if I figure out my life and what I want and who I am and I realize I made a huge mistake by letting you go, I'll let you know. But in the meantime, I don't want you to wait for me. You know how I am. I may never figure my shit out."

I swallowed the lump in my throat. It wasn't really up for discussion, so there was no point in arguing. I could beg for her to stay with me, but if she didn't love me by now, I couldn't change that.

"There's something else," she said tentatively. "Even though Luca said the guys that came after my won't be a problem anymore, my…"

"Won't be a problem anymore?" I repeated, interrupting her. "Like he killed them?"

"Jesus, no! Of course not, Adrian. They're in jail, where criminals belong."

"He said that?"

"Yes."

I blew out a sigh. It was amazing that Giada couldn't forgive me for a few lies of omission, but she ate up Luca's bullshit like it was Cheerios.

"Anyway, my father is still worried about my safety, and he thinks if we pretend that I'm back with Luca, his enemies will back off."

I rolled my eyes, trying to pinpoint the exact moment my life became a soap opera.

"I just thought you should know that in case you hear something, it's not true. It's all for show. I'm not dating Luca again. I mean it when I say I'm focusing on me right now."

"Okay, Giada. Sure thing." My voice sounded as jerky and skeptical as I felt, but that was all I could muster. "Take care," I said, hanging up before I lost it.

Giada

*B*etween the awkward discussion with my parents and the crushing conversation with Adrian, I was depleted. I felt like I had the flu. I alternated between hot and cold, and I was achy, tired and so utterly defeated by the world that I could barely drag myself out of bed to use the bathroom. On Sunday, I perked up a little only because I was eager to return to school that night. I ate some toast and soaked in the bath before dressing and styling my hair.

By the time I emerged from my bedroom shortly before dinner, I was confident I appeared normal and that no one would know how empty and alone I felt. I barely acknowledged my parents, and when Angelo climbed into the car along with Enzo and me, I popped in my earbuds so I wouldn't be expected to converse. My plan worked, but by the time we arrived at my apartment, I was desperate for true solitude. It was almost as though I realized I wouldn't feel even-keeled again until the loneliness in my heart was matched by the emptiness of my surroundings.

Angelo walked me into my apartment, carrying my bags, then left. I warmed a can of soup and then crawled into bed before eight pm, praying I'd feel normal again when I awoke.

When I peeled my eyes open, it was still dark outside, and I didn't feel any better. I glanced at the clock and realized why. It was only 12:15, closer to my normal bedtime than to morning. I groaned loudly, then noticed a light coming from under the bedroom door. Sitting up, I listened carefully and realized I must have left the television on.

I stumbled out to the living room then stopped abruptly. Luca was stretched out on my couch, sound asleep, his phone clutched tightly in one hand and the TV remote in the other. He was dressed casually, in faded jeans and a navy tee shirt, and his face was more relaxed than I'd seen it in ages. Asleep, Luca seemed a decade younger than awake. I reached for the remote, ready to click off the television without even pulling the remote out of his hand, but the movement woke him. His hand snapped shut around mine.

Luca released me a moment later, looking confused as he sat up.

"I was going to turn off the TV. You were asleep."

"*I* was watching TV. *You* were asleep."

I snorted at the ridiculousness of his insistence. "Why are you in my apartment?"

"I came here to talk with you, but you were asleep. Since it wasn't even 8:30, I figured it was just a nap and you'd wake up."

"I was tired," I said, now feeling the exhaustion again. I sunk onto the couch where his legs had been.

"You look like shit. Are you sick?"

"Thanks. No. Just…" I exhaled and shook my head. I didn't know how to explain what I felt. He gazed at me for a moment, then rubbed my shoulders with his hand.

"It's normal to be rattled after someone shoots at you."

"Yeah, I guess. I also broke up with Adrian this weekend, so that didn't help."

Luca frowned. "I thought you broke up with him weeks ago."

"No, we were on a break. But I didn't feel right stringing him along after…"

"After you ravished me in my own bed and then left me high and dry?" he interrupted.

"Okay, *I* did not leave *you*, and second, no, that is not what I was going to say. After two weeks apart from Adrian, I still wasn't sure what I wanted to do with him. That didn't seem like a good sign," I said. Although, now that Luca brought it up, fooling around with another guy while technically still "on a break" from Adrian was a pretty clear sign I wasn't ready to be a committed girlfriend to Adrian.

Luca didn't say anything.

"I'm a fucking mess. I have a great boyfriend that I keep messing things up with, and I have less than two months until I'm in the real world, and I have zero job leads or interests, really. Oh, and sometimes, people shoot at me, apparently."

He shrugged like that last one was no big deal. "Giada, you're twenty-one. Follow your dreams. Try of several jobs and figure out what makes you happy. Or don't work at all. You could take some time and travel. I know a guy with a fabulous beachfront villa in Sicily."

"Yeah, you'd just love to lock me up there for a year."

"I would," he agreed, smiling as though he wasn't admitting to being a creepy possessive stalker. He stroked my hair gently. "And about Adrian…you don't love him the way he loves you. You can try to deny it, but you know that's the truth. And the fact that you don't love him that way doesn't mean there's anything wrong with you, just that he's not the right man for you."

I was still so groggy that Luca's words actually seemed wise. But then I remembered that he was generally motivated to get in my pants or manipulate me to some other selfish end.

"Let me guess. You are the right man?"

He shrugged again. "That's for you to decide. In the meantime, your papà is still worried about your safety."

"Why?"

"Because he's paranoid, and he has no clue how scrappy and capable you truly are."

"So you don't think I'm in any danger?"

"No more than ever. Look, Giada, your father deals with many unsavory characters in his line of work, and your family has loads of money. That combination will always make you a target."

I yawned. "So why are you at my apartment?"

"I thought I'd drop by and see if you wanted to finish what we started Friday."

I stood and rolled my eyes. "Not tonight. But you can sleep in the bed if you keep your hands off me."

Luca appeared to consider the conditions of my offer, then followed me into the bedroom.

When my alarm woke me the next morning, Luca was gone. Surprisingly, I was bummed by that. I needed to talk with him, but I supposed it wasn't a great time anyway since I had class in an hour.

I bypassed the shower and had just finished dressing and fixing my makeup when there was a sound at the door. Rounding the corner, I saw Luca coming in, his arms loaded down with a box of donuts and a bag on top.

"Craving carbs?" I teased.

"It's for you. You have no food in your apartment," he said.

I flipped open the lid to the donut box to see that it held

muffins. "Mmmm," I groaned, grabbing one and yanking the paper off of it. I poured myself some coffee while savoring the buttery goodness and ignoring the curious stares from Luca.

"I presume you have classes today?" he asked, selecting a blueberry lemon muffin for himself.

I nodded and hoisted myself onto the counter.

"Should we maybe talk at some point?" he asked.

Now I shrugged. He stared expectantly.

I supposed after what happened between us following the near-death experience, I owed him some sort of explanation. "Like I told you last night, I don't know what I want. I'm sorry if I gave you the wrong idea on Friday. I think it was just the adrenaline."

Luca shook his head. "Call it what you want, but you always come back to me."

I stared at my muffin wrapper, now empty save for a few crumbs too small to eat. I didn't disagree with what he was saying, but I was confident in my assertion that I wasn't ready to make a major life decision now.

"My dad wants me to date you. He thinks being associated with your family will keep me safer. He actually said I should just pretend to be your girlfriend if I didn't want to have a real relationship with you. But it doesn't seem right for me to use you."

"You didn't mind using me the other night," he reminded me.

Heat rushed to my cheeks. "I'm sorry."

Luca stepped forward, wedging his firm body between my legs. "You may always use me in that manner," he said, his mouth so close to mine that I could feel his breath on my lips. "I'm only sorry we were interrupted. I planned to make you come at least two more times."

I swallowed nervously, the sound of it drowning out the pounding of my heart for the briefest of moments. I inhaled through my nose, taunting myself with his delicious scent.

"Tesoro, you can't tell me you don't feel the connection between us."

At that moment, I couldn't tell him anything. Having his hips between my thighs was so distracting that I'd forgotten how to speak. *Damn him.*

Luca gazed down at me, a cocky grin plastered on his face. He knew exactly how he affected me. He raised his thumb and ran it along my lower lip before dipping it into my mouth. I resisted the urge to groan.

Luca exhaled roughly. "I have to go. I have a meeting in the city tonight, but I am free tomorrow evening. Will you join me for dinner?"

I nodded, and before I registered what had just happened, he left.

I sat on the counter for a few minutes to gather my wits, then I smeared some cream cheese on one of the bagels and dropped it into a paper sack to take for lunch. Something told me I'd need all the carbs I could get to prepare for a night with Luca.

CHAPTER 12

Giada

$\mathcal{D}$inner with Luca was fun, and we stayed at the restaurant for close to three hours eating, talking, and laughing. I probably would've let him stay the night after, but he walked me to my apartment, told me to get some sleep, then left after only a peck on the cheek.

The next weekend, Luca invited me to a wedding back in Connecticut. His friend Giovanni was the groom. I'd never met Lauren, the woman he was marrying, and I had no recollection of ever speaking to Giovanni, but Luca assured me they anticipated my attendance.

In typical Luca fashion, he offered to pay for my dress, but I opted to wear the navy blue one he'd bought me in Italy. Luca had also arranged for me to meet him at the church. As Luca was apparently in the wedding, he needed to arrive early for photos. As Enzo slowed to a stop in front of the large Bronx church, I thanked him for the ride.

"No problem. So…you're going home with Luca, right?"

"Unless we're fighting," I replied, scooting towards the door.

I'd meant it as a joke, but as Enzo's eyes met mine in the rearview mirror, I assumed I had the same cringey expression on my face as he did. I laughed to brush it off, and was about to climb out when he spoke again.

"Why don't you text him and let him know you're here," he suggested.

"I think I can handle walking in alone." I gazed over to the church. It was large, but not that large. And churches were my comfort zone.

Enzo swiveled around in the seat. "I'd feel better if he came to get you. These are his people, not yours."

I wasn't sure what to make of his last statement. I hadn't expected to know any of the other guests anyway. But, it also wasn't worth picking a fight with Enzo over my entrance to some church.

"Do you want to walk me in?" I asked certain that would appease his concerns. Instead, he shook his head vehemently.

"Not a chance. You can go with Luca, or you can go on your own, but I am not leaving this car. Salvatore Marino's guys will eat me alive."

I chucked at his tone, then winced. "Oh God, do you think Mr. Marino will be here?" I hadn't mentally prepared to see Luca's parents.

"I don't know, but Giovanni works for him, so maybe."

Before I could fully process that possibility, Luca exited the front doors of the church. He glanced side to side before focusing directly on the car, which told me that someone had let him know I'd arrived. As I drank in the sight of Luca, wearing a crisp black tuxedo complete with bowtie, I forgot all about his parents. He looked so hot I practically forgot my own name too.

"Have fun," Enzo teased as I reached for the door handle.

Luca met me right as I swung open the door. He leaned into the car, his dark eyes gleaming as he scanned my attire. "Tesoro," he breathed, kissing my forehead. Then he gripped my hand to pull me to my feet. He thumped his fist on the top of the car. "Grazie Lorenzo," he called before shutting the door behind me.

"You look…handsome," I said, having to stop myself before saying "scrumptious," the first word that came to mind.

He grinned. "And you look stunning, but I'm not sure how I feel about that dress."

My hand fell away from his, and I stopped moving forward. "What do you mean?"

Luca cocked his head to the side and chuckled. "You hated me the last time you wore that. You flirted and teased me all night, and then you broke my heart."

That didn't exactly match my recollection of that night in Italy, but I was pleased that he at least remembered the dress. Most men were oblivious to a woman's attire. "Well, I can't promise I won't flirt, but I can tell you that what happens after the wedding depends entirely on your behavior."

He quirked an eyebrow. "Duly noted," he said. He wrapped his arm around me and leaned in, lingering by my neck before kissing my cheek. "You even smell amazing."

"I thought you'd approve of this scent. It's Dolce and Gabanna," I said, letting him guide me towards the entrance of the church. "Hey, will your parents be here?"

"Just my papà," he replied.

I supposed that was better than seeing both of Luca's parents, but I didn't have time to consider it before Luca began introducing me to a bunch of people on our walk up the aisle. As far as I could tell, everyone knew him. I supposed that made sense since he was such good friends with the groom. What surprised me, though, was that I didn't recognize a soul. Everyone on the groom's side of the aisle looked Italian, but apparently, none of them were in the same group of Italians who frequented my family's gatherings.

Luca stopped at the third pew from the front. "I need to go

offer Giovanni some last-minute advice, but the ceremony will start shortly, and I'll pick you up right here after. Okay?"

I nodded and scooted into the aisle. I watched as Luca shook hands with several more guys before disappearing off to the side of the sanctuary. I smiled, gazing around the church, happy for the chance to see the sanctuary of another parish. I'd come to learn that no two churches looked alike, but they all offered the same soothing elements, and they were all beautiful in their own way. I was so distracted by the architecture that I didn't notice anyone right beside me until a hand clamped down on my shoulder.

I jumped and turned, coming face to face with Salvatore Marino.

"Buon giorno, Giada. You look beautiful. How are you doing this lovely afternoon?"

"I'm um, good, sir. Thank you. And you?"

"No complaints." He smiled warmly, and an awkward pause ensued. I glanced nervously at the men flanking him on both sides, wondering why they were all still standing there if they weren't going to say anything.

"Did you, um, would you like to sit here?" I asked, motioning to the pew.

For some reason, that amused Mr. Marino, but thankfully he shook his head. "We'll talk later," he promised.

I watched as they walked to the front of the sanctuary then made their way to the opposite end of the row ahead of me. Salvatore scooted into the pew beside a much younger woman, whispering something in her ear as he did. One of his guys sat behind him, and the other leaned against the wall on the side of the sanctuary, looking every bit the part of a creepy bodyguard. I wondered what the bride would think of having armed goons lining the aisles on her special day.

The song changed abruptly, signaling the start of the ceremony, and Luca appeared at the front of the sanctuary along with two friends I recognized, one I didn't, and then the groom. I couldn't take my eyes off Luca. He appeared so commanding, standing there by the altar. And as his gaze locked on me, my insides turned to mush. I felt naked under his intense stare, and I couldn't help but let my mind wander, seeing him at the altar like that.

Back in high school, I would've bet my life that I'd marry Luca Marino someday. Even after we'd dated for a while, I still staunchly planned to remain a virgin until my wedding night. When I'd finally changed my mind on that topic, it was mostly just because I was so confident that Luca would be my husband that I fully justified sex with my (future) husband as a valid exception to the rule prohibiting premarital sex.

Now, I didn't have as strong of a vision for my future. I could clearly picture the wedding, and there wasn't a doubt in my mind that Luca would make a dashingly handsome, doting groom. I was equally confident that our wedding night would fulfill my every fantasy, but the rest of it was fuzzy. Would I spend my life as a married woman home alone while Luca worked nonstop and jetted around the country? Would Luca attend weddings with other women like his father seemed comfortable doing? Would the silence of his secrets grow so unbearable that we couldn't even stand to be in the same country as each other much of the year?

Luca winked, jolting me from my thoughts. Then, as his grin widened, I realized the rest of the congregation had stood to welcome the bride. I quickly rose to my feet and turned to the back of the sanctuary.

I hadn't met Lauren, but she made a beautiful bride. She was a petite woman, and her over-the-top chiffon dress probably outweighed her, but even under the many layers of lace and tulle, she stood out. Her light brown hair was twisted on top of her head, covered with a sheer veil, and her face displayed a calm confidence I envied. Lauren clearly had no doubts about what she was about to do. She didn't just love Giovanni; she knew marrying him was the right decision.

My stomach clenched as envy flooded my system. I couldn't envision ever being that confident about such a permanent decision. I mean, I was sure I wanted to get married, and probably sooner than later. I didn't doubt that my dad would continue to treat me like a child until he'd successfully passed me off onto another man. While I didn't love that old-fashioned approach, I also recognized I didn't have the independence or career prospects I'd need to live for long as a single woman .

Some days, I told myself I'd be happy marrying either Adrian or Luca, but I never really believed that. Adrian would be an amazing husband. Of that, I was sure. He wouldn't cheat, he wouldn't hurt me, and he probably wouldn't keep any secrets. Any woman would be lucky to end up with Adrian. Even me.

Except, I also recognized from experience that even when I was with Adrian, Luca still filled my thoughts. The moment anything at all was less than perfect with Adrian, my body started craving Luca like he was a gallon of water in the middle of the desert.

Logic—and Gabriella—told me that might be a sign that neither Luca nor Adrian was the man for me. Maybe I'd meet a third man, someone who I felt comfortable committing to—someone who made me forget all about Luca and Adrian. But I doubted it. With my luck and my history, I'd just be in love with all three at once.

I glanced over at Luca's dad, not surprised to see he appeared bored out of his mind. I did enjoy weddings, but then again, I tended to enjoy every church service. The wedding did not include a full mass, so it was short. The couple had already exchanged rings and recited traditional vows. I eagerly anticipated their first kiss, not knowing either of them well enough to guess whether it would be a simple, chaste peck or a fully indulgent makeout session. In the end, it was somewhere in the middle

—closed mouth and tasteful, but longer than the wedding etiquette books might recommend.

Everyone stood, and applause filled the sanctuary as the couple sauntered down the aisle. I couldn't help but smile, inexplicably happy for these people I didn't even know. I turned back to the front in time to see Luca offering his arm to one of the bridesmaids. Jealousy whipped through me, even as I realized it was likely just a part of the ceremony. I noticed Sal head off with his guys towards the exit and was about to follow suit, when Luca returned.

"Shall we?" he asked, offering me the same arm the blonde had just clutched.

"I don't know how I feel about being the second woman you escort," I said, feeling childish even as I rejected his arm and started down the aisle on my own.

With cat-like reflexes, he tugged my hand, pulling me away from the crowd and towards the front of the sanctuary. He led me out a side door into a mostly empty hallway.

"Stacy is married," he said.

"Stacy?"

"The bridesmaid you're ready to murder," he explained.

"I'm not…" I began, but then I stopped. He was right. I was strangely jealous. "I hate seeing you with blondes," I finally said.

Luca backed me against a wall, planting his palm beside my head. "Good. Because I prefer brunettes," he said, gradually inching his face closer.

It was impossible to feel anything but lust with his body inches from mine. Especially when he was wearing a tuxedo. Everything about him ratcheted up my desire for him.

"I would love to know what you were thinking during the ceremony," he said. "The look in your eyes…" he grinned.

"I was thinking all sorts of church-like thoughts," I said, my fingers reaching out to stroke the silky material of his jacket.

His gaze intensified, and my insides melted. His head dipped even closer to mine, and I could almost feel the electric charge of his lips on mine. But then a throat cleared, and Luca jumped back.

I turned to the side and saw Salvatore Marino. Heat flooded my cheeks, and I glanced away quickly.

"Apologies for the intrusion, but could I borrow my son for a moment?" he asked me.

Luca had already stepped away with his father, so I didn't respond. They walked to the end of the hall, then stopped. I gazed at them, able to hear their conversation but still forced to decipher its meaning solely based on their body language since they spoke entirely in Italian. Salvatore's two guards had remained closer to me. I wasn't entirely sure why, but I felt better not paying them any attention.

I could tell Luca was resistant to whatever his father was saying, but after a moment, he nodded. His father reached into his jacket and retrieved a gun, then passed it to Luca. Even from a distance, I could see Luca's eye roll, but then he simply wedged the gun into the back of his pants and then smoothed his vest and jacket back over it. Salvatore then patted his son on the shoulder and walked back to where his bodyguards stood. He tipped his head in my direction then kept walking.

Luca stayed where he was for a moment then walked back to me. He draped his arm across my shoulders and started walking me back towards the door. "We are supposed to ride with the rest of the wedding party in a limo."

"Okay," I said. I reached my arm up around his waist, feeling the distinct outline of a handgun against my wrist. "Are we expecting a shootout at the reception?"

Luca shifted my arm off of him, clasping his hand around mine. "No. But my papà is paranoid. He doesn't like having so many people who work for him in the same room. I'll give it to Alessio when we see him," he promised.

I hadn't expected that response. Honestly, I'd grown accustomed to Luca always being armed. "Won't you feel naked without it?"

I was teasing, but he lifted his pants leg to reveal a holster and handgun around his ankle.

"It's all good, sweetheart. Don't worry."

I suppressed a cringe.

The reception was held in the ballroom of a hotel about fifteen or twenty minutes from the church. The happy couple rode in a different limo, but Luca and I sat across from Thomas, his girlfriend Rebecca, and Alessio's date Ashley. Alessio rode on the other side of Luca, and the two of them chatted in Italian the entire drive. Ashley was focused on her cell phone, and Thomas and Rebecca seemed caught up in their own little world. I would've felt ignored, except that Luca kept his hand on my leg, and his fingers traced tiny circles on my thigh.

Once we were inside, Luca was much more attentive. He made sure I had a drink in my hands at all times, and he hand fed me several of the appetizers. Before the main course was served though, he was called away for photos. I could tell he was trying to find someone for me to talk to, but I quickly shook my head.

"I'm going to the restroom anyway."

He narrowed his gaze. "No more lipstick, okay?"

I laughed and rolled my eyes. "Not really your concern, is it?" I taunted. I wasn't sure where the restroom was, so I just headed out the closest of the three exists from the ballroom. I wandered down the hall a bit before reaching the bathroom. I'd barely gotten through the door when I stopped dead in my tracks. The bride stood there, along with the blonde Luca had accompanied down the aisle.

"Sorry," I mumbled, starting to back out of the restroom.

"No, it's fine!" Lauren called. "We were just pinning up my dress."

The blonde was frowning at the back of the bridal gown,

shaking her head. It was obvious she had no idea what she was doing.

"Here, do you want a hand?" I offered, dropping my purse on the counter and coming closer. "There should be a small fabric loop inside the bustle that you can latch around these buttons."

The blonde backed out of my way, and I began gathering the lengthy train of the dress in my hands. Once I had folded it against Lauren's back, I lifted until I spotted the loop. "It should fasten right like this," I said, securing the first part. With the weight of the dress, I wasn't surprised that the train affixed in three separate spots.

"I'll go get you a drink," the blonde said to her friend, leaving us alone.

"Alright, I think you're all set," I told the bride. "Gorgeous dress!"

"Thank you. I'm impressed you were able to figure that out."

"I minored in fashion design," I explained. "I'm Giada Conti. I'm not sure if we've met before. I'm here with Luca."

The bride chuckled. "Of course. Giovanni talks about you all the time. I'm surprised we haven't met before. It sounds like we might have a lot in common."

She didn't elaborate, therefore leaving me wondering what exactly those shared interests might be. I also wasn't sure why Giovanni would've ever spoken of me or what he'd said. I knew he was one of the main guys who worked with Luca, but we'd never been close. To be honest, I'd found him a tad scary.

Lauren groaned and fanned herself. "It's a million degrees inside this dress."

I smiled. It looked uncomfortably warm, although the outdoor temperatures were still low enough to offset the thick fabric.

"Well, seems like you and Luca might be next, huh," she continued. "I should get back out there, though. It was nice meeting you. We'll have to get to know each other after the honeymoon."

I touched up my makeup, reapplying both pressed powder and lipstick just to show Luca I could, then washed my hands before making my way to the door. When I swung it open, I nearly slammed into Luca.

"Geez! You startled me," I said. "Were you stalking the women's restroom exits?"

He grinned. "The bride told me you were in there. I was debating whether you were waiting for me to come in and ravish you."

"Nope, just fixing my lipstick," I said proudly. "And for future reference, I'm never waiting to be ravished if I'm in a public bathroom."

Luca started to let me pass, then reached for my hip and swung me back to face him. He dragged his thumb roughly across my lips but then, before I could protest, his mouth was covering mine. He kissed me until I'd forgotten all about my lipstick. Then, we walked hand in hand back to the reception.

The dinner was delicious, and then there was lots of dancing and drinking. They served wedding cake, but in true Italian form there was also an oversized table of other sweet treats. Luca and I both drank too much, but the dancing helped offset it.

"It's weird seeing your creepy friends all relaxed and having fun," I mused as we danced arm in arm.

Luca crooked his head down to gaze at me. "Did you just call my friends creepy?"

I winced. I hadn't meant to say that part out loud, but it was true.

He shook his head and held me close. "Lauren seemed impressed with you. Giovanni suggested we double date sometime."

Luca didn't seem like the type to ever participate in a double date, but I didn't feel the need to comment. The music had changed to a more upbeat song, but with my head pressed against Luca's chest and his arms wrapped around my back, I had no interest in moving any faster.

"Yeah, she mentioned getting together after their honeymoon. Any idea where they're going?"

"Sicily."

"Oh!" I didn't know why that surprised me, but it did. Giovanni was clearly Italian, but Lauren didn't seem to be. "What part of the island?"

"Palermo. The exact villa you were in the last time you wore this dress, actually."

"You let people stay in your villa?"

"No, not people. Giovanni."

"He's a person," I pointed out. "Wait, for free?"

I heard the rumble of Luca's chuckle in his chest. "Si."

"Wow. I'm not criticizing. It's super generous. I'm just surprised because you always struck me as being a tad protective of your personal spaces."

"Well, I wouldn't let just anyone stay there. It's a short list."

"I'm on it," I reminded him.

He chuckled. "That you are."

"Is Alessio?"

"Of course."

"Thomas?"

Luca nodded.

"What about their girlfriends?"

"I'd trust them to supervise anyone they invited."

I smiled. "There's no one else on the list, is there?"

He shook his head. "No. I trust three men in the world, and one woman, on a probationary basis."

"Probationary? What does that mean?"

He shrugged. "You keep me on my toes. Most people don't surprise me, but you…I've known for ages, and you still continue to stump me. I just can't tell what you're thinking."

For some reason, that amused me. Resting my hands on his biceps, I gazed up at him. He'd folded his suit jacket over the back of a chair after dinner, so now he looked even hotter, wearing just the vest over his white button-down. "Can you tell what I'm thinking now?" I asked.

His eyes seemed to darken as he stared at me. His head dipped lower and lower until our lips were nearly touching. "I have an excellent guess what you are thinking now, and the best part is, for once we are on the same page."

His soft whispers sent shivers up my spine, and he kissed me before I could ask for clarification.

Luca's father left the reception fairly early, and Luca relaxed considerably once he was gone. Watching Luca laugh and joke with his friends reminded me of high school. Back then, Luca had been the life of every party. Since he graduated, he always seemed stressed and tightly coiled when in public. I'd known he was friends with Alessio, although I couldn't honestly say why they were so close, but this was the first I'd seen Luca interact with Giovanni and Thomas as anything but work associates.

I liked the laid-back version of Luca. A lot. And somehow seeing that other people liked him, too, made me feel better about my inability to get him off my mind. Maybe current day Luca was just as charismatic as the old Luca.

We cheered for the couple as they exited the reception, then slowly made our way to the door. We shared a limo with Alessio and Ashley, but Thomas and Rebecca didn't join us this time. Ashley was so drunk that she slumped across Alessio's lap, but he didn't seem to mind. He and Luca joked some in Italian while he stroked his date's hair like she was a cat.

"How come you missed that bouquet?" Alessio said, switching to English and turning to me.

I hesitated, unsure what the proper response was. Obviously, I was in no position to be the next one married, seeing as how I'd been with a different man earlier that same month. But I didn't want to make Luca look bad by telling his best friend I just wasn't that into him.

"Contact sports have never been my thing," I finally said.

Alessio laughed, but Luca shook his head, rubbing my thigh in an increasingly distracting manner.

"Giada has every detail of her wedding mapped out except for the groom," Luca said, sneaking a sideways glance at me before continuing. "One day it's Adrian, the next day it's me...just all depends on which way the wind blows."

"Luca," I began, but Alessio interrupted.

"Not everyone can obsess over the same person from age sixteen on," he said.

"I don't obsess," Luca insisted.

Alessio leaned forward as though telling me a secret. "He's been in love with you since your second day at that godforsaken boarding school. Don't let him fool you with his bad attitude and controlling demeanor."

I opened my mouth to respond, but no words came out. I turned to Luca, but he simply sat there, expressionless.

A moment later, the limo pulled to a stop. Alessio turned to his date, who was clearly unconscious. He mumbled what had to have been a swear word under his breath, then tried unsuccessfully to wake her.

Luca laughed so hard that he snorted, but then he crawled out after his friend and helped him lift the girl. Once she was out of the car, Alessio hoisted her up over his shoulder. Her skirt rode up high enough to reveal most of her ass to anyone walking by, but at this point, I figured she probably didn't care.

Luca, still laughing, at least had the sense to caution his friend. "Don't slam her head on the door when you go in."

Alessio nodded. "Come on, amico, you of all people know this is not my first time carrying an unconscious woman into my apartment."

They both laughed way too hard at that, and then Luca started to turn back to the limo.

"Oh, hey, your papà's Beretta!" Alessio shouted, as though just remembering a greeting card or some leftovers and not a deadly weapon. "Left hip, I think," he said.

Luca reached around his friend, pulling out a large black handgun. He glanced at it and then shook his head. "Nope." He squatted down and raised Alessio's pant leg, revealing yet another gun. "Still no."

Alessio shifted his date further to his shoulder and lifted his arm slightly. That revealed yet another holster, this one several inches below his armpit. "Third time's a charm?" he said hopefully.

"Yep, night man," Luca said, gripping that gun and hopping back into the limo with the weapon still on his lap. He relaxed back against the seat and slung his arm over my shoulders as the limo pulled away from the curb.

"Umm, should I be concerned that your friend somehow had three guns at a wedding?"

Luca frowned at me. "He only had the third because you didn't like me with it."

"Yeah, but the other two?"

"Second Amendment, baby. I don't know what you want me to say." He slipped the one from his lap into the back of his pants and turned to me. "I would've thought you'd be more concerned by Alessio's comment about unconscious women."

I couldn't help but smile at that. "No, he's never struck me as a guy who has the best taste in women. Have he and Ashley been together long?"

"They're just friends," Luca replied.

He must have noticed the confusion on my face because he then offered a more detailed explanation. "They're friends who fool around. I think she's a stripper. Anyway, he brings her to events when he needs a date."

That didn't answer as many questions as it raised, but I let it drop as we'd reached Luca's apartment. We were both tired and starting to lose our buzz from the alcohol, so I had fully anticipated us both just going to sleep. Instead, we'd ended up in the shower together.

The next morning, we slept late then binged on bagels and coffee from the corner deli. We spent the entire weekend together. It reminded me of our time together in Italy, and it was magical. Nothing extraordinary happened, and we barely left his apartment, but everything just felt right. I still hadn't fully straightened out my own feelings in my brain, but I decided not to question my arrangement with Luca as long as it was running smoothly.

The next weekend, we went back to my parents' house. The last time Luca and I had both been at my childhood home at the same time, Adrian had been there as well. Everything had been awkward and strained. But now, I wasn't with Adrian. This time, the man I was bringing home to my family was already familiar with them and well-liked by them. When we arrived at the house, Luca carried his own bags up and paused by my bedroom.

I gazed up and, quickly interpreting the look on his face, shook my head furiously. "You are staying in the guestroom. You can't seriously think my dad would be okay with you sleeping in my room."

Luca raised an eyebrow but deposited his bags in the room across the hall from my room.

No one in the house commented on our sleeping arrangement, so I considered that perhaps my parents didn't know that Luca and I had sort of been dating again for real. Or whatever we were doing.

But then at dinner the next day, Luca mentioned he was moving out of his Stamford apartment. "I need to be in Syracuse to get a new project off the ground this next month or so anyway, so I guess the timing is just as well," he said.

My dad immediately recommended Luca stay with me.

"I thought you were concerned about my virtue," I reminded my dad. "Don't you think people might get the wrong impression if Luca is living in my apartment?"

There was a stretch of silence at the table, and then my dad chuckled. Everyone else at the table joined in on the joke except me.

After dinner, Luca followed me to my bedroom.

"Didn't you just move into that place?" I asked.

He nodded. "Yeah, but it was never mine. It was just one of the places my papà owned, and now he wants it open so someone else can move in." He paused and made a face. "One of his women, I assume."

"Oh God, I'm sorry," I said.

"I don't have to stay with you," he said, sitting on the foot of my bed.

"Your parents' home in New York isn't very convenient to Syracuse."

"It's extremely convenient for virtually all of my other work, though. More so than upstate, especially."

"Yeah, but your parents live even farther from me."

"Think you'd miss me?"

I turned away, uncertain of what the answer to that was. Sure, Luca and I were getting along great now, but that's always how it started with us. Soon we'd be at each other's throats, or he'd do something horrific to remind me what a pig he could be.

"It would only be for a month or so, but I mean it. If you're uncomfortable with me staying with you, I won't."

Hearing that it was such a short amount of time did make my hesitation seem unreasonable. "Are you sure you want that? Wouldn't you rather live with Alessio or Thomas or someone?"

Luca wrinkled his nose. "Grown men shouldn't live together. I'm not a vagrant. I have other options. Your father just wants me close to you because he's still scared for you. That shooting terrified him."

"If you want to stay in my apartment, you're more than welcome," I finally said. Maybe more time with Luca was exactly what I needed.

He reached for my hands, smiling. He tugged me until I was seated on his leg, and then he kissed me. "How welcome do you think I'd be in here tonight?"

I laughed against his lips. "I'd say it's fifty/fifty whether my dad kills you."

"Aww come on. I'd bet more than seventy percent chance he lets me live."

"Are you a betting man?"

"Usually, yes. With you, I'd never gamble." He kissed my forehead. "Sogni d'oro, amore. Sweet dreams," he translated.

I stayed in bed for several minutes after Luca left but then decided I wasn't even that tired yet. I crawled out from under the covers and peered out my door, but the guest room was clearly unoccupied. I wondered if I should be offended that he'd apparently gone downstairs to hang out with my brothers, then dismissed it. I always questioned everything when things in my life went smoothly. It was like I'd try to scrounge up problems where there weren't any.

Obviously, I just needed to chill out and accept that life was actually going okay.

Adrian

*B*etween law school and my now painfully awkward job for the judge, I managed to keep busy the first two weeks after Giada dumped me. Thanks to the proximity of Giada's apartment to the law school, I couldn't help but notice Luca coming and going from her apartment on a few occasions. It sickened me to think about that monster getting close to her again, but there was nothing I could do.

The next Saturday night, Ryan—the guy from my study group who'd quickly become my closest friend in law school—invited me out to a bar. We'd tried to round up a whole group of guys, but the law school party scene wasn't like the undergrad one. Some of the guys were already married or settled down, a few worked other jobs at night, and even those who weren't otherwise occupied weren't as enthusiastic about a night out at the bar as the undergrads I'd known.

Still, I was glad to be out on the town. Between school and studying, I rarely saw the world outside of the law building or my apartment. We picked our favorite bar, grabbed a table, then played a round of pool before settling back into our seats. Ryan was a New Yorker and had a girlfriend back home, so he'd be an excellent wingman if the opportunity arose. Unfortunately, every woman I noticed fell far short of the standard I'd set by dating Giada.

There were several women at law school who met all of my requirements as far as being smart, kind, and funny, but none of them were as interesting as Giada, and none of them were even in the same realm as her in terms of physical assets. Outside of school, a fair number of attractive women would flirt with me from time to time, but they were all either dumb, boring, or self-absorbed.

"I see why you're still single," Ryan mused as I blew off a blonde that came by our table with a lame pickup line about having seen me around before. "She was hot."

"Yeah," I agreed. "But not my type."

"What is your type?"

"Giada."

"Your ex isn't a type. She's a person."

"It's more of an on-again, off-again sort of thing. I'm optimistic," I said, feeling anything but.

Ryan chuckled, and we moved on to discussing sports.

Halfway through my beer, the conversation lulled, and I scanned the bar for ideas for our next discussion topic.

"Oh shit," the words left my mouth the second I spotted Luca, and about a nanosecond before he spotted me. I jerked back to my drink, suddenly eager to see the bottom of the glass.

"You okay?" Ryan asked, glancing around to try to spot what had set me off.

"Nope. Not really." I finished the rest of my beer, and Ryan offered me his. I chuckled. "No thanks, but if we stick around for another round, it needs to be something stronger."

"Does this have to do with the tall, dark-haired guy walking this way?"

"Fuck."

"Adrian," Luca greeted me, slapping me on the back in a way that probably resembled a friendly greeting to those who didn't know our history and dynamic.

I sighed and reminded myself I could be mature and polite for the two minutes it would take to get rid of him. "Luca Marino, this is Ryan Marchetti. Ryan, Luca." I said, in what had to be the least enthusiastic introduction ever.

Luca extended his hand to Ryan. "Nice to meet you. Are you Italian?"

"No!" I said at the same time as Ryan.

Luca shrugged and glanced around. He spotted an empty chair at a nearby table and dragged it to ours, straddling it backwards. I rolled my eyes then looked around to see which of his cronies he'd brought. Seeing none, I turned back to him.

"You're not here alone…" I began.

"Nope. Thomas and Alessio are here. Figured we needed a guy's night after a long day of work."

"What are you doing in town?"

He cocked his head to the side, a bemused expression spreading across his face. "You didn't hear the news? I'm moving in with Giada."

Every muscle in my body tightened. I casually reached across the table and grabbed the beer Ryan had previously offered me. Luckily, the waitress came by then. Ryan ordered another beer, and I switched to whiskey. When she turned to Luca, I quickly assured her that he wasn't staying. Luckily, he agreed and pointed to a booth in the corner where he would be seated.

"What do you do, Luca?" Ryan asked, clearly sensing the tension and trying to add some normalcy to the conversation. "Are you in school now?"

I turned to Luca, intrigued as to how he'd answer that first question. To my disappointment, he brushed it off with a generic response.

"I'm in business."

"So, um, how do you two know each other?

No way was I letting Luca frame that relationship. "Mutual friend," I said quickly. "Remember the ex-girlfriend I told you about? He's the guy she left me for. Twice," I added, sounding significantly less bitter than I felt.

"Oh, come on, Adrian. She said you broke up with her the first time. And this last time, what did you expect? The best thing you had going for you was that you weren't under her papà's thumb."

"I think your friends are missing you, Luca."

He glanced over at them then turned back to us. "Listen, I know you and Giada still talk, so I wanted to be mature about this and let you know before anything is official."

I waited, praying he wasn't about to tell me that he was moving Giada to Italy or something equally insane.

"I bought her a ring. I got her father's blessing, of course, and um, I'll probably ask her in the next week."

I blinked several times but had no response whatsoever for what he'd just told me. He'd at least lost his normal douche tone when speaking, but no intonation whatsoever could soften the blow of his words or erase the image now etched into my brain of Giada in a wedding dress next to Luca the sociopath.

"Right," he finally said. "So, um, no hard feelings. She'd like if we could get along, especially if you'll be working for her father."

"I'm not," I said.

"Sure you're not," he said, in a placating, almost mocking tone. He stood and turned to Ryan.

"Nice to meet you."

Ryan nodded, and Luca started to walk away.

"She will never marry you," I said, my voice level and filled with certainty that, in reality, was more of a wishful prayer. "She's just scared now. When things calm down, she will come to her senses, and when she does, I'll be waiting."

Luca leaned over, placing a hand on the table in front of me. "Look, Adrian, I'm being nice because I promised Giada I would, but you would be well advised to watch yourself. And as for Giada, you don't know her as well as you think you do."

He turned and nearly bumped into the waitress as she returned with our drinks. "Put anything they order tonight on my tab," Luca said, smiling politely then walking off.

Ryan cringed. "Well, in that case, keep 'em coming."

The waitress nodded and left us alone.

"So, he's a dick," Ryan said.

I nodded.

"But a rich one, I guess?"

I nodded again. Then it hit me. If Luca was here, he wasn't

with Giada. I started to stand. "I've got to go talk to her while he's not with her."

Ryan flew out of his seat and nudged me back down. "Noooooo. Man, come on. Think about it. That is a terrible idea. You're drunk, and it's late. Nothing you say to her now is going to be persuasive. Second, if you like her, I'm guessing she's smart. So if he's really the creep you say he is, she'll figure that out, and she won't agree to marry him. Third, if you're wrong and she actually does like him even a little, she'll never forgive you if you fuck up his proposal."

I sighed and sunk into my seat.

Ryan peered over my shoulder. "Also, he and his friends are scary as fuck."

I had to laugh at that. If only he knew the half of it.

Ryan distracted me for a little while, and then an attractive brunette named Debra came by our table and distracted me even better.

She wasn't in the same category as Giada, but she was sexy and flirty and managed to make me laugh. Plus after the night I had, thanks to Luca and his big mouth, the attention from a beautiful woman was more than flattering. So, a little while later, when Ryan said he was heading out, Debra suggested I show her my place, and I didn't say no.

CHAPTER 13

Giada

Living with Luca wasn't much different from dating Luca. He took over half of my already-limited closet space, filled the bathroom with his various grooming devices, then promptly disappeared for a few days. I was busy with school, though, so it didn't much matter. And on Wednesday, Angelo surprised me.

Historically, a surprise visit from my oldest brother wasn't a good thing, but this time, he said he just wanted to take me to lunch. As we ate and chatted about purely amicable topics, I got the impression he legitimately wanted to get to know me better, which was sweet. He even came inside the apartment for coffee after lunch.

"You sure you have time before your next class?" he asked, settling onto the couch.

"I'm a second-semester senior. Classes are kind of optional at this point, but yes. Plenty of time." I pulled out a few of the sketches I'd done for my last fashion design class, and he even pretended to be interested.

"These are amazing, Giada. Why did you decide to major in interior design instead?"

"Because I can't sew," I admitted. Besides, I wanted to wear the high-end fashion, not stitch it together behind the scenes.

I followed his gaze to the corner, where one of Luca's suit jackets was draped over the back of a chair.

"It's weird seeing his stuff around here and knowing it was Dad's idea. I still remember in high school when you'd have to sneak around to make out with him."

I laughed at the memory, then stopped abruptly. "What do you mean, Dad's idea?"

Angelo shook his head. "Not his idea, just that he was on board with you two living together. You know, he's been so concerned about your safety since that incident at the shipyard and then with the drive by... When Luca came to talk to him about your future, he was more than happy to give his blessing."

I considered all of that, but it was nothing new to me. I eyed my brother suspiciously. "So, really, what brought you by today? You sure you just wanted to see your baby sister?"

He nodded. "Yeah. I had some free time and was near this part of town, and I realized I might not see you as often if you move to Italy so I didn't want to take this for granted."

"Why would I move to Italy?"

Angelo frowned, "I figured you would live there with Luca when you're married. Isn't the majority of his business there?"

"Married? Geez, I'm not even out of college yet."

Angelo sipped his coffee like it was no big deal. "Honestly, I'm surprised you aren't already engaged. Wasn't that the whole point of him moving in?"

"I thought you said it was to keep me safe."

"Don't twist my words, Giada. I'm not trying to pick a fight. I don't want to argue. I just don't get why you're hesitating. You've got the man. Why wait?"

Wow, what a loaded question. I blew out a sigh. "I'm not even twenty-two yet. I'm not ready to make major life decisions. If I have the right man, there's no hurry. And besides, what if I don't?"

My brother suddenly looked flustered. "Is this about Adrian?"

"I don't know, maybe. Or maybe there's someone else out there that I'm supposed to end up with that I just haven't met yet. I like Luca, but he isn't perfect. I'm not sure we could survive each other in the long run."

"If you're waiting for perfection, you will die alone."

"So says my perpetually single older brother," I said with an eye roll. "Besides, I'm not one hundred percent sure that I'm *not* supposed to end up with Adrian. He is a good man, too."

"He's hardly perfect," Angelo said. He pulled out his phone and began scrolling.

"No, but he's less likely to end up in hell than Luca."

"That's not your place to judge, Giada," he said. "And maybe you should see this."

My phone binged with an image Angelo texted to me. On the screen was a picture of Adrian with a brunette. For a second, I thought it was me, but on closer inspection, it was obvious she was less pretty and significantly sluttier. Her arms were wrapped around Adrian in the picture. I winced, hoping my lunch wouldn't come back up.

"Swipe to the next one," Angelo said.

I did but wished I hadn't. The next image showed Adrian leading the woman by the hand into his apartment. I swallowed the bile rising in my throat and set down my phone. "We're not together, so it's not my business if he's seeing someone else," I said, wishing I actually felt that way. We'd spoken just days before, and he hadn't mentioned a new girlfriend. "Besides, are you having him followed?"

"You know Dad has guys watching you to keep you safe. Sometimes they check in on other people in your life, or his. This caught their attention because they know this girl. Her name is Debra."

I cringed, wishing I didn't know that information.

"She's a prostitute."

"What? That's ridiculous. Adrian would never…"

"Well, he did."

"How do you even know about her…occupation? Are you a client?"

"Jesus, no. I just know. And I thought you should know what Adrian is up to when he's not with you." Angelo stood. "I'm sorry to end our visit on such a sour note, but I have to head back to town. Thank you for the coffee. Give Luca my regards when you see him tomorrow."

I nodded and hugged my brother.

~

Adrian

It took some convincing to persuade Giada to meet me at the student union building after her last class that evening. I wondered if she was nervous about seeing me in light of Luca moving in, but when I'd pestered Enzo earlier, he'd finally blabbed that Luca was out of town. Even if his goons were watching her, they couldn't find fault with us meeting in a public building on campus. Besides, I wasn't afraid of Luca Merino.

We made small talk for a few minutes, but it was obvious Giada was annoyed with me for some reason, so I decided just to skip to the point.

"I ran into Luca over the weekend, and he told me he's planning to propose."

That clearly surprised her, but not as much as I'd expected.

"When did you see him?"

"Saturday night. I was out with a friend, and he was out with his usual crew."

"Yeah, I think I know about your friend," she muttered.

I wasn't sure what she had against Ryan, but that was completely beside the point. "Giada, you can't marry him. You know what he's like. Have you completely forgotten what he did to Enzo? How he treated you? He cheated on you, Giada. God, he could be off with another woman right now for all you know."

"Oh and you're one to talk," she quipped.

"What does that mean? I never cheated on you. I would never cheat on you." I shook my head. "We're not even together, and I can't even bring myself to be with another woman because I only want you."

"Bullshit!" she said, her sudden increased volume causing a few other patrons to glance in our direction. She rummaged around in her purse, pulled out her phone, and slid it across the table to me. I glanced at the photo displayed on her screen and instantly felt sick.

"Tell me that's not you," she said.

I searched for the right words to explain.

Giada looked me in the eye and then took her phone back. Tears formed in the corners of her eyes, and my head ached with the awareness that she'd clearly hoped it wasn't true.

"Giada, you and I weren't together then. I didn't even…"

She held up her hand to shush me. "Debra, is that her name?"

I nodded, then started to tell her again that I didn't even sleep with that woman, but then it hit me. There was no rational reason for Giada to have a photo of me with this woman. And it wasn't a coincidence that I was photographed shortly after I'd seen Luca.

"Giada, don't you see what he's doing? Luca sent someone to spy on me and take this picture so you'd feel pressured to stay with him. He's manipulating you, and you're letting him get away with it. He doesn't want to be with you; he just wants to win! He wants control."

Giada stood abruptly. "Just shut up, Adrian. I never thought Luca was perfect, but I expected more from you. I mean, seriously, a prostitute?"

My jaw dropped, her last statement so utterly confusing that I almost didn't respond to set her straight before she took off.

"Giada, wait!"

She swiveled to face me. "No. We are done here. And for what it's worth, I didn't get this photo from Luca. He doesn't know anything about it."

She scurried out of the building before I even realized what had hit me.

~

Giada

Luca was in the apartment when I returned after my last class Thursday. I greeted him warmly, almost surprised at how relieved I was to see him after a few days apart. He smiled and pulled me onto his lap in the wide upholstered armchair. I would've been happy to kiss him till my lips went numb, but after only a few minutes, Luca pulled back.

"Come to the city with me," he whispered before I had a chance to pout.

"Sure," I said, perplexed as to why such a silly request required us to stop kissing. "When?" I pressed my mouth against his again.

Luca swept his tongue across my lips before darting it into my mouth.

"Now," he answered, still teasing me with his tongue.

I moaned at the eroticism of his expert movements, and then I realized what he just said. I pulled back abruptly. "What?"

Luca grinned. "If we leave within a half hour, we can be there in time for a late dinner."

"I'd have to pack."

"If you can pack in under ten minutes, we'll still have time to finish what we started. I was thinking I could try that move I did there with my tongue on other parts of your body."

My mind went blank at the suggestion, and suddenly, I wanted nothing more than to drag him into my bedroom. But I couldn't pack that quickly. "We could eat later."

"We could, but it's fun to make you wait," he teased. "I'd been planning to drive, but I suppose if you're really eager, we could ask Lorenzo to drive us, and I could attempt my magic in the backseat."

I cringed at the thought of fooling around in front of Enzo, even though I was fairly sure Luca was kidding. I slid off his lap and went into the bedroom to pack. "What are we doing in the city?"

"Casual dinner tonight, sightseeing and then obscene amounts of kinky sex tomorrow, then brunch and church with my parents Saturday, and if you survive that, a fancy dinner out Saturday night."

I was so distracted by his inclusion of kinky sex on our itinerary that I nearly missed the part about his parents. I assumed that was his plan. I started out of the bedroom to call him on it, but he met me halfway, with a dress in hand. He held it up and raised an eyebrow.

"For brunch?" he asked.

I smiled and stepped closer to touch the fabric. The marigold dress was strapless and featured pink peonies and a matching satin bow just under the breasts. It was gorgeous, and the bright, warm colors were perfect for a dreary early spring day.

"I'll probably need a sweater," I said. I rose to my toes. "Thank you. It's lovely." I sighed and returned to the closet to pack more items. "It's too bad you're happy in your current line of work because you'd be a great personal shopper."

He laughed and lounged on the bed. "Only for you. I'm happy to report that I have not memorized every inch of any other woman's body, so I'd have no clue what size or style to buy them."

As I finished packing my clothes and moved on to toiletries, I asked another question that had been weighing on my mind. "When you were out of town this week, did you have someone watching me?"

Luca laughed as though he hadn't previously done that multiple times. "I personally did not, but I know for a fact your papà had Lorenzo follow you like a hawk while I was gone. He's not spying on you so much as trying to keep you safe."

I frowned. "Promise?"

"Yep. Although if this is your way of asking if I know you met up with Adrian last night, your loyal driver did tell me about that, but only after I asked."

"You asked if I saw Adrian? You still don't trust me?"

"I was curious if you'd seen him because I ran into him last weekend. I thought he might try to talk with you after that."

"Why didn't you tell me you saw him?"

He shrugged casually. "It wasn't exactly an eventful evening. He was with some guy at a bar, and we just talked for a couple minutes. I forgot about it until after I was out of town."

His answer was innocent enough, so I focused on my packing. We talked and listened to music while we drove, arriving in the city just in time to change clothes at the hotel before our dinner reservations. That night, he kept his promise about showing me some expert work with his tongue, and the next morning, I awoke a very happy girl.

We stopped for bagels and coffee near the hotel and then, we hit up a few touristy sites, starting with the Statue of Liberty. Despite growing up in the region, I'd never ridden the ferry to Ellis Island. With Luca by my side, telling me stories of various Italians immigrating to America, it was fascinating.

Our next stop was Central Park. It wasn't super warm out yet, but with our jackets, it felt refreshing as long as we kept walking. We paused in front of the bow bridge, admiring its simple beauty.

"Did you know that thousands of artists have painted this exact bridge? There's more paintings of it than almost any other bridge in America," I said, wishing I could recall more of the specifics from my American art history class.

Luca smiled and squeezed my hand. "Come on, let's walk across it."

We paused again at the top, and I turned to look out over the railing. It was gorgeous. When I turned back to face Luca, he had a goofy look on his face. He reached for both of my hands and pulled me close, kissing me on the mouth in a way that made me forget we were in the middle of a busy park. When he ended the kiss, he stayed close.

"Will you marry me, Giada?" he asked, his voice barely more than a whisper.

I froze, uncertain whether I'd heard him correctly. Despite my hesitation, Luca continued staring into my eyes peacefully, apparently content to wait for me to remember how to speak.

"I...I..." I finally stuttered.

He raised his hand to my face, gently stroking my cheek. "It's alright, Giada. I've put you on the spot. I just...I've been carrying the ring around with me for ages, and looking at you now, I realized I don't want to wait any longer."

"Did your father put you up to this?" I asked.

"No," he replied quickly, looking slighted.

"Did *my* father?"

He raised an eyebrow. "Your father gave me his blessing and

mentioned that our engagement would help ensure your safety, but I bought the ring ages before he said any of that."

I considered his words. "So, you want to marry me?"

He breathed a laugh. "Yes. Very much so."

"Because you love me, not because someone told you to?"

A gust of wind hit us and blew my hair over my eyes. Luca tenderly lifted the strands up and smoothed them back into place. "If you haven't noticed, I'm not awfully compliant about doing what people to tell me to do. And yes, ti amo tanto. Senza di te non sono niente." He paused, then translated the last part for me. "I'm nothing without you. Sposami?"

He fumbled around in his pocket for a moment, then dropped to his knee.

Despite harboring a multitude of fantasies wherein I married Luca, I'd never once guessed he'd be one to assume the traditional proposal position.

"Yes," I said. "Si."

He rose up and wrapped his arms around my waist, kissing me firmly. He slid the ring onto my finger, kissing my hand as he did so. Only then did I get a good look at the ring. It was a platinum band with a large, clear round cut diamond in the middle and three smaller round diamonds on each side forming a triangle. It was gorgeous and sparkled more than any jewelry I owned.

"You could pick something else if you don't like it," he said.

"I love it."

We kissed again, and I texted a picture of the ring to my mother and Gabriella. Then, I switched my phone to silent the rest of the day and celebrated the engagement with Luca in bed.

I didn't have a chance to panic about brunch with his parents until we awoke the next morning. Though I hadn't seen Luca's mom in ages, I wasn't nearly as worried about her as I was his father. Luca assured me they'd both be thrilled, but that didn't mean they'd be nice.

"You have the most beautiful shoulders," Luca said, dropping soft kisses all over my shoulders and collarbone. "It should be illegal for you to cover them with sleeves."

"Mmmm," I said, squirming at the tickles from his breath. "I'll freeze if I don't wear something over this."

Luca pouted as I reached for a sweater. I considered my options and then draped a cream-colored chiffon scarf over my shoulders instead. He smiled contentedly.

We were a few minutes late arriving at the restaurant, in the lobby of a hotel on the east side of town. My future inlaws had already arrived. Luca's father stood as we approached, nodding politely. Camilla smiled warmly at her son, then turned icy as she greeted me.

I glanced at Luca, but he seemed oblivious. He held out my chair for me to sit while he spoke. "I hope you haven't been waiting long. I guess we were a few minutes late."

"It's fine," Mr. Marino said.

At the same time, Camilla turned to me. "You'll have to plan ahead better, or you'll always have my Luca running behind."

Luca turned to the passing waiter and ordered us coffee, and then we all focused on the menus for a minute. He held tightly to my hand under the table, probably to ensure I didn't inadvertently flash the ring too soon. Once we'd ordered, though, he turned to me and grinned.

"Well, we have some news," he said. Then he lifted my hand up and placed it on the table. His parents both immediately spotted the diamond.

Mr. Marino stood and hugged his son warmly, then walked around to me. He kissed each of my cheeks, then turned back to Luca. "Congratulazioni ai nuovi fidanzati! Tanti auguri per una vita felice insieme," he said.

Luca smiled, then turned to me. "Congrats to the newly engaged, many wishes for a happy life together," he translated.

Camilla cleared her throat. "She doesn't speak Italian?" she asked, her expression filled with disgust.

"She's lived here her whole life, mamma."

"Still," she said.

I bit the side of my cheek, not having anticipated such resistance from Mrs. Marino.

Luca changed the subject, complimenting his mother on her hairstyle and dress and asking about their activities lately, but by the time our food came, the discussion turned back around to our engagement.

"Wasn't it only a month ago that you were dating that Greek boy?" she asked me.

"He's not Greek," I said, dodging the question.

Camilla turned to Luca. "She's changed her mind more than once about you lately. Aren't you concerned the wind will blow a different direction again, and she'll leave you in the dust?"

I waited for Luca to jump to my defense, but instead, he just laughed. I shot him a dirty look.

"Baby, you have to admit, you weren't so fond of me for a while there." He squeezed my hand then turned back to his parents. "Can't say I blame her. That Adrian guy is pretty dreamy."

His father snorted, and even his mother mustered a smug grin. I suppressed an eye roll and focused on my coffee. Luckily, our food arrived promptly and the discussion shifted again.

As we finished our meal, Camilla pushed back her chair. "Giada dear, why don't we stop off in the ladies' room before we head out."

I flashed Luca a subtle help-me look, but he simply smiled.

I dawdled behind his mother, and ducked immediately into a stall at the end. I didn't have to pee, so I pulled out my phone and quickly typed out a text to Luca. This was his mother I was dealing with, and he needed to support me more. If he thought I was going to accept being the number two lady in his life, well he had another thing coming.

I flushed the toilet so Camilla wouldn't know what I was up

to and then made my way to the sink. Camilla was already there, reapplying lipstick. She eyed me warily.

"Do you have a sweater to put on at church, dear? That dress is a tad revealing for mass, don't you think?"

"It was a gift from Luca for today," I replied, flashing my fakest smile.

She frowned. "So tell me about your wedding plans? Have you decided on a date or a general color scheme?" She paused, blotting her lipstick. "I assume you're planning for the ceremony to take place in Connecticut, right? But you know Luca will surely want a reception in Sicily. And you're going to have to learn some Italian."

"We've been engaged less than twenty-four hours. We haven't discussed anything."

Now her face contorted into a confused look of disgust. "What have you been doing? I mean, what could possibly be more important?"

Facing the mirror, I watched my face turn red at the vivid recollection of how we had passed the last twenty four hours.

She clearly caught the look in my eye but luckily didn't comment. "I thought all young ladies planned their weddings."

"I figured Luca might want a say in it all."

"Hmm. That's thoughtful," she said, in an incredibly unappreciative tone.

I offered the least fake smile I could muster and started towards the door.

"Giada, just a moment. I hope you don't take any of this the wrong way. As you know, Luca is my only son, and so his happiness is paramount. I understand your parents have raised you to be a wholesome and virtuous Catholic, and since everything with you and Luca feels so rushed, I have to wonder if the reason you're in such a hurry to marry him when you only just got back together is so that you can…consummate the relationship."

I froze, considering the possibility that there were hidden

cameras somewhere recording this conversation solely to see how far I'd let this crazy woman go without snapping. But as she stared at me, patiently awaiting a response, I realized she might actually be serious.

"Yeah, um, I appreciate your concern about us rushing into things. Luca and I haven't discussed it, but I sort of assumed we'd have a longer engagement."

Her face relaxed. "Oh, good. So there will be lots of time for us to get to know each other before things are official."

My soul cringed at the thought. "Sure. And, um, just for the record, I lost my virginity to Luca back in high school, so that whole consummating thing is not a concern."

I quickly exited the bathroom before she could reply. I made a beeline for Luca, who caught me and pulled me close for a chaste hug. "Your mother is insane," I whispered.

"Yes, she is a saint," he replied, the look in his eyes telling me he heard exactly what I'd said.

I pulled my phone out under the table and texted him the last part of my conversation with his mother. His phone buzzed right as his mother returned, and as soon as he read what I'd written, he stood.

"Can I talk with you outside for a minute, Giada?"

I nodded and thanked his parents for brunch. He told them we'd meet them outside in a few minutes, and then he escorted me out of the restaurant with a hand pressing gently against my lower back. Once we were safely out of the hotel, he swiveled to face me.

"Please tell me you are joking, Giada."

"I wish I were. It was awful being trapped in that bathroom with her."

"Giada, my mother is an angel. I don't understand how her worrying that we are rushing things leads to you telling her about our teenage escapades."

"I could reenact the entire conversation for you now if you'd take me back to the apartment."

"We promised my parents we'd go to mass with them."

"You promised. I knew nothing about it."

"Baby."

I pouted. "Your mother said my dress was too slutty for church."

"She did not."

"Okay, she didn't use that word, but…"

"Giada, seriously. You can gripe about my papà all you want, but my mother? She's as sweet and kind as they come."

"All she's done is criticize and attack me."

He shook his head, then glanced down at his phone. "I think you're being a little overly sensitive is all."

"Are you going to take her side over mine the entire time we're married?"

"I don't know. Are you going to whine and nag the entire time we're married?"

I lifted my foot and slammed it into his shin. He grunted and reached for my elbows, pulling me closer. He kissed my forehead and then lingered.

"You know it just turns me on when you're feisty like that, but if you think my mother is hard on you now, just wait till she sees you attacking me," he whispered. He then roped his arms all the way around me in an all-encompassing bear hug. It was one of his typical moves that he used to restrain me when he worried I was going to beat the shit out of him. As much as I wanted to stay mad, though, the gesture always calmed me.

When he finally relaxed his hold on me, I realized it was because his parents were coming.

Mass always grounded me, and simply being inside a church, even if not my usual church, calmed me. By the time we left, I was focused on my many blessings and tuned out any further unwelcomed commentary from Mrs. Marino. As soon as we reached the hotel, I called Gabriella. I recounted the full proposal details to her, right down to the weather description and the outfits Luca and I both wore, and after squealing with excitement together, we then discussed my concerns about his mother. As I knew she would, Gabby reassured me.

When I finally finished my phone call with Gabby, the Thai food Luca had ordered had arrived, and we ate hungrily, exhausted by the day. I then took a bath, which was relaxing until Luca burst into the bathroom, eying me mischievously.

"Do you need something?" I asked.

"Funny you should phrase it that way," he replied, stripping off his shirt.

I watched as he unfastened each button, moving from the top down and barely even pausing as he finished the final button and transitioned to his belt. He set the belt on the counter, then, slipping out of his shirt, he let it fall to the floor. Wearing just his black suit pants and a ribbed white sleeveless undershirt, Luca was undeniably an attractive man. My heart fluttered a little at the sight of him, tall and lean, with just the right amount of muscle. He was the epitome of masculinity, and he was mine.

"Are you going to join me?"

He appeared to consider this, then shook his head. "I was hoping you would join me, but I can wait until you're done, as long as you let me watch."

"I'm not exactly doing anything. Baths are more like a relaxing thing. It's hard to relax with someone watching."

"I can relax you in less than five minutes," he reminded me, his eyes twinkling with promise.

I crooked my finger towards him, motioning for him to come closer. "Prove it."

He was completely undressed in twenty seconds, lowering himself into the tub facing me. He winced as the water sloshed over his groin. "Are you trying to cook yourself like a lobster?"

I smiled. I liked my water hot.

Once he'd adjusted to the temperature, he reached for me, lifting me onto his lap, my knees on either side of his legs and pressing against the marble walls of the tub. Luca dipped his head down and quickly captured my nipple in his mouth, raking his teeth along it and biting gently before lapping his tongue across it and then suckling. The contrast in the sensation, from rough to gentle, took me from fully relaxed to panting with need and ready to explode in under a minute. By the time he switched to my right breast, I was gripping his head tightly, holding him to me.

His hand slid between our bodies, tracing along my aching core. I was so turned on by this point that I wasn't ashamed of the way I rocked against his hand, desperate to increase the pressure. When he pulled his hand free, he shifted our legs some, then positioned himself at my entrance. I took over from there, lowering myself onto him slowly, appreciating the slight variance in sensations due to the water. He let me control the pace, so I lifted up and down slowly a few times, then sped up. Luca fondled my breasts with his hands for a minute, ensuring the pleasurable sensations assaulted me from all angles. Then just as the intense warmth started to build and spread from my core throughout my entire body, he gripped my hips, using his hands to move me quicker. My orgasm swept over me hard and fast, and it was like the waves of the water around us had taken over my body, filling me and surrounding me.

Luca's grip tightened on me. "Sto per venire," he groaned. Before I could think of the translation, it became obvious, as he moaned louder then thrust into me harder, emptying himself into me in hot spurts.

The water around us didn't still until several moments after we did, and then Luca slowly hoisted me off his lap, stood, then lifted me out of the tub. He haphazardly rubbed a towel across each of our bodies, then carried me into the bedroom. He dropped me onto the bed, then crawled in beside me.

"Will you teach me Italian?" I asked. "I'd like to know all the things you say in the heat of the moment."

He laughed. "If you know what they all mean, I'd have to stop saying them. I kind of like having my secrets. Besides, I thought your father described you as unteachable."

I feigned insult, but really, it was the truth. I'd studied more for Italian than my other classes and still ended up with a GPA-destroying C.

Laying on Luca's chest, our damp bodies still entwined, I felt more relaxed than I had all day. I'd had too much coffee to sleep this early though, so I opted to talk instead.

"Gabby said to tell you congratulations as well."

He made a deep growl of acknowledgment as he continued stroking my hair.

"She also said all Italian men are momma's boys. She said I should cut you some slack and that it's better I learn now that you'll always choose her over me."

"I am not a momma's boy," he insisted, bending his outer leg in a way that shifted me onto my side facing him instead of directly on top of him. "And there's no reason I'd ever have to choose either of you. Men have mothers and fiancées. They're not mutually exclusive."

"Come on, you won't even admit she was a little harsh with me today?"

He relented slightly, his lips twitching so I realized he was conceding, at least some. "Maybe, but think of it from her perspective. She didn't know I was going to propose, so this all seemed sudden and out of the blue to her."

"But your father was aware?"

"Of course."

If he hadn't stiffened immediately after answering, I wouldn't have thought twice about it. But since he had, well, I revisited my earlier question.

"Your father wanted you to propose now, didn't he?"

"Yes," he said after a lengthy pause. "He's always liked you. And he says I'm a better person when I'm with you."

I tried to piece it all together. I appreciated that my dad wanted me to be formally tied to Luca so that whoever was after him would know I was under the protection of the Marinos and stay away from me. But my dad would never actually…would he? I looked Luca in the eye, hoping at least if he lied that I'd be able to tell by his expression.

"Did my dad tell you to propose to me?"

"No." He answered quickly and without any flicker of emotion that would indicate dishonesty. Just as I was about to relax though, his eyebrow twitched.

"Luca, please just tell me the truth."

"I am." He sighed. "Your papà approached mine."

"And then your father told you," I supplied. It all made sense now. "But why would your father agree to pressure his only son to get engaged?"

He shook his head. "I don't know exactly, but there was some sort of compensation or business deal."

I cringed. "So my dad paid your dad to convince you to marry me?"

Luca squirmed then shifted to sit up. I followed suit, too angry and hurt to lay down. How had I been so stupid to think any of this had been real?

"What did you get out of this whole arrangement?" I demanded.

Luca lowered his eyes to me. "You."

I rolled my eyes and climbed out of the bed. I couldn't sit still anymore. I needed to go somewhere. "I asked you this morning if you were doing this because of our fathers. You lied right to my face."

Now Luca rose to his knees and tugged my arm until I tumbled back onto the bed. I tried to move again, but he firmly held my arms and swung his leg over my waist, effectively pinning me. I tried to ignore the eroticism of the position, with it being the exact reverse of how we'd been mere minutes before, with both of us still nude. I drew up my knee to try to knock him off of me and tried to swat at his face, but he was bigger than me and stronger than me. I suspected I could fight him all night and never gain an inch, but that didn't mean I wasn't going to try.

"Stop trying to claw out my eyes, Giada. I'm not letting go of you until you listen to me."

I made one last-ditch effort to slap him, freeing my hand for a moment, but he caught it before my fingers contacted his face.

"Had my papà told me to propose to anyone else in the world, I would've said no. Nothing he could've promised me or threatened me would have made me agree to marry anyone but you."

I wanted to believe him,. He seemed to be telling the truth, but who was I to know for sure?

"I always planned to marry you sometime. Without my papà's prompting, though, I probably would've waited until Adrian had been out of your system for more than a month." He paused and laughed. "I can take a beating from you, but I doubt my ego could take it if you said no when I asked you."

I had to laugh at that. "Get off," I said, calmer now.

He grinned mischievously and inched his groin towards my face. "I would love to. You won't bite, will you?" he asked, stroking his erection.

I rolled my eyes at his play on words. "Not what I meant, but it's nice to know that watching me struggle turns you on."

He winked and slid off of me. "It's a good thing since you're always attacking me lately."

He had a point. I'd been told by others that I had a temper, but I couldn't think of another person who infuriated me as often as Luca. It didn't make sense, and besides, it was confusing, especially at times like now, where I wasn't completely sure if I wanted to slap him or fuck him. Further compounding my uncertainty, Luca began flicking his tongue across my nipple.

I moaned involuntarily, then nudged him off my breast, but he just moved to the other one. I felt my body react to his touch, my back arching towards him.

"Luca, come on. We aren't done talking. Are we even really engaged? I mean, are we actually planning a wedding, or are we just pretending to be engaged until my father calms down about his business enemies?"

He traced his tongue down my abdomen, dipping it into my belly button until I giggled at the tickle. He peered up at me and grinned, looking so adorable and sexy that my mind went completely blank.

"That is entirely up to you, tesoro. I'm just along for the ride," he said. Then he stroked his velvety tongue along my slick core, and I cried out at the intensity. I was still sensitive from our activities less than an hour before, and somehow, with one well aimed kiss, my body was on fire and ready to go. He sucked my clit into his mouth, and I screamed his name. He gripped my hips, holding me in place while he devoured me, as though anything could have possibly pulled me away from his magical tongue.

Just when I was about to fall over the edge, he stopped, quickly covering my body with his own. He grinned proudly, clearly aware of what he did to me.

"You are infuriating, Luca Marino," I said, panting with need.

"And you love it," he replied. He thrusted sharply into me, filling me to capacity, and I dug my teeth into his shoulder as jolts of pleasure shot through my body in wave after wave. Luca came shortly after, his warm seed spurting into me as he groaned my name.

We were both too exhausted to continue our discussion now, but as we fell asleep, I had to wonder what the future held for us. I couldn't deny our chemistry was off the charts, but I was equally sure it wasn't normal for all of our fights to lead to amazing sex.

CHAPTER 14

Giada

We dropped by my family's home on the way back upstate, and everyone there had offered us the enthusiastic congratulations I'd expected from Luca's parents. Several of my relatives also wished Luca good luck in dealing with me, but that didn't bother me. I found it endearing that Luca knew I could be high maintenance and still wanted to marry me.

Back at school, it felt like business as usual. Luca staying in the same apartment as me reminded me of our time in Italy. Well, except that I was in class most of the day, and he was commuting to Syracuse for some new business venture each day. Still, we'd succeeded at being a normal, happy couple for several consecutive days, so I decided to attempt another mature step.

"Hey Luca, will you be late again tonight?" I asked.

"Probably."

"Okay. Well, I was going to try to meet up with Adrian after my last class today. I thought I should tell him in person about our engagement."

Luca set down his phone and stared at me. "Why? He already knows."

"I'd feel better if I told him."

"I'd feel better if you didn't see him again."

I sighed and headed back into the bedroom. Why had I even mentioned it to Luca?

Instead of meeting up with Adrian that evening, Gabby and I went to the gym after class and then ordered takeout and chilled at my apartment. When she finally left around ten, I was surprised that Luca still wasn't back. I texted him, and he replied that he was still working.

Nearly an hour later, I'd changed into my short, silk night-gown, certain Luca would regret staying out so late when he noticed my attire in the morning. When I heard a ruckus at the door, I grabbed my robe and went to investigate right as someone began knocking. Glancing out the peephole, I spotted Luca, with three other guys behind him. I sighed and unlocked the door.

"Thank you, baby, my key is so hard to turn," he mumbled, dropping it on the floor and stumbling in. Alessio, Giovanni, and Thomas followed, all as drunk as Luca.

"Which of you drove home?" I asked. They all snickered.

Luca stepped closer, looping his finger over the tie holding my robe shut. He tugged, probably meaning only to loosen it but instead yanked it fully open. His eyes widened with glee. I quickly yanked it shut, but not before giving my fiancé's buddies a lovely view of my skimpy attire.

Luca turned to them. "Damn. I pro'lly would've gotten lucky if I'd gotten back sooner."

Alessio said something in Italian, and they all laughed again, probably at my expense, but I no longer cared what they were saying. A familiar, pungent scent lingered over the guys.

"Is that gasoline?" I asked.

They all glanced at each other.

"Why do you guys smell like gasoline?"

The guilt was obvious in their expressions. I leaned closer to Luca and inhaled sharply, realizing another offensive odor was mixed in with the gasoline. "And smoke?" I considered the options. It didn't smell like cigarettes so much as a full blown campfire. "Were you guys by a fire?"

Luca's eyes narrowed. "Tesoro, don't worry about it. It's not your business."

He reached for my arm, and I swatted his hand away. "Not my business? You show up late at night drunk and smelling like an arsonist, and I'm not supposed to ask questions?"

Suddenly, the guys were all more somber.

Luca had the nerve to look disappointed in me. "That's right, Giada. You are not supposed to ask questions," he said, his voice lower, but still within range of his friends.

I shook my head and started back to the bedroom. It was all ridiculous. "I have class in the morning. I'm going to bed."

Luca reached for my hand. "Hang on. I need a shower. Why don't you join me, and we can talk there?"

He gave me a pointed stare that I assumed meant he had something to tell me that he didn't want to say in front of his friends. I could handle that.

"I'll meet you in there," I said.

As I walked out, I heard Luca turn to his friends and tell them to leave so he could shower with his lady. They cheered for him like a bunch of high schoolers. As mortifying as it was to think of these guys picturing me in the shower, I was more focused on figuring out where Luca had been and why.

I started the water but didn't undress until he had joined me in the bathroom. I watched him undress, and then he paused.

"You coming?" he asked.

I nodded, slipped out of my nightgown, and joined him in the water. He shampooed his hair and let the excess drip down his body so that by the time he rinsed, there was only the slightest residual scent from earlier. I noticed it had been stronger on his friends, so I assumed they had been the ringleaders in whatever mischief had occurred.

"Okay, talk," I said.

Luca stared blankly back at me.

"You said if I got in here with you, you'd tell me what you did tonight," I reminded him.

"I did not say that."

I gritted my teeth together. "You did too," I insisted. Although, now that I thought about it, he hadn't actually said that. I'd just assumed that was the deal.

"Baby, I can't tell you a damn thing about my night."

"Is this because I said I was going to see Adrian? Are you trying to punish me? I didn't even go to see him!"

"I'm not trying to do anything. I needed a shower and thought it would be more fun with you in here, too."

"Then tell me why you smelled like fire?"

"Why do you think?" he snapped back.

I sighed. "Was there an accident?"

"No."

"Did you hurt someone?"

Luca stared back at me, the water pelting his face.

"Did you do something illegal?"

"Giada, stop! You're going to have to get used to not having all the answers if this arrangement is ever going to work."

"This arrangement?" I stepped out of the shower before I strangled him. I wrapped my towel around me, even though it was still wet from my post-gym shower only a few hours before. Then I wrung out my hair in the sink and slipped into the bedroom. I had learned all I needed to know.

The next day, things were noticeably different between Luca

and me. He was so distant and cold that I nearly missed the heavy-handed possessiveness he'd shown earlier in the week. We ate breakfast in silence, both of us feigning interest in our phones. He wore a business suit, and I almost asked why, but stopped myself. I didn't want to ask him questions that he wouldn't be willing to answer.

The next time I glanced up at him, he was glaring back.

"I don't know why you're annoyed with me. You're the one who stayed out late and got drunk and did God-knows-what."

"Giada, do you realize I'm of no use to you or your father if I don't keep doing my job the way I've always done it?"

"What does that have to do with anything?"

He dropped his phone onto the table. "You want me to be someone I'm not, and then you're pissed at me when I don't meet your impossible expectations. If the whole reason we're together is so I can keep you safe, then I need to do that. You can't interrogate me every time I miss curfew."

I stood and turned away before he could see my eyes gloss over. His statement answered every question I had about our relationship, if not his whereabouts the previous night. I was a fool for ever thinking our engagement was real.

Once alone in my bedroom, I texted Adrian and asked if he could meet sometime during the day. Then, I went to church. There wasn't a mass until evening, but sitting alone in a quiet sanctuary always helped me think. Apparently, I had a lot to sort out.

Adrian

*G*iada hadn't specified what she wanted to talk about, but I couldn't help but feel optimistic at the fact she wanted to meet. After the way our last conversation went, I wouldn't have been surprised if she'd chosen Luca for good, but I reassured myself that he'd never let his fiancée meet up with her ex. If she was coming to see me, she must have come to her senses and turned him down.

As soon as she walked into the café, though, all optimism whooshed out of me like I'd taken a punch to the gut. The sparkles from the diamond on her left hand lit up the entire damn room. Aside from the ring, she looked great, as always. Her hair fell in loose, shimmering waves across her shoulders, and her outfit accentuated all her finer assets while still remaining classy and casual.

I stood and offered her a half hug when she arrived. "I see congratulations are in order," I said, focusing all my effort on not sounding bitter.

She seemed surprised by my statement, so I reached for her hand. Glancing at the ring, I shuddered at everything it represented.

"It's beautiful," I said. "I would've never been able to afford one like that."

"I wanted to tell you myself," she said, taking the seat adjacent to me.

The waitress came by and asked for drink orders, but having dined there with Giada many times before, I just placed the full order for us both.

"I never meant to hurt you, Adrian, and I appreciate all the times you've been there for me."

Her sincerity should've meant more to me, but it didn't. Sure, she never meant to hurt me, but she still did.

"I know, Giada." I gazed at her again, drinking in her timeless beauty. "I honestly never thought things with us would end this way."

The waitress delivered our drinks, momentarily breaking the tension.

"Me neither," she said.

A flicker of doubt crossed her eyes. "You deserve to be happy, Giada."

She stared into her iced tea, looking anything but happy. "Thank you. That's nice of you to say in light of, well, everything."

"Hey," I said, reaching my hand across the table to cover her hand. She quickly yanked her hand back.

"Sorry," I mumbled. "I just wanted to make sure you knew that I meant that. And, I mean, you are, right?"

Gia gazed up at me, bewildered. "Am I...happy?"

I waited for her to answer, but instead, she turned back to her drink. I decided to be bold. "You're engaged to the love of your life, Giada. You should be ecstatic. You have your whole future ahead of you. Anything you want in the world can be yours. You're marrying your best friend, the person you know better and trust more than anyone else. No matter what happens the rest of your life, he'll be by your side."

She breathed a soft laugh.

"I'm serious. That's how it's supposed to be when you get engaged. If you're not feeling that, something isn't right," I stared at her until her rich brown eyes locked on mine then flitted the other direction again.

"This isn't a fairy tale, Adrian. Real life is complicated."

"You know you have options, right?" I asked, lowering my voice. "Say the word and we'll go away. I'll keep you safe."

"That's not your job."

I winced. I'd give anything to have that job again. She had to know that.

"Do you love him?"

"I do," she said.

She sounded convincing, and she hadn't hesitated. So, that was that.

"Okay then."

She peered up at me through her eyelashes. "I might still love you too, though."

She spoke so softly that I couldn't be certain I'd heard her correctly.

"I'm sorry. That's not fair for me to say. You deserve to move on without any of my baggage," she continued.

"If you still have feelings for me, I don't want to move on."

"Shh," she cautioned. "I don't think Luca would ever hurt you, but I'd rather not test him."

"I'm not scared of him, Gia. But I am scared for you."

"He only proposed because his father told him to. I mean, I guess my dad offered his dad some business deal in exchange for marrying me, so…"

"He told you that?" Having seen the way Luca looked at her, it was hard for me to believe anyone would have to persuade him to marry her. He was obviously in love with Giada.

"Not exactly. But I'm a little fuzzy on the terms of the arrangement. I don't think we're engaged in the sense of planning an actual wedding in the near future. It's more just that my father is terrified something will happen to me, and he thinks I'll be safe if everyone thinks I'm with Luca. It's more business arrangement than romance, and I'm not sure exactly how long it'll last."

I considered what she was saying, unable to shake the optimism now coursing through my veins. "I'll wait for you," I said.

"I can't ask you to do that. It's not fair." Giada quickly said.

"Gia, I love you. I tried to move on, and I couldn't. I didn't sleep with the girl in that picture. I couldn't even…" He sighed and paused. "We kissed some, but that was all."

The waitress delivered our food, but I was too focused on the possibilities to eat.

"You're graduating soon, Gia. I could transfer to a law school in Chicago for next year. We could get far away from here, and you could have the fairy tale life you deserve."

She smiled and picked at her salad. "I mean it, Adrian. I don't want you to wait for me."

I nodded, but clearly, she did want me to wait and only felt bad asking. "How about this…if I decide I'm ready to move on with someone else, I'll let you know. If you wake up one day and realize you're one hundred percent certain that Luca is the only man for you, you'll let me know. In the meantime, we'll be friends. And if you ever need someone to whisk you away from it all, just call me.

"I can do that," she agreed.

Giada

$\mathcal{L}$uca texted that he'd be staying in the city until the weekend, so I took the opportunity to live as though nothing had happened between us. I hung out with Gabriella, studied, and ignored the giant rock on my finger and all of its implications.

Knowing Luca would return Friday night, I went to a party with Gabby instead. When I got home, Luca was there, and he was pissed. He'd texted me over the course of the evening, and I hadn't replied, so I'd known he wouldn't be happy. I let him yell for a minute and then said I was tired. I was still awake a half-hour later when the bed shifted as he settled in beside me, but I didn't say anything.

When I awoke the next morning, I continued the silent treatment. I left for the gym after breakfast, but Luca was there in the bedroom as soon as I emerged from the shower.

"I don't understand why you're so mad at me," he said. "Did you not want me to go to New York?"

I brushed by him to select my outfit from the closet.

"Is this about Adrian? I know you met him for lunch while I was gone."

I swiveled to face him, but as I gauged his expression, all my words left me. He didn't look jealous or mad, but more like confused, or maybe even sad.

"Gabby is leaving for spring break tomorrow, and I told her I'd help her pack. I'll be back by dinner," I promised. I couldn't avoid Luca forever anyway. My dad had insisted we attend some stupid anniversary party for my aunt and uncle the next day. Probably it was best if Luca and I talked at some point before then.

He nodded.

That night, I was craving homecooked Italian, so I warmed up a spicy arrabiata sauce and some penne. Luca came home just as I was plating up the food, so he joined me for dinner. We made terse, distant conversation. The meal was so awkward and uncomfortable that indigestion settled in before I even finished chewing. When I stood to return the dishes to the kitchen, relief flooded my system.

When I turned back around, Luca was watching me, looking the opposite of relieved.

"Giada, please! We can't go on like this. Tell me what I can do to make you happy!"

His damp eyes pleaded with me, and the desperation in his voice was unsettling.

"You could let me go," I said, surprised at how cold I sounded.

"You've been gone for years, Giada. Don't you get it? I never wanted this with you. I wanted something real." He shook his head. "I could've stuck around after boarding school, could've made sure you never met Adrian or any other guys, but I didn't. I wanted you to live, to experience, and then to choose me anyway. I don't want you to marry me because Papà says you have to. I want you to do it because you want to. Because you actually love me as much as I love you."

I swallowed the lump that kept creeping back up my throat. "You don't love me. You just love power and convenience."

"I've loved you since I was seventeen, Giada," he said, his voice sounding weirdly raw. I searched for the words to dismiss what he was saying, but he continued.

"I love your laugh. I love the way you sigh in your sleep. I love the dresses you sketch. I even love your off-key singing." He reached for my hands and sat on the couch beside me. "But mostly I love the way you make me want to be a better person. I'm constantly striving to do better so I can become the man that you deserve."

"Oh, Luca," I sighed, squeezing my eyes shut so the tears wouldn't fall. The man was a master of deceit, but his words, his emotions, were sincere. In a different world, maybe we could work out as a couple. I didn't doubt that I loved him, but without trust, without security or confidence, love just wasn't enough.

But it also wasn't fair that our fathers were manipulating our emotions for their own gains.

"You're just as much a pawn in this as I am," I reminded him after several breaths.

"Don't you get it, Giada? We don't have to be pawns. Neither of us do. Let them think we're still together because they want it and not because we're in love. We're stronger together, Giada, and once we're married, we are unstoppable. I can give you the world if you let me, baby."

"I don't need the world. I just need someone I can trust.

Someone who can tell me how his day at work was without lying, and without me wondering the gory details of the events that he omitted. It doesn't matter that you treat me like royalty if I'm always wondering if you're a monster."

"I'm not perfect, Giada. I'm not pure and good like you. But I'm not a monster. And you know exactly who I am."

I shook my head. "I don't. You don't tell me. You keep me at a safe distance, on a need-to-know basis. You hide away the rest of your life with a series of passcodes and locks. I don't know who you are."

Luca's gaze narrowed, and his voice dropped. "I don't have to tell you, Giada. You know who I am. Just like you know what I do."

"I don't!" I repeated, frustrated that he wasn't hearing me.

He squeezed my hands sharply, forcing my eyes to lock on his. "You do, Giada. That's what we're arguing about. That's what you're scared of. You know. Say it!"

The intensity of his stare now was frightening, but I didn't want to play dumb anymore. I wanted the secret out in the open every bit as much as I now sensed he did. "You're in the mafia," I whispered.

Luca didn't acknowledge my words at all, but instead kissed me. The word that terrified me to speak aloud somehow offered him relief.

I broke away after a few seconds. "Luca, if you love me as much as you say you do, then leave. Stop working for them."

"I'm not working for them, Giada. I *am* them. Don't you get it? This wasn't a choice for me. I didn't just happen into this line of work." He shook his head. "They don't call me Il Principito because of my good looks. This is my destiny. My papà is a boss."

I wasn't sure how to respond to this information. I had suspected his father was involved, but hadn't confirmed he was a part of it, let alone the boss, whatever all that entailed. "Okay, well, if your father is the boss, just tell him you want out."

"There's only one way out, and that's in a body bag."

I shuddered. "How is that supposed to make me feel better?"

He frowned. "You said you wanted the truth. You didn't want secrets. So, here it is. The truth."

"Am I supposed to just be okay with marrying a criminal?"

"I'm the same person I've always been. Nothing has changed."

I wasn't sure what to say.

"It isn't that bad, really. I like the people I work with. I'm good at what I do."

I snorted. "You're a gifted thief."

Luca shook his head. "I don't steal."

"What do you do then? Why do you have so much money?"

"I was born with money."

"You know what I mean, Luca."

"Most of it is legit business. You live in this society where everyone just assumes the government is good, that they have your interests at heart, and that's just not always the case. Politicians are corrupt, lawmakers are corrupt. They use average businesses to line their pockets, and we don't let them get away with that. And we offer protection. Business owners pay us to help keep their businesses safe and successful. If you look at the history of the mafia in Italy and the United States, you can see how it has shaped economies and helped the little people."

I suddenly felt exhausted. He was right that I'd had my suspicions before, but I'd never expected him to admit it all. And now, for him to just talk and talk, it was like a flood of confession that I just wanted to stop.

"I need a few minutes alone, Luca," I said, dizzy.

"Why?"

I flung my arms in the air. "Because you've just told me all this insanity, and I need some time to process it all."

He didn't say anything else, but simply stared at me as I walked into the bedroom and shut the door. I pulled the rosary out of my nightstand drawer and sat on the bed while I ran my fingers across the smooth beads, letting the familiar words soothe and comfort me. By the time I finished the full series of prayers, the sun had set, bathing the room in darkness.

When I glanced up, I noticed a shadow standing in the light cast from beneath the bedroom door.

"Luca?"

"Si," he answered. There was a long pause before he asked if I wanted him to go.

"Go where?"

"I don't know. Away from here. Away from you."

I considered that then shook my head. "No, but I'm tired."

He nodded but didn't move when I went to the bathroom to brush my teeth.

Later, he was still tentative as he crawled under the covers beside me. Neither of us spoke for several minutes, and then I was the one to break the silence.

"You should've told me sooner. When you're keeping secrets from me, I can't trust you."

"Those are the rules, Giada. I wasn't allowed to tell you. I'm still not, and I didn't tell you anything you didn't already know. Besides, it's not all my secret to tell. A lot of people would be affected if certain information got out."

I slowly drew in a breath, feeling the air spread throughout, filling the emptiness in my chest. Then I exhaled, and the relief was gone. "You wanted me to marry you without knowing any of this about you?"

"If we're married, it's different. When we're married," he said, shooting me a pointed stare, "I can tell you more, anything that involves me, really, just nothing implicating others."

"Why is that?"

"Spousal privilege. They can't compel you to testify against me in court."

I cringed. I hadn't even thought about the legality—or lack thereof—of it all. I had been focused solely on the morality side, and the mortal danger of it. "God, the things you could be charged with," I mused.

"Don't think about it," he said.

I ignored him, already too focused on the horrifically long list of crimes I knew from my earlier research were associated with the mafia. "Fraud, embezzlement, money laundering, racketeering, extortion, drug trafficking, prostitution, assault, murder…"

"I've never killed anyone," Luca interrupted.

I hadn't realized I was thinking aloud, so his comment startled me for a moment. Then, I realized what else I'd said. "Prostitution?"

Luca rolled his eyes. "Giada, come on. I've never paid anyone for sex."

I must not have appeared too convinced because he continued.

"I've never slept with anyone who has ever been paid for sex. I just…well, I'm aware that there are some ladies who will provide those services to our business associates for a price. And they give us a small portion of their fee in exchange for their safety."

I sat upright. "So you're a pimp?"

"No. It's not like that at all. I'd love to live in a world where no woman has to make a living like that, but that isn't our reality. And women who choose to do that—well, it's dangerous. They have no way of finding customers or ensuring they'll treat her with respect and follow the rules. So we do that for them. We ensure they're paid upfront, that they have as many customers as they want, and that the customers never cross any lines."

I squeezed my eyes shut. It was too much. Everything Luca was saying was ridiculous—I knew that. But somehow, the way he said it made it sound okay.

"Baby, this is a lot to take in. Let's get some sleep, okay? You don't want to look tired at the anniversary party tomorrow, do you?"

I should have had so many more questions, but it was all

jumbled in my brain. I'd never expected answers to any of it, and the onslaught of details from the confession was too much to take. I tried to fight it, but sleep consumed me within minutes.

CHAPTER 15

Giada

The next morning, Luca was already awake and making pancakes when I finally crawled out of bed. He wore sweatpants but no shirt and was casually sipping his coffee and thumbing through the newspaper while waiting to flip the pancakes. He looked completely normal, like nothing had happened the previous night. He was acting like things were normal between us, like he hadn't just admitted to being a career criminal deeply entrenched in organized crime on two continents.

"Morning, sunshine," he said, handing me an empty mug. He filled it with steaming coffee before kissing the tip of my nose.

I eyed him warily. "Did I dream it all? Everything we discussed last night?"

Luca laughed. "You did not."

"So why are you acting like everything is fine?"

"Because it is. Nothing has changed. I'm still the exact person I have been the last five years."

I considered his words and realized that under it all, I did still feel the same. "I'm a fake."

He raised an eyebrow.

"Before, I pretended you and I were on the same page, that I knew enough about you to make an informed decision. Now, I have to pretend you're not a criminal mastermind. I appreciate the honesty, but I still feel like I don't know anything about the real you."

Luca was quiet for a moment. After he slid the pancakes onto a plate, he turned to me. "Pack a bag, and we'll head out right after the party. Bring enough for two nights."

"Where exactly are we going?"

"Surprise," he said, planting a kiss on my forehead. "I want to show you something, or someplace, rather, that will help you get to know the real me better."

That idea intrigued me. I could definitely use a getaway. "What kind of things should I pack? Do I need a bikini? Cocktail dress?"

He laughed. "Jeans, tee shirts, and maybe a hoodie. Tennis shoes and boots would be good, too."

I wrinkled my nose. "Are you taking me to a baseball game? You know I don't *play* any sort of sports, right? Oh God, and it's not a ranch, right? I don't do horses, either."

Luca shook his head. "No hints. You'll just have to trust me."

With my entire family at the party, I didn't have time to think about Luca or anything he'd said. Mostly, I just fielded questions about my plans after graduation. When someone asked how my job search was going, I told them I'd been so entrenched in wedding planning that I hadn't focused on my career yet. If they asked about the wedding plans, I insisted I was prioritizing final exams and job hunting and then would set a wedding date. If someone pressed for more details on either of these endeavors that I hadn't forced myself to put any effort into, Luca would whisk me away with some faux excuse.

He was the perfect fiancé the entire time. But by the time we left, I realized I was a tad nervous about this mystery road trip. I was excited to get away and have a couple days of fun, especially since all the chaos and my dad's paranoia as of late had robbed me of any real spring break vacation, but also, I couldn't help but feel a little stupid for agreeing to go away with a man who'd just told me he was a career criminal.

I soothed my nerves by fidgeting with the radio in the car and scrolling through all of my social media accounts while Luca drove.

"Enjoy that while it lasts. We will not have WiFi or cell reception where we're headed," he said.

My phone slid out of my fingers. "Umm what? You didn't mention that before. That's a dealbreaker."

"Too late to turn back now," he teased.

My pulse shot up. The WiFi alone wasn't a big deal, but I was trying not to panic over the prospect of being totally alone with this man who I barely trusted with no cell service to bail me out.

"My dad knows I'm going away with you," I reminded him.

"Yep," he agreed. "So he won't expect to hear from you for a couple days."

As we drove out into the middle of the woods, I realized we'd gone more than ten minutes without seeing a single house, person, or car. I started to panic. My palms were sweaty, my limbs felt all jittery, and I was breathing like I was running a race.

But then, Luca pulled to a stop on a gravel drive. In front of us stood a small but charming log cabin. Its porch spanned the entire width of the house, with the front door in the center and a wooden two-seater swing suspended from the ceiling on one side of the door. The cabin appeared new and well maintained.

"Where are we?"

"My secret hideout," he said with a boyish grin, tugging my hand.

When we stepped inside, a fresh, woodsy scent greeted me. I blinked several times while my eyes adjusted to the dimness of the main room. To my left was a small galley kitchen, and to my right was a living room complete with a sofa, coffee table, chair, and end table. Straight ahead was a table for two, which appeared to have a side that could be raised to permit seating for one or two more people.

"Bathroom?" I asked, suddenly panicked that Luca had taken me somewhere without indoor plumbing.

He slipped the duffel bag off my shoulder and motioned for me to follow him. Just past the kitchen was a small bathroom, housing a sink, toilet, and shower stall—the only storage being a mirrored medicine cabinet. At the end of the cabin was a bedroom. A large bed with wooden bedposts that mimicked the style of the cabin nearly filled the room, but there was also a matching dresser, nightstand, and small stone fireplace.

I noticed the lamp on the nightstand and frowned.

"How is there electricity, gas, and water way out here?"

"Generator, propane tank, and well," he explained. "It isn't completely off the grid, but close."

He set our bags on the bed, then kissed the top of my head. "I have some more things to unload, so make yourself at home, and I'll meet you on the porch in a bit."

I explored more thoroughly before making my way to the porch. I sat on the swing and rocked back and forth, noticing that we were perfectly positioned to watch the sunset in a bit. Luca joined me on the porch but remained standing. He handed me a stemless glass filled with white wine.

"Who lives here?"

"No one, usually."

"I mean, whose cabin is this?"

"Mine."

"You bought this cabin?"

Luca nodded.

"Why?"

"I mean, it's like Money Laundering 101, buy lots of property with cash," he said.

I raised an eyebrow, uncertain if he was teasing.

He turned towards the horizon and sighed. "I've had a good decade or so to think about where my life was headed, and I haven't always liked it. I don't want to become my papà. But every day, I see my alternatives narrowing down until, pretty soon, that's all that will be left. This place is my Plan B."

"How so?"

"Well, until now, no one else knew about it except me."

"No one?"

He shook his head. "I bought it a little over a year ago, and I've come up here a few times, but mostly I'm maintaining it just in case."

"In case what?"

"In case Plan A for my life isn't turning out the way I want. As long as I have this place, I can just slip away, and no one will know. I figure I could lay low here until I get set up to move further away and go totally off the grid."

"Why?"

"Because then no one can find me. No one can control me. No one will have any expectations whatsoever. It'll just be me and the wild, and I can build whatever life I want from there."

"Where on earth did you come up with this idea?"

He took his time answering. "When I was younger, my Uncle Samuele took me camping a few times a year. We'd sleep in a tent, build our own fires, fish, and hunt. It was fun, you know? Like the typical adventure that every little boy wants to experience. But it also taught me some useful survival skills and built up my confidence. Every trip, Uncle Samuele expected me to do more and more of the work by myself, and I did. By the time I was ten, he had me convinced that I could survive on my own in the wild with just a knife and a pack of matches. There wasn't anything else in life that I was really good at."

I tried to picture a young Luca trudging through the woods, covered in dirt. "I never realized you went camping as a kid."

"See, you're learning new things already."

"I also didn't know you had an Uncle Samuele. Have I met him?"

"Maybe when you were younger, but probably not. You would've liked him, though."

"Would've?"

"He's gone now."

"Like living off the grid gone?"

"No, like swimming with the fishes gone."

"Oh. I'm sorry."

Luca shrugged. "Occupational hazard in the family business." His expression showed he mourned the loss, though.

I stood and reached for his hand. I gradually tightened my grip until he turned to me, and then I rose up onto my toes to kiss him.

He looked surprised by the kiss. "No one is around to see you doing that, so you don't have to pretend," he said.

"Ouch. I guess I deserved that. I was going to thank you for bringing me here."

Luca offered me a half smile. "You're welcome."

We cooked dinner together, using the groceries he'd packed in an oversized cooler. Then we returned to the porch to talk after we ate.

Watching the sunset from our cozy porch swing, a fuzzy blanket tossed over our laps, I felt a level of peacefulness that I hadn't experienced for a while. I still couldn't wrap my mind around the fact that Luca—the man who'd been manipulating my emotions for years—apparently had this whole other side to him. Suddenly, he was real. He was this multidimensional person with interests, and fears, and hopes. It was a tad unsettling.

"For so long, you've been a fixture in my life, but you've never really been a human in my mind. I've never seen a hint of fear or weakness or sorrow or loneliness or anything from you."

"Really?" He shook his head. "I could say the same about you."

"Oh, please. I'm an open book. An emotional mess."

"Hardly. You never compromise, not your morals, not what you want, never. And you're not afraid of anything. I, on the other hand, wake up every morning terrified that I'm becoming my papà. I feel like I should be scared of being shot or stabbed or drowned, but honestly, that stuff doesn't scare me nearly as much as ending up all alone because I'm a greedy bastard incapable of love."

"You're not your father."

"Not yet."

I didn't have a response to that. We sat outside for a few more minutes, then as soon as I yawned, Luca led me inside to bed.

The next morning, we ate bagels and drank coffee on the porch, and then he dragged me out on a hike in the woods. I had low expectations, assuming we'd get muddy, pricked by brambles, and swarmed by bugs. But as it turned out, Luca led me along a path that wasn't muddy or overgrown with foliage. I heard birds chirping happily, but didn't notice many insects. The air was still but refreshingly cool.

We didn't talk much as we walked, but I appreciated the opportunity to be alone with my thoughts. I'd slept surprisingly well the night before, and woke feeling optimistic about Luca and life in general. Luca's greatest fear was being perceived as weak, so for him to show me this cabin—his personal retreat, his hiding spot if the world got too scary—well, that was huge.

It seemed we'd walked for hours, entirely uphill, when we

reached a clearing. We were at the top of a massive hill, looking down over a gorgeous vista. There were smaller rolling hills beneath us, all dotted with trees and spring flowers, and a massive field of golden wildflowers in the distance.

"Wow," was all I could muster.

"If you ever want to feel small and insignificant, this is a great place to stand. The first time I came here, I realized how unimportant I am. It occurred to me that if I were to disappear, the whole world would just keep going. No one would really be affected."

"That isn't true."

He didn't answer immediately, so I turned back to take in the view until he spoke again.

"I don't know how I keep messing things up so badly with you, Giada. It doesn't make sense because you're honestly all I need."

I turned to face him, but he was still gazing out over the vista.

"I feel like I won't become a monster as long as you're by my side. You won't let me step over the edge. And as long as you're in my life, I can deal with all the other shit. Whatever I have to do during the day, it'll be okay because I can come home to you."

Finally, he turned to face me. "And I'll never have to wonder if I'm worthless because you'd never stay with me if I were. I'll spend every day trying to be worthy of your love."

"You could never be worthless, Luca."

He was skeptical. "The way you looked at me these past few days. There's nothing worse than knowing I've disappointed you, or than thinking you hate me."

"I could never hate you, Luca."

He reached for both of my hands. "You have, and it's fine. I earned it. I didn't know how to be the man you deserved and still be the man my papà expects me to be. I still don't, really. But I want to do better, Giada. I love you. I always have."

Luca paused his soliloquy, but I was too stunned to speak, so he continued.

"I want to spend my life making you smile. I want to make you happy. I want to be the type of man you can be proud of. And I want you to love me so much that if I said I wanted to go off the grid and live in the woods, you'd start packing. I want us to be so happy and so in love that none of that other shit out there can even get to us." He dropped my hand to gesture off into the nothingness.

I wasn't sure if it was his words, the gorgeous view, or even the look in his eyes, but something completely took my breath away. I felt dizzy, and the sensation of falling overwhelmed me. But then I focused squarely on the man beside me, and gradually, I regained my footing.

"I want you," he said after a long pause.

"You have me," I said.

He reached up and wiped a tear off my cheek. "No, Giada, I want you for real. Not because you're scared to leave me. And I sure as shit never want you to be scared of me."

"I'm not."

His eyebrow shot up. "When you found out about Enzo… You were terrified of me."

He wasn't wrong, so I didn't try to argue. "That was ages ago."

"I saw the look in your eyes when I told you we wouldn't have cell reception."

"That wasn't because I was scared of you. I was scared to be unplugged, disconnected from everyone else. What if someone needs to reach me? Or if I need to reach them?"

"No matter what happens between us, Giada, I will never let anything happen to you. I will always keep you safe."

It stressed me out to hear Luca talking that way. "Luca, stop. I know that. Why can't you see yourself the way I do?"

"I do, Giada, and it isn't good enough. I'm going to be better."

I hardly recognized the desperate, insecure man pleading with me. Physically, he still resembled the dark-haired, chiseled man I'd fantasized about since high school. But now, it was like he'd shed an invisible layer and revealed this complex, sensitive and transparent man.

A man who, it now seemed, was irrevocably mine.

"I want this—you and me—to be real. I want us to have a real life together because it's what we choose, not some arranged marriage. I want to make *you* happy, not just your father."

Luca gazed at me from glistening, hooded eyes. Everything about him, from his words to his stance, was so uncharacteristically vulnerable. He was finally showing me all of his cards. He'd told me who he was that week, and now, he'd given me the rest— what he wanted for us.

I had never desired Luca more than at that precise moment. I reached my arms around his neck and tugged his head down to mine, planting my lips against his with such fervor that we both stumbled backwards. After a moment when I still hadn't regained my balance, Luca lifted me, nudging my thighs around his waist as though I weighed no more than a child.

I kissed him on the hillside, with that gorgeous vista in the background, until my lips went numb. I kissed him like there was no tomorrow. I hadn't imagined ever feeling that loved, that overjoyed, with Luca. It was like all the pieces of our lives were finally falling into place together.

He was the one to break off the kiss, setting me back on the ground but steadying me with his arms before separating our lips. His eyes were searching for something in my face, but I didn't want to make him wait any longer.

"I love you, Luca. For real. With all my heart."

He grinned. "I love you too."

This time he initiated the kiss, and I was the one to end it. I wanted more than kissing, and I needed him to know that.

"How private is this hill?" I asked.

"I've never seen anyone else out here. Why?"

I bit my lip. "I want you," I said. "And your cabin is too far."

He hesitated, and I imagined a billion different thoughts floating through his brain. I decided to simplify things for him. I leaned in to kiss him again then reached for his fly and unzipped his pants.

"Giada, no. We can't. If someone came up here and saw... I don't want to share you."

I groaned. "Then hike fast."

He laughed then motioned for me to follow. He led me by the hand the first twenty minutes or so, and then the path narrowed so we had to walk single file. I enjoyed the view and squeezed Luca's butt a few times as he hiked ahead of me. After the third time, he groaned and turned. He kissed me hard then carried me to the other side of a tree. A massive trunk had split and was resting sideways across the grass, and Luca nudged me backwards until I was leaning against its sturdy base.

While still kissing me, Luca slid his hand up my tee-shirt. He tugged the cups of my bra down below my breast and teased my nipples until I groaned loudly. He continued working his magic until I felt like I was going to combust. I grasped for his zipper again, but instead, he pulled his hands free and unfastened my jeans. He slipped them down just below my butt, tugging my panties with them, then knelt in front of me.

My breath caught in my throat at the awareness of what he was about to do, and I figured the civilized thing to do would be to stop him. Sure, the tree offered a slight shelter from the main path, but we were technically still out in plain sight where anyone hiking by could see us. My heart was racing, and my body was aching for him though. So instead of nudging him away, I thrust my fingers into his hair, stroking the soft strands as he leaned forward, parted my thighs, and licked my fiery core.

I cried out at the first contact, the sensation alright already so exquisitely intense. Luca persisted, though, returning one hand up my shirt while the other served to steady me. The pressure built quickly, and within a minute, I was about to burst. Luca must have sensed it too because he brought both hands to my thighs, steadying me as he delivered one last stroke of his powerful tongue, sending me shattering into a billion pieces. He held me in place, devouring me still as I rode the aftershocks of pleasure. And then, before I caught my breath or even opened my eyes, he'd pulled up my jeans, fastened them, and re-positioned my bra cups.

He pulled me to him and hugged me then, and finally, I started to snap out of it and remember where we were and what we'd just done.

"I love you so much, Giada," he whispered, holding me tight.

We made it the rest of the way back to the cabin without any other delays, but once we arrived, I followed through with my plan to have my way with him. It hadn't been that long since I'd last had sex with Luca, but this was different. Now we were making love, and it was better than ever.

The next twenty-four hours we lived as I suspected newly-weds would, alternating between slow, lazy bouts of lovemaking with quiet cuddles and long stretches of talking. We had no television, no internet, no phone, even, and that was fine. I didn't even miss technology.

I awoke on what was supposed to be our last morning in the cabin with a heaviness in my belly that I immediately recognized as dread. After a year of trying—and failing—to succeed as a couple, Luca and I had finally figured it out. We were happy. We were in sync. We were complete. But what if all that changed when we returned to the real world?

"What if we stay another day?" I mused while we finished up our morning hike.

"Your family is expecting us back later today."

"So? We are adults. I have nothing on my calendar tomorrow."

Luca appeared to consider this, but then he shook his head.

"You have school. I have business I need to attend to. Besides, your father will be angry if he doesn't know where you are."

"It's spring break. And my dad will realize I'm still with you," I pointed out. "Please?" I thrust my bottom lip out in a dramatic pout.

Luca stared at me for less than a minute before his expression softened, and I knew I'd won. "I can't say no to that face," he said, kissing me.

He taught me to fish that day—or attempted to, and then we stayed up well past midnight playing random card games in front of the fireplace. By the time we finally went to sleep, I was exhausted and fully expected to sleep till morning.

I awoke to a gentle tickling on my thighs and slowly opened my eyes to find that Luca had ducked beneath the covers and was slowly peppering my body with butterfly kisses. I startled when his tongue reached its goal, then moaned, my hips bucking towards his mouth. I let him continue his magic a minute more, then tugged him up my body. He worked his way up my body, pausing to lavish adequate attention on each of my breasts, and then he settled on top of me.

"Couldn't sleep?" I asked, smiling as his dark eyes twinkled in the night.

He thrust into me slowly in lieu of answering. He raised my arms above my head, continuing his luxuriously lazy pace, gazing into my eyes instead of kissing me.

"I had this dream that you said you loved me for real. I couldn't fall back asleep without hearing your voice, without knowing if you were actually mine."

It melted my heart, hearing how much this tough, seemingly emotionless man needed my love, how he depended on my approval for his most basic needs. I tried to touch him with my hands, but he held my arms in place. So instead I wrapped my legs around his waist.

"I am yours, Luca. Always," I said, my breath growing erratic now as his pace increased and brought the tension increasing deep inside me right along with it.

I wiggled my arms again, and this time, he released them. I roped them tightly around his neck, pulling his face close to my own. "I love you, Luca," I whispered right before he captured my mouth in a fierce kiss.

"Oh, Giada," he murmured.

CHAPTER 16

Giada

Luca wanted to get an early start the next morning, but for some reason, I was tired.

"I slept great. Can't imagine what your problem was," he said with a wink, reaching over to grab my duffel bag from me.

"I can handle a ten-pound bag," I said.

"You can handle a two-hundred-pound man, so I don't doubt it."

We were only about fifteen minutes into the drive when both of our phones began buzzing with countless alerts.

"Guess we're back into cell range," Luca joked, trying to check his phone while driving.

I snatched the phone out of his hand. "I'd rather not die today."

"Giada, don't," he said, his expression severe.

I glared back until he glanced over and noticed.

"Tesoro, I'm sorry, but sometimes guys text me info that isn't mine to share."

I rolled my eyes but set his phone down. "Fine, but if you want to read your messages, you'll have to pull over."

"Can I at least listen to my voice mails?" he asked.

I handed his phone back to him and turned my attention to my own phone. "Oh my God. I have eighty-four missed calls!" I started to scroll through them right as my phone rang. It was Adrian. Certain something major had happened to justify that many calls, I answered.

"Giada? Oh, thank God!" The relief in his voice was palpable. "No one has been able to reach you. We weren't sure if…" His voice grew muffled, and I heard him tell others in the background that I was okay.

"Adrian, what is going on? I have like a million missed calls."

"Are you with Luca?"

"Yes, we were out of cell service for a couple days."

"You need to come to the hospital. Matteo has been shot."

The phone slipped out of my hand onto my lap. As I picked it up, I glanced at Luca, whose face had turned ashen grey. He swallowed loudly and squeezed my leg, signaling that he too had just learned the same message.

I placed the phone back by my ear to get the address from Adrian, but he wasn't able to tell me much about Matteo aside from the fact that he was in critical condition and had been rushed into surgery. When I hung up, I wanted to tell Luca to drive faster, but my voice was completely gone.

"He'll be fine, Giada. Matteo is tough and strong. He will pull through this."

"I should've been there," I finally mumbled.

"There's nothing we could have done. I'm hurrying, though."

I glanced at the speedometer and realized he was pushing ninety miles per hour. I prayed we wouldn't get a ticket because it would only slow us down.

The rest of the drive was torture, with Luca silently focused on getting us there as quickly as possible without killing us while I was overwhelmed with guilt. I couldn't have stopped Matteo from getting hurt, but I still should've been there. I should've been there to hold his hand as they wheeled him into surgery, to donate blood, to pray for him. I should've been there to comfort my parents.

And… God, my poor parents. They had expected us back the day before, so when I hadn't returned, they must have feared the worst. For all they'd known, two of their children were in danger.

Enzo met us at the hospital entrance so we could rush inside while he parked the car. My legs were so jiggly with terror that I leaned on Luca as we walked. When we reached the right floor, we were immediately flooded with a crowd of familiar faces. My entire family had gathered in the waiting room.

"I should've been here," I mumbled.

"You're here now," Luca replied, pressing a kiss against the side of my head. He gave me a comforting squeeze and then released me into the arms of my mother who was rushing towards us.

She hugged me so hard I thought my eyes might pop out, and then she began lecturing me about staying away a day longer. I tuned out of her arms, not because the lecture wasn't warranted, but because my dad was shouting at Luca a few feet away. I'd never seen my dad look so angry or use that tone with anyone other than my brothers. I cringed, half expecting Luca to shout back, aware that his temper and pride made it near-impossible for him to let anyone else talk down to him, but he didn't. He just shook his head and apologized.

"What happened?" I asked, turning back to my mother.

"He was shot," she said, her eyes swollen and red.

"But why? By who?"

"We don't know. Probably random. Maybe an attempted car theft."

Done with his lecture, my dad placed his hand on Luca's back and walked him across the waiting room and around the corner. My uncles Leo and Vinny went with them. I frowned, certain there was more to the story than my mother was giving me. I couldn't help but wonder if she even knew the whole truth.

My mom went over everything the doctors had said so far, with my aunt nodding to confirm each detail as she spoke. And then I sat in silence with my mother and aunt in the waiting room. I was suddenly exhausted, all the events of the day weighing on me like a ton of bricks and the lack of sleep over the weekend piling on. I probably could've fallen asleep if the silence had ensued, but after about a half-hour, my dad returned.

I stood and cautiously approached him, my arms extended. He held me tight for a moment, then shook his head. "Your mother was terrified. We didn't know if you were alive or dead."

"I'm so sorry," I said.

He dismissed me with a curt nod and returned to my mother.

I gazed to Luca, who subtly motioned for me to follow him.

We walked to a private corner at the end of the hall. The moment we both stopped moving, I fell into his arms, burying my head against his firm chest.

"I'm so sorry about my dad," I said, his body muffling my words. "He should've yelled at me, not you."

"He was right to blame me. I should've known better." He kissed the top of my head. "It just didn't occur to me that…"

I squeezed my eyes shut. "What if he isn't okay?"

"He will be, Giada. Have faith."

If only it were that easy.

I let him comfort me for another minute before pulling back. "My mother said it may have been a random car-jacking," I said, trying to convey my incredulity with my tone.

Luca glanced to the left, then the right, then ducked his head. "A few weeks ago, some Colombian dealers tried to smuggle a shipment of smack in through the marina."

"What?"

"Heroin," he clarified, pausing to make sure I followed. "Your father stopped it, and they're pissed. A few of the guys came after him and made some threats, and then when they realized they couldn't get to him, they came after you."

"That's why you were protecting me," I realized.

"Yeah, and that's why it was so important that we went after them and made sure they couldn't try to hurt you again." He blew out a sigh. "We thought that was all of them and that the threat was gone, but it turns out they had some connections to one of the larger cartels in Colombia. They're still pissed, and they went after Matteo."

"Jesus! Did the police catch them?"

Luca shook his head.

"Was Matteo alone, or did someone else see them? I mean, surely someone has to know who did this to him."

"*We* know, Giada. And we will get them."

"If you know who they are, then why isn't someone talking with the police?" I began brainstorming all the connections we had who could help. Surely Adrian still knew some people at the prosecutor's office who could rush things, and my dad must have friends in the police department.

"And say what, exactly?"

"That they shot Matteo and tried to shoot at us!"

"Shh! Keep your voice down." Luca squeezed my hand to calm me. "You're not thinking through this. If we tell the cops anything, they're gonna want to know what happened to the hundred and fifty pounds of heroin."

I shrugged. "So tell them it was destroyed."

"They'd never believe that."

"It's the truth, isn't it?"

Luca frowned. "It doesn't matter. Baby, trust me. We will find whoever did this to Matteo, and we will make sure they never threaten anyone in your family ever again. This whole thing ends now."

I blew out a sigh. It was all so insane. I felt like I was trapped inside of some ridiculous TV show. I was furious with my father because clearly he set into motion all the events that resulted in Matteo fighting for his life, but at the same time, it wasn't entirely unpredictable. My father had always lacked trust in "the system," as he called it. The government and all of its entities, especially the police, were corrupt.

My father preferred to handle things on his own, and he'd always said that was why he liked having all my tough, well-armed, male relatives working with him instead of strangers or, gasp, women. He wanted people he could trust but also people he could count on to defend themselves and the business when the police failed. And however I examined the current situation, I couldn't deny that the police had missed the boat. They should've intercepted the drugs before they even arrived at my father's dock. It shouldn't be his job to weed out the criminals abusing his property.

"Giada," Luca's voice snapped me back to the present. "I need you to keep this between the two of us, okay?"

I nodded.

"I'm so sorry we weren't here. I never meant to keep you away from your family."

I reached up and stroked his cheek. It was scratchy from stubble, but just touching him comforted me. He leaned against my hand, then turned and kissed my palm.

"I'm not mad about this weekend," I said. "I'm so glad we went, and I appreciate you opening up to me so much." I let my hand drop, and Luca caught it, holding both of my hands in his own.

He tilted his forehead down to meet mine. "I love you, Giada."

Despite everything, I couldn't help but smile. "I love you too," I said.

He ducked down further and pressed his lips to mine. It was a slow, sweet kiss, and it was exactly what I needed.

"I should go talk with the guys more, see if we have any more information to go off of. I'll let you know if we hear anything else."

I nodded and watched him go.

Adrian

When Angelo called to tell me his brother had been shot, I'd genuinely felt bad. Matteo had always been kind to me, and he was as good of a person as possible, given his family circumstances. But when Angelo asked if I'd seen or heard from Giada, I was terrified. I'd envisioned losing her to Luca, not actually losing her. In my warped mind, there would always be a future where she could come to her senses and choose me once and for all.

I'd joined the family at the hospital out of support for Matteo but also because I was too anxious to do anything else. With her family surrounding me, there was a slight distraction from my worry, but also, I'd be the first to learn updates once Giada was located if I stayed at the hospital.

After we learned Giada was safe and Matteo was taken down for surgery, I left the hospital. I headed back when I figured Giada would arrive, but after a brief search, I couldn't find her. I guessed that she might have gone somewhere with Luca, but Giada's father shook his head, saying Luca was making a phone call.

I took off to look again. Finally, I spotted her, at the end of the corridor, nestled in the nook by the ice dispenser and coffee maker. She was upset and crying visibly, but she wasn't alone. Luca was with her, not making a phone call like he'd claimed. His arms were around her, slung low on her back. His head was angled down, and he was whispering something to her. She nodded her head, and he wiped her tear.

My stomach clenched as he kissed the top of her head, but I still couldn't walk away. He was her fiancé. Of course, that required him to comfort her when her favorite brother nearly died. Maybe Luca was telling her some story, what she should say to her family to cover up for their absence so that no one saw what a jerk he really was.

I waited, my heart thudding uncontrollably, for their embrace to end. Finally, it did, but not the way I'd wanted. Luca said something else to Gia, and she laughed. I heard the distinct sound of her beautiful laugh through her tears. She swatted him playfully and then lifted onto her toes, reaching for his cheek as he bent to kiss her.

I couldn't stomach the kiss, but I couldn't tear my eyes away. It wasn't an over-the-top, soap-opera style makeout but an intimate, comforting kiss of two familiar lovers. It was not the type of kiss for putting on a show. It was the type of kiss partners might share when they assume they're alone.

I was nauseous, and now I also felt like a peeping Tom for watching them.

I turned down the hallway, desperate to escape the stuffy hospital, but nearly smacked into Giada's mom, Martina.

"You're not leaving, are you?"

"I was just going to get some air," I said, then realized the stupidity of my statement. "But I probably should leave now that Giada is here."

"I'm sure Marco would appreciate if you could stick around at least until Matteo's out of surgery. You're practically part of the family."

I cringed at the implication of her words. Once upon a time, I had longed to become a part of that family. But I'd wanted to be a part of the family by virtue of marriage to their daughter, not in the same way half those guys in the waiting room were considered to be family.

I couldn't say no to a woman who nearly lost her son though, so I nodded. "Sure, Mrs. Conti, I'll stick around. Can I get you some coffee or anything?"

Her face relaxed. "Coffee would be great. Thank you, Adrian." She hugged me tightly then took off towards the waiting room. I winced, remembering where the coffee was. I considered looking for a different coffee kiosk but then saw Luca walk quickly out the exit at the opposite end of the hall.

I had nearly reached the coffee when Gia emerged from the corner. Her head was down, her hair blocking her eyes, so she would've slammed right into me had I not caught her with my hands.

"Adrian!" she said, as though she hadn't realized I was there. "I'm sorry. I wasn't looking."

"It's alright. I was just getting some coffee for your mom. She asked me to stick around until—"

"No, of course. It's fine. You should be here."

"Do you want a coffee?"

She shook her head. I started to move past her since there was nothing else to say, but she caught my arm.

"Adrian, wait. I...about Luca," she began. Her face transformed from sorrowful distress to anxious discomfort.

"It's okay," I said, eager to escape the awkwardness. "You love him."

She opened her mouth as if to protest, then shut it, her eyes searching mine. "I'm so sorry," she finally said. "We've been talking more, and I understand now. He's not the person you think he is."

I wanted to shake some sense into her, to slap her out of whatever spell she was under and scream that she was wrong, that I recognized exactly the type of person he was. But I didn't do anything.

How could I? Luca was the type of person who had a half dozen goons waiting down the hall who'd eagerly beat the pulp out of me if I moved in on his girl. Besides, it wasn't the time or the place, and clearly, Giada wasn't my problem anymore. I couldn't convince her to see what was right in front of her, and that couldn't be my burden. Eventually, she'd have to figure that out on her own.

"Neither are you," I finally said, hating myself for sounding so bitter.

"I'm so sorry, Adrian," she said.

"Me too," I said, offering her an awkward side hug. "And Matteo will be just fine, Gia. Don't worry."

~

*G*iada

*M*atteo was out of surgery around six p.m., but he went straight to the ICU. My parents were allowed to visit him, and then Angelo and I could. He wasn't awake, and seeing his battered body supported by bandages, IVs, and tubes was more traumatic than relieving. The doctors assured us the surgery had been a success, but they said they didn't want to wake him until morning. Apparently, he had some swelling in his brain and the rest would help relieve the pressure more quickly.

My dad insisted Luca take me home to rest, but I resisted. There was no reason for me to leave the hospital, and I hated the thought of being away if something happened. Then my dad said

I could head out with Luca or I could go with Angelo, but either way, I was leaving. Obviously, I chose Luca.

We were silent as we drove, and once we reached Luca's family home on Staten Island, I retreated to his bedroom. His parents were back in Italy and the house was empty, but I just still felt more comfortable staying in his private space.

Luca tried to get me to eat something. Not surprisingly, I had no appetite. He ate while watching me push food from one side of my plate to the other. I could tell my stress was making him miserable, but I didn't know how to think about anything else. Until Matteo was fully recovered and safely at home, I would worry.

"Giada, come here," Luca said, holding his hand out to me. "How can I keep your mind off this? How can I help you feel better?"

I considered his words, tried to think about what really would make me feel better. "Make love to me," I finally said.

He gazed at me like I was crazy, but he complied. He undressed me slowly, touched me softly, and made love to me with tender, deliberate movements. Afterwards, he stretched out behind me and held me tightly. I was beyond exhausted, but I couldn't sleep. I tried to keep my mind off things, but the longer I lay there in the dark, quiet room, the more emotional I became. I tried to stay still as I cried, not wanting to wake Luca, but his arms tightened around me, signaling that he was already awake.

"Shh, sweet Giada. It's okay. You're safe, and Matteo will make a full recovery."

I believed his words but couldn't stop crying. He kissed my shoulders over and over, shushing me softly.

"I'll never let anything happen to you," he promised.

I focused on the sensation of his solid body pressed against mine, the rhythmic patterns of his breathing, and the light tickle of his breath on my shoulders. I was almost asleep when Luca's phone rang. He stiffened behind me.

I reached around and gripped his arms, holding him in place. "Let it go to voice mail," I said.

He kissed my shoulder then easily escaped my grasp. "I can't, baby." He reached over me and answered the call. He didn't say anything, but I heard the caller on the other end speak.

"Got it," Luca said, disconnecting.

Instead of settling back against me, he rolled the opposite direction. I instantly chilled, the absence of his body against mine leaving me vulnerable, cold, and sad.

"I have to go," he said, his tone conveying his awareness that I wouldn't like his words.

"No you don't," I said, sitting up.

He was already dressed from the waist down. I watched as he secured a handgun near his ankle, then reached into his drawer again and slid another along the back of his pants before tugging an undershirt over his head.

"Please don't leave me, Luca," I begged. "I don't want to be alone now."

"I'm sorry, sweetheart. I love you, but this can't wait. Don't leave the house."

"Don't leave me!" I repeated.

"I'll be back before you know it," he promised. I heard the click of the door as he left, and another click as he locked it behind him.

I sighed, defeated. I squeezed my eyes shut, determined to fall asleep to pass the time more quickly until he returned. But I couldn't sleep. By the time the sun began peeking through the thick wooden blinds, Luca still wasn't back.

I rolled out of bed and tried his phone, but after four rings, it went to voice mail. Sighing, I texted Enzo. Apparently, I needed a new ride to the hospital.

On the ride over, Enzo pretended not to know where Luca had gone, but I was certain he had at least an idea. When we arrived at the hospital, my dad was there along with Angelo, but my mother and aunts had gone home to rest. A few of my uncles were standing around, but no one seemed too concerned with my arrival. I approached my dad but waited till he turned to me to speak.

"Any guesses where Luca went last night?" I asked.

"He left you alone at his father's house?" my dad said, instantly making me cringe.

"No, he had Alessio come to the house before he left," Enzo said.

I turned to him, bewildered.

"He didn't leave until I arrived," Enzo clarified.

"If you talked with him, you obviously know where he went," I said.

Enzo shrugged. "He sent a text. I didn't ask."

I rolled my eyes, certain he was lying.

"Giada, darling, you should head home and rest. We will call you when your brother awakens."

"I'll wait," I said, annoyed. I took off in search of coffee.

CHAPTER 17

Adrian

Marco texted me after his son woke from surgery and asked me to come by the hospital. I wanted to refuse but decided this was not the time to challenge his authority. Manipulative asshole or not, he was suffering watching his son in pain. Giada was with her brother when I arrived, and I was pleased to see he was not only awake but talking and smiling. He was apparently doing so well that they moved him to a regular room.

Shortly after I arrived, Luca returned. As soon as Angelo saw him, he rushed towards him and patted him on the back. Marco followed behind, and much to my surprise, pulled Luca in for a long, tight hug. He said something quietly to Luca, who then nodded, and then he patted Luca on the back.

I turned in confusion to Enzo, but then Marco came over to Stefano, who was seated beside me.

"Luca has done it. That bastard who hurt my son is no more," Marco said, tears forming in the corners of his eyes.

My eyes widened as I turned to Stefano, unsure how he would respond to such a wild statement.

Stefano's lips widened into a broad smile. "He avenged our Matteo?"

Marco nodded.

Stefano slapped me on the back and jovially exclaimed, "Justice has been served!"

From the looks on everyone's faces, they assumed I shared their joyful sentiments. Honestly, I was more disturbed by the fact that they had no problem discussing it in front of me than the fact that everyone seemed chipper to accept that Luca was a cold-blooded killer.

I gazed around in search of Gia, but she had disappeared into her brother's room with her mother. *How convenient.*

I watched as she left his room a minute later. The celebratory mood persisted, but the volume level had decreased some at least.

Gia was alone as I approached her, but she already looked bewildered and annoyed before she even spotted me.

"What is going on?" she asked.

The sardonic grin felt natural on my face as I answered her. "Didn't you know? Your fiancé is the man of the hour." I paused to ensure the rest of my statement wouldn't be lost on her. "He went after Matteo's shooter and killed him all by himself. There's a picture going around if you want to see the body."

The transformation on her face was so rapid that I could practically feel the whirlwind of emotions zipping through her. I saw Luca approaching out of the corner of my eye, and I patted her on the arm. I had to get out of there before either of them noticed the satisfaction in my smile as Gia focused the full wrath of her emotions on Luca.

"What did you do?" she asked, lunging towards him. I almost

hoped she'd hit him, just because she was probably the only one who could do so and survive.

His face was eerily calm and cool as he gripped her arms, holding her at a safe distance. "Giada, we'll talk later. Now is not the time," he said, effectively cutting off all her protests. He had an audience, though, so of course he couldn't let anyone see him show emotion or especially weakness just to comfort his beloved princess.

He bent to kiss her forehead, pulling back quickly before she could spit on him. Then he nudged her towards Thomas.

"Can you take Giada for some coffee and fresh air? She had a rough night, and I need to talk with Marco."

Thomas nodded and placed his hand on Gia's back, nudging her along down the hall. I watched as she shook free of his hand and marched herself off down the hallway. I almost felt sorry for her but, then again, she made her choice.

Giada

*I*f Luca thought spending time alone with his minion would calm me down, he was wrong. If anything, it only gave me time to think of all the horrible things I wanted to shout at him. I was so mad at him, but frankly, I was disgusted with everyone. They all seemed so excited and proud. It was nauseating.

I guessed Luca was coming back when Thomas checked his phone, shook his head, then offered a lame excuse to leave. When I saw Luca, I was torn between wanting to walk away from him and wanting to punch him. I went with the latter, but he grabbed my hand before I made contact with his gut. Clutching it tightly, he led me down the sidewalk towards an empty corner of the parking garage.

"Let go of me!" I snapped.

"Are you going to hit me?"

"Maybe," I said.

He released my hand and offered a half smile.

"I'm sorry I left last night. I expected a different reaction, though."

"Seriously? You treated me like a fucking child in there. I'm not some subordinate you talk down to."

"No," he interrupted. "That's how this works, Giada. You can say whatever the fuck you want to me when we are alone, but when we are in public, you act the way you're supposed to. Treat me with respect, and be supportive. Don't embarrass me in front of both of our families."

I shook my head.

"No, we agreed that this," I said, pausing to gesture back and forth between us, "This is real now. That means I act however I want to act. If you want me to treat you with respect, you better earn it. And don't talk to me about being supportive. I begged you to stay last night. Didn't you see how much I needed you? You just left me."

"I left *for* you. It was your brother I avenged, not mine."

"Bullshit. You left for you. You want the attention and the fan mail."

Luca frowned and shuffled his feet. "Do you know what keeps you safe at night?" He paused for effect. "This. The fact that anyone who would ever consider doing you or your family harm knows without a doubt that they won't live twenty-four hours after. They don't fear the police. They don't worry about the justice system. They fear *me*. I'm the deterrent. Our family is the deterrent. Our justice is swift and certain, and we don't pause to ask questions."

"Jesus, Luca. Do you hear yourself? You killed a man last night. How is that not a big deal to you?"

His expression hardened. "I never said it wasn't a big deal, just that I did what had to be done."

"Did it?"

"Yes, Giada. You know it did. And if it hadn't been me, it would've been someone else."

"So why not let someone else do it then? It didn't have to be you."

"How is that any better? How can I ever be a respected leader if I order others to do what I won't? How can I force someone else to live with that guilt?"

I snorted at his mention of guilt. The deceased was nothing more than a notch on the bedpost to Luca. Luca didn't care about him, about his family.

"He wasn't a good man, Giada," Luca said, as though he'd been reading my mind. "He shot your brother. He tried to murder Matteo."

I shook my head. Luca didn't get it. He probably never would. "For all you know Luca, he came home yesterday and had this exact same argument with his girlfriend. You really think he just woke up and decided to shoot Matteo? No! Someone told him to do it. For some reason, he thought he had to do it. He did the only thing he thought he could do to keep his family safe. He is no different from you, except now he's dead."

I ignored the hurt expression on his face as I turned and stomped back into the hospital. Once inside, I forced my most convincing smile onto my face. Hopefully it would at least fool the people who didn't know me well. Luca didn't follow me back in, and almost everyone else had cleared out as well, including my dad. Angelo and Enzo were both in the waiting room, along with two of my uncles. My mother was seated at Matteo's bedside.

I poked my head into his room. I confirmed that he was awake, then said hello.

My mother turned. "Ah, good. I am headed home to take a nap and a shower. Can you keep your brother company?"

I nodded, and she left.

Matteo seemed groggy, but we made small talk for a few minutes. Apparently, even in his highly medicated state though, he recognized my moods.

"What crawled up your ass and died?" he asked crudely. "Everyone else seems to be celebrating. You look like you're at a funeral."

"I'm sorry. I am glad you're doing better. You scared us there." I paused. "Did you hear that I wasn't here when they brought you in?"

He nodded, and I was about to apologize, when he shushed me. "I was unconscious, Giada. I didn't know who was and wasn't here, so don't feel bad. You came as soon as you could."

"Thank you, Matteo," I said, grateful he was so understanding.

"What's really bothering you?" he asked after a minute.

I laughed, not wanting to burden him with my problems when he was confined to a hospital bed. "You probably have more important things to think about than my love life."

"Actually, I'm bored to death, so as long as you don't say anything to ruin my vision of you as a good, innocent Catholic girl with your virtue still intact, I'd love to hear it."

I cringed. "Don't say 'bored to death' when you almost died less than twenty-four hours ago."

"Too soon?"

I nodded. He was still staring expectantly, so I spilled. "Luca and I went away this weekend. We talked, and I thought we worked everything out and were on the same page again."

"So now you have to let down Adrian?"

"Adrian's known for weeks. It's not like Luca kept the engagement a secret."

"Yeah, but were you really planning to marry him?"

It felt weird opening up to my brother. We'd always been close, but not in the frequent heart-to-heart discussion sort of way. I supposed I had no one else to talk to, though. I couldn't exactly tell Gabby all about my latest problem with Luca.

"I would've married him in a heartbeat yesterday if we'd run into a priest."

Matteo looked shocked. "Oh. Wow. I hadn't realized things were that serious with you two. I sort of thought you just agreed to marry him to appease Dad."

"Maybe initially," I said. Then I shook my head. "Anyway, it doesn't matter now."

"Why not? Did something change?"

I was surprised they hadn't told them. "The guy who shot you is dead. Luca killed him."

Matteo tried to sit up and doubled over in pain. I leaned closer to help him.

"Shit, Giada, watch your mouth. If Dad or Angelo heard you say that..."

"They already know. They were proud of him."

His expression tightened. "Right, but they don't know that you know. Jesus. Did Luca tell you that?"

I figured it was safer to throw him under the bus than Adrian, and Luca certainly hadn't denied it when we spoke. I nodded. "He doesn't tell me anything about any other guys, but he tells me things about him."

That revelation appeared to stress out my brother. He didn't speak for a long moment, and when he did, he'd switched over to his wise older brother tone. "Listen, Giada. You don't want to hear everything that goes on in Luca's life. Let him have his privacy. Trust him to tell you what you need to know, and don't get hung up on the rest. Loving someone like Luca will take its toll on you if you're always worried he won't make it home at night."

"I'm not sure I can love someone like that at all."

He frowned, then took his time answering. "You can. You already do. You have your whole life."

Even counting our time together in high school, Luca and I had been together less than four years. "A few years is hardly my whole life."

Matteo's expression changed, almost as though he were trying to read my mind. Finally, he gave up and spoke. "I don't mean Luca. Now get out so I can take a nap."

I hesitated, still pondering the meaning of his last statement, then stood. I gave him a gentle hug, careful not to crush him, then left. Enzo was waiting to drive me home.

Adrian

I stared ahead at the altar, unsure of proper protocol for sitting in a church outside of an actual service. I'd never done it before, but at the moment, it seemed an appropriate place to be. I appreciated the silence, the somber atmosphere, and the potential for some sort of penance, if only I could pinpoint where I'd gone wrong. I'd made so many missteps along the way that I wasn't sure how far I needed to go back to alter the path I'd taken.

A familiar voice interrupted my thoughts. "Can I sit here?"

A dozen different sassy quips rolled through my brain, but instead I just nodded. Giada sat several inches away, and though she remained quiet, her mere presence distracted me. I could smell her cinnamon gum, could hear her soft, uneasy breathing. I turned towards her and realized her eyes were closed, but her lips were moving slightly. I guessed that made sense. People came to church to pray, not just think in a quiet space.

She looked sad and tired. As soon as her lips stopped moving, I spoke.

"How's Matteo doing today?"

Her eyes flew open. "Huh?"

"I wasn't sure I should go by the hospital. Doesn't really seem fitting now that you and I aren't—"

"Oh, right. He's okay. He's eating and talking and fully milking the attention. They say he'll make a full recovery."

"That's good," I said, and I meant it. "Is your fiancé at the hospital?"

She frowned, and her fingers stroked the rosary beads in her hand. "I don't know. I haven't seen him."

"Don't you live with him?"

"Not this week. We had an argument last night. He left and didn't come back. I'm staying at my parents' now anyway, at least for the rest of spring break."

"Huh. Guess we'll have to check the papers to see who else got murdered last night."

Gia didn't answer, which only made me feel worse about having said it. Still, I was too pissed and too hurt to be the bigger person.

"You chose wrong," I said.

"I always do," she replied, still looking straight ahead.

I wasn't sure what that meant, but she didn't elaborate or turn towards me. I waited a few more minutes, then stood. She pulled in her legs to let me pass but said nothing.

The church was still mostly empty, but as I started out, I noticed another familiar face several rows back. It was Luca, glaring at me. I shuddered at the intensity of his stare, wondering how Gia could ever look at him and see anything but a cold, heartless killer. Still, I didn't feel right leaving her unaware of his presence in there.

"Gia," I said, my voice barely above a whisper.

She turned to me, and I motioned towards Luca, then slowly walked out.

Giada

I gazed back at Luca, then turned straight ahead. I waited a moment to see if he would come to join me, but when I glanced back, he was still seated several rows back, his head hung.

I rose and walked back to him. He scooted down as I neared, making room for me at the end of the row. As I sat, the only other people in the sanctuary stood to leave.

"I assumed you'd be in the hospital chapel," he said. "Your brother said you just left."

"So you were trying to avoid me?"

"I thought you wanted space." He paused. "Besides, I'm not sure how to make things right with you and God at the same time. I suspect He'll be more forgiving than you, though."

I peered closer at Luca. I could tell he was tired, but it was more than that. It was a defeated weariness. Right now, Luca looked like a man who could just as easily give up and accept the loss as press onward. I supposed I should be relieved that he at least felt remorse, but instead, it seemed like a bad omen. He'd done what he had because he felt he had no choice, not because he thought it was the moral thing to do.

"I don't know how to help you," I said finally. "No one can absolve you of guilt when your plan is to keep doing horrible things and just asking for forgiveness later."

He bent forward. "No, I suppose not."

I let him think in silence for a few minutes before speaking again. "I needed you with me that night. You could've let someone else take care of it if it really needed to be done. They would've understood."

Luca breathed a laugh. "Sure, this time they would've. But next time? Eventually I'd have to stop delegating. And besides, is that any better? Does your God spare the man who gives the order as long as he doesn't pull the trigger?"

It wasn't really any better, but I suspected he'd feel better at the moment if he hadn't literally gotten his hands dirty. I knew I'd feel better anyway.

"I told you this would happen," he said. "I said I'd do terrible things over and over, and you said you'd stay with me no matter what. You promised."

Shit. I had sort of said that. But at the time, I hadn't anticipated him running off and killing someone twenty-four hours later.

"I needed you to do that, to give me the benefit of the doubt. I needed you to pull me out of it. I needed to hear you say it was okay, that I did what I needed to do. I needed to hear that you still loved me, that I'm not a monster." He paused, his voice cracking. "You let me down, Giada."

I bit my lip. Luca was mad at me? That was a twist I hadn't anticipated.

Luca was still leaned forward, his elbows on his knees and his head in his hands. He rubbed his hair with his hands and then closed his eyes.

I watched him in silence for several minutes, the strong, sensitive man who was so deeply conflicted. He had screwed up, and he wasn't even pretending that he wouldn't do it again. Was that truly what I had agreed to? Could I really love him through it all, knowing this was what the future held?

I clutched the rosary in my lap, tracing my fingers along each bead, the path long since smoothed from overuse. As a young girl, I'd relied on my beads to pull me through each long, tedious mass. Back then, religion seemed so basic to me. I didn't understand why there were so many nuances or rituals. Back then, there was no ambiguity between good and evil. The line between right and wrong was distinct and bold.

As I'd grown, the lines blurred, and the questions arose. I wondered if it was ever okay to do a bad thing for a good reason, whether a good person could do a bad thing and still not be evil. Now I had to decide where the new line should be drawn. How many times could someone act badly before crossing over into the realm of evil? Did intentions even matter, or only actions?

With or without me, Luca would continue on the same path. There was no doubt of that in my mind. Maybe if his father were out of the picture, or maybe if he moved somewhere far, far away, maybe then he'd be a different person. As long as we lived in a world with Salvatore Marino, Luca would remain under his thumb.

But with me on his side, maybe Luca would have a chance at redemption. Maybe together, we could find another way.

I placed my hand on his leg. "You're right," I said, startling him from his own silent reflection. "I'm sorry, Luca. It was too much too soon, and I was mad because I needed you that night."

I paused as he slowly turned to me, but then I continued. "But I see now that you needed me too, and I'm sorry I let you down. I do love you."

Luca squeezed my hand.

"And you're not a monster."

He raised his eyebrow, but didn't speak anymore.

CHAPTER 18

Adrian

The downside of the location of the law school was that I inadvertently caught glimpses of Giada all the time. Somehow, I saw her more now than ever. If I was in the library trying to study for finals, I'd glance out the window, and there she would be, stretched out on a blanket on the lawn of her apartment building with Gabriella, laughing and studying. When I ate lunch at a table on the veranda of the law school, I'd see her walking into her apartment with her backpack slung over her shoulders.

The worst was when I saw her with Luca, which was often since he apparently now lived with her. Whenever they were together, his arm stayed so tightly wound around her that it was as if he realized she'd run if given a chance.

I reassured myself that she would graduate soon and move away, somewhere. I'd be left alone with my memories of her then, and after time, those would fade. I hoped by next fall I would look back on my days with Giada and feel only happiness and not the deep stabbing pain of emptiness that now gripped me whenever I saw her.

A clean break—cutting her whole family out of my life—was the only way I could move on. But I had to say goodbye first. On the day before her graduation, I'd glanced at her apartment throughout the day and hadn't once seen Luca or his car or any of his usual group of suspects that followed him around.

I'd wrapped up a book for her—Dr. Seuss' Oh the Places You'll Go, and taped a store-bought card to the front. It was hokey and cliché, but perfect for graduation. It wasn't the gift I'd ever envisioned giving to the love of my life on her college graduation, but since she'd made it clear I was nothing more than a friend to her, it seemed appropriate.

I was nervous as I rang her bell, certain the anxiety would increase with every passing moment. Fortunately, the door swung open quickly. It was Luca.

"Adrian," he said, nodding his head politely. He didn't seem even the slightest bit surprised by my appearance, but I was shocked and thrown by his.

It took me a moment to recover. "I wanted to give this to Giada," I said, lamely lifting the present up.

"She's not here," he said without appearing bothered that I brought a gift for his fiancée. "I can take it. Or if you want to give it to her yourself, she's just up at Gabriella's."

I couldn't say goodbye to her if I left the present with Luca, so option B was my best bet. The fact that he even offered me the choice was depressing, though. Months ago, he would've never given me an opportunity to speak with her alone. Then, he controlled her every move, certain that if given the freedom, she'd run from him. Now, he clearly didn't even feel threatened by me. Now, he was confident that Giada was his, no matter what I did.

That realization nauseated me.

"Thanks," I mumbled, eager to get away from him. But then I stopped myself, realizing this may be my last chance to ever speak my mind to him. I turned to face him, emboldened by the knowledge that I had nothing left to lose.

"I know you love Giada, but you'll never make her happy. She's a good person. You're not. Every time you two get back together, I see a little more of that light inside her get sucked away. You're only going to bring her down until she's no better than you. Is that really what you want for her?"

Luca's expression hardened, but he said nothing.

"And I know you paid a prostitute to seduce me so Giada would feel pressured to accept your proposal. I also know you murdered a man in cold blood to try to win her affections." A sardonic laugh escaped my lips. "Did you really think that would work? Any of it? The fact that you even thought Giada would approve of that behavior shows how little you understand her."

I paused, but Luca didn't even acknowledge my rhetorical questions, so I forged ahead. "I didn't sleep with the hooker, and Giada learned exactly what type of a man you are when you went after her brother's shooter. She's a forgiving person, and trusting too. But even Giada will hit her limit someday. Eventually, you'll cross a line you can't undo, and she won't forgive and forget. And every day you toy with her emotions and make her fall for you, you're just ensuring it'll be that much harder for her to pick up the pieces of her life after you're out of it for good."

As my words ended, silence spread between us.

"She's in apartment 434," he finally said, his face void of emotion.

"You're going to ruin her life. If you really loved her, you'd let her go. Or show her your true colors and let her decide how much she can handle." I told him, turning just as he closed the door in my face.

～

Giada

Luca began acting strangely the day before my graduation. I wasn't sure if he was just anxious about the transition or excited about our trip to Palermo the following week, but the shift in his behavior was palpable. He'd gone from attentive and loving to distant and quiet. When I asked him about it, he said he was merely stressed about some work stuff he needed to finish in New York before we left.

I knew he'd seen Adrian, so when I'd returned home from Gabby's that evening and Luca had immediately pounced on me and dragged me back to the bedroom like a lion devouring his prey, I figured he was just marking his territory. Luca wanted to make sure I understood I was his, so he claimed every inch of my body, over and over until we were both exhausted.

His insecurity was endearing. It amused me to realize this amazingly sexy, confident and powerful man could even think I might choose someone else.

But the next day, he became distracted and cold. He joined my family for brunch in the morning, but after the actual graduation ceremony, he surprised me with the announcement that he was heading back to his family's Staten Island home immediately. I'd assumed he would be going out that night to celebrate with Gabriella and me, but instead, he simply left Enzo to keep tabs on me.

Still, I cherished the time with my best friend, acutely aware that our relationship was changing drastically, too. Even though we both planned to move to New York over the summer—me with Luca and her with a new roommate whom I feared would replace me as her closest friend—we weren't naïve enough to think everything would stay the same.

Enzo drove me to the Marino house the day before Luca and I were scheduled to leave for Italy. He helped me in with my bags, then hugged me before leaving.

"It has been my pleasure to drive you around these past few years, Giada," he said.

I pouted, not having realized that anything would be changing with him now too. "You're still going to see plenty of me," I reminded him.

He smiled and nodded, but something in his eyes told me he knew something I didn't. Luca had never fully regained trust of Enzo after the…incident…so I wondered if perhaps my husband-to-be had replaced my driver with one of his own—and forgotten to tell me.

"Have an amazing trip. And congrats again on your graduation."

He waved at Alessio, who was just pulling into the driveway, as he trekked back to the car. Ignoring Alessio, I went into the house. I expected a warm greeting from Luca, but instead, he merely nodded in acknowledgement of my arrival. His phone was pressed tightly to his ear and he was pacing nervously, so I gave him his space.

I contemplated unpacking but decided to get a drink and relax in the kitchen instead. Luca had just hung up the phone when the doorbell rang.

"You expecting company?" I asked. He was back in the bedroom, and I wasn't even sure he heard me, so I started towards the door. "I'll get it," I said.

"Giada, wait!" Luca called, rushing out towards the foyer just as I swung open the door.

Standing in front of me were two scantily clad women. They looked every bit as confused as I did. I gazed at the first girl's low-slung jeans and midriff-bearing bra top before taking in the tight leather skirt and halter top on the other one. Any doubts I had about their profession were cleared up when they spoke.

"Are you here to party with Luca?" the blonde asked.

I turned to Luca, my temper flaring already.

"Hey, um, ladies I think you might have the wrong address," he said.

"Oh no, I would never forget a face like that," the redhead purred, brushing past me. "When you called and said you changed your mind, we were so excited."

The blonde glanced at me again. "The price goes up if we include her."

That was it. I grabbed my bags that were still in the foyer where I'd left them, pushed by the blonde, and stormed to the curb. I noticed Luca running after me in his socks.

"Wait!" he shouted.

To my surprise, I did stop. As much as I wanted to kill Luca right now, I was eager to hear how he'd explain two hookers showing up at his house saying he'd called them.

"Come on Luca, I'm waiting. I am so eager to hear you talk your way out of this one. Let me guess. It's not what it looks like?"

"I..." He shook his head, stammering like a fool. "Giada, I'm sorry. You know I'm a jerk, though. I'm not the kind of guy that always does the right thing."

"No. No you're not."

"I can't live this way, with you always holding me up to his standards."

"Oh please, Luca. You've set the bar pretty low, even for you."

He sighed and ran his fingers through his hair. "You know you'll come back to me soon enough. You always do, once you get bored of him."

Suddenly, everything became so clear. I tugged off my ring and pelted it at his face. "Fuck you, Luca." Then I started off towards Alessio's car.

"Please take me home," I said to Alessio, still seated behind the steering wheel of his car, pretending not to be watching all of the drama.

"Don't leave like that," Luca said, sounding like a whiny baby at this point.

I swiveled abruptly on my heels. "Like what, Luca? Pissed off? Hurt? Wishing that I never met you?"

He winced and startled as though I'd hit him. "You don't mean that."

"I wish you were dead," I said.

Alessio's eyes widened like he couldn't believe Luca was just going to stand there and let me talk to him that way. But for once, I didn't care about his stupid reputation or any ramifications.

It didn't matter anyway. It was the last time I'd ever let Luca Marino get close enough to hurt me.

I climbed into the car, watching as Luca nodded at Alessio, probably signaling he could drive me home.

I didn't speak a word to Alessio the entire drive home. It was mortifying, having anyone know that my fiancé chose prostitutes over me. How could I be so stupid? I bought into it all, again. This wasn't the first time he'd manipulated me into falling for him. It wasn't even the second or the third. What was wrong with me?

My brother Matteo greeted us outside. Alessio didn't even step out of the car, but instead wordlessly dropped me off and pulled away. I was sure my eyes were swollen and red, and my cheeks were probably splotchy from crying, so I had to explain something to Matteo. I took a deep breath, and spit it all out.

"Luca and I broke up, for good. I am not going to Italy with him, I am not moving in with him, and I am not marrying him. I do not ever want to see him again, and if he's ever invited back into this house again, I will leave and never come back. I don't even want to hear his name uttered again. Do you understand?"

Matteo stared at me slack jawed.

"I'm serious, Matteo. And please let everyone else know as well. I can always go live with Gabby if you guys can't abide by these simple rules."

Matteo nodded curtly, and I brushed past him to head to my bedroom.

Matteo left me alone until the next morning, when I felt surprisingly better. The last few times I'd broken up with Luca, the sadness lingered longer. This time, there was only regret. Not regret at having lost him, but regret at having fallen for his tricks in the first place.

"You look nice today," Matteo said, timidly approaching as though I might lash out.

"Makeup," I replied. I tried not to look at him. He'd healed remarkably, but he still walked with a heavy limp that demanded the assistance of a cane. Everything about him reminded me what Luca had done—not just to avenge Matteo's injury, but how he'd manipulated me into falling for him and kept me away from my brother when he needed me most.

Matteo grimaced as he slowly lowered himself to a chair, propping his cane up beside him. "I, uh, spoke about your rules with the whole family, so I think you're safe. Dad especially wanted to know what happened though. You seemed pretty happy when we saw you before graduation."

I shook my head. Nothing could make me spill the embarrassing details to my family. I pulled an individual bottle of kale/mango/apple juice out of the fridge and unscrewed the cap. Despite the horrific color, it tasted okay. I figured to fully detox my life, I needed to detox my body too.

"So, um, it's probably too soon to say this," Matteo began.

I glared at him, certain he was about to speak the name that I'd forbidden anyone to say, but he ignored me.

"But Luca told us not to give you a hard time. He asked that we not pressure you to go back to him. He actually told Angelo you'd be better off with Adrian."

My eyes widened but I still said nothing. Matteo continued.

"Adrian is a good guy. I don't know how you left things with him, but I did gather that you were pretty upset when you heard he gave Dad some information about that judge he was working for. If it's any consolation, I don't think he wanted to lie to you. He was adamant that he didn't want that car, but Dad insisted. And the only reason he agreed to even help out in the first place was to pay for his mom's cancer treatment."

I was still staring at my brother, trying to decide why he was telling me all that.

"I saw him on campus, when I was there for your graduation. He still loves you. It's pathetic, really. But anyway, I just thought you should know he's a good guy, and I think Dad could leave him alone if you insisted."

I opened and shut my mouth several times before finally deciding there were no appropriate words for my brother. Instead, I took my detox drink and cell phone and made my way to the patio.

Gabriella's family was hosting a graduation open house for her that afternoon. When I'd originally sent in my RSVP, I'd told her Luca would accompany me. Of course, that was no longer the case. I didn't want to ruin her fun day by telling her we broke up, so I quickly texted that he'd had some work thing come up and wouldn't make it.

She replied immediately, asking me to come over early if I was solo anyway. I considered the invitation. The longer I was with her, the harder it would be to conceal the truth, but maybe it was better that way. Maybe I was fooling myself thinking I could conceal it from her just for the duration of her party. Besides, being with my bestie always cheered me up.

I stood and headed back inside, nearly slamming into my dad.

He eyed me warily as though shocked to see me out of bed. "Where are you off to in such a hurry?"

"I'm going upstairs to change for Gabby's graduation party.

Now that I have no date to the party, I'm going to help her set up."

His lips pursed together. "I'll have to see how soon Lorenzo can get here. He had some errands to run today."

"I can see if someone else can drop me off," I said, realizing that since I'd planned to attend the party with Luca, there had been no need for my overprotective father to arrange for Enzo to drive me. Given that my brother had been shot, I wasn't foolish enough to even attempt to convince my father I didn't need a driver.

"Drop you off?" He shook his head. "Giada, Lorenzo will be accompanying you the entire time you are at the party, or anywhere else for that matter."

"That's not necessary."

"I disagree. Anytime you leave this house, you will have Lorenzo or Angelo or one of your uncles with you. And that's not up for discussion."

I sighed. I supposed this was my punishment for breaking up with Luca. "What happens when I go back to my apartment?"

"I assumed that since you are no longer planning to move to New York with..." he paused, thankfully remembering my rules just in time, "anyone, that you would move back here."

I grimaced at the thought but realized he was right. There was no reason for me to stay on campus. All of my friends had graduated and were moving on to wherever their jobs or lives would be.

"My lease isn't up until the end of the month," I reminded him. I'd planned to move to New York after our trip to Italy. Of course, now that I wasn't taking that trip, I could, theoretically, move sooner.

"We can arrange for you to move sooner. And if you need to go to your apartment for any reason, Lorenzo will go with you."

"I'd like to spend a few days on campus before moving away."

My father looked annoyed by that but didn't argue. "Tell me

the dates, and I'll clear it with Lorenzo. Although I'm sure he would appreciate if you could keep your time there brief. Since your apartment has only one bedroom, I assume he would be sleeping on the couch."

My jaw dropped. I decided to ignore any implication that I'd welcome Enzo into my bed and to focus on the larger invasion of privacy. "He could stay at a hotel. Or a different apartment. I am an adult. I don't need a babysitter inside my own apartment."

"I disagree, and it's not up for negotiation. You knew the ramifications of your decision to end your engagement. If you didn't—"

"Seriously?" I interrupted. "You're punishing me for dumping Luca?" I flung my hands in the air. "This is ridiculous. He's not the man you think he is. Do you have any idea what he did?"

My father's brows narrowed until they formed a point above his nose. "I know that he rearranged his work schedule countless times to accommodate your whims. I know that he sacrificed his freedom to move in with you and keep you safe. I know that he risked his own safety to ensure you weren't hurt. And I know that he put up with it when you humiliated him with your fickleness and your inability to choose between him and Adrian Patras."

He blew out a sigh. "I don't agree with your decision to end your engagement so abruptly, but I will respect your choice. But until I am completely satisfied that there is absolutely no threat whatsoever to your safety, you will be escorted by someone I trust at all times."

He turned on his heel, leaving me fuming in the kitchen. I waited a moment, then gazed over at Matteo, who was desperately trying to pretend he hadn't witnessed the entire debacle. I shook my head and stormed upstairs.

Enzo arrived an hour later to drive me to Gabriella's. We were both quiet the majority of the drive, but as we neared her family's home, I remembered how, just a short time ago, Enzo had essentially said goodbye, assuming his days of babysitting me were over. He couldn't possibly be happy about the fact that now, thanks to my single status, he was back on babysitter duty twenty-four seven.

"I'm sorry you're stuck driving me again," I said.

He startled as my voice shattered the silence in the car. "I don't mind."

"Well, it sounds like my dad plans for you to babysit me constantly. That will get old quickly. I'm not that interesting."

"I disagree," he said with a sly grin.

"You know he intends for you to sleep on my couch when I return to my apartment?"

"It's only for a few days, right? I'll be fine."

I sighed. "Okay. I just feel bad. I didn't realize how much my decision about…you know, would affect you."

"You deserve to be happy, Giada. If that isn't with Luca, you were right to end things with him."

"You don't think I should've, though," I guessed.

He chuckled. "Answering that question is definitely above my paygrade. I don't know what all happened with you two, and I don't want to know."

I didn't blame him for that. We were both quiet for a few more minutes before Enzo spoke again.

"It's maybe not my business, but just since it seems we may be spending a lot of time together in the near future, it might be helpful for me to know…" he paused, visibly uncomfortable about whatever he wanted to say. "Are you seeing Adrian again?"

"No. I haven't spoken to him since the day before graduation."

Enzo seemed to accept my answer as the truth. "Your father called him after Matteo's injury. He was hoping Adrian had seen you or knew where you were, at least. But he didn't ask Adrian to come to the hospital. Adrian showed up on his own, and he stuck around until you arrived."

I frowned, uncertain of whether Enzo was trying to tell me Adrian still cared about me or what.

"Your father respected that, him showing up for the family when he didn't have to. Adrian was never his first choice for you, but I don't think he'd fight it now."

"Oh," I said, as the larger significance of Enzo's words hit me. It brought back what my brother had said too. If my dad actually accepted Adrian now, maybe that was a sign. If my family's meddling had been the problem for us in the past, maybe we could push past that.

I wouldn't pretend I didn't still have feelings for Adrian. Yes, I'd been infatuated with Luca, but everything with him was just such a fantasy whirlwind. Adrian was real life. He was the one constant in my life. He was the one with the potential to ground me. He would be a stable partner in life for as long as I let him.

Assuming I could somehow regain his trust.

CHAPTER 19

Giada

I'd stayed home for four days after the breakup before returning to campus. The responsible thing to do would be to look into possible job prospects while I still could access the career counselors at the university, but instead, I spent two days sorting all the crap from my apartment.

Sifting through photos and notes and even old homework assignments and invitations brought back so many memories. I loved the college experience, and now that I was done, I felt crippled by the absence, especially since I had absolutely nothing else planned for my future.

I'd always viewed college as a time to experience life, a chance to try new things, make friends, heck, even make mistakes. I'd done all of that.

But now, I could finally see the big picture. I'd been so completely blind the past year. Luca had never been the man for me. It had been Adrian, all along. Sure, Luca and I had passion, but that wasn't healthy. We were too…volatile together. He made me crazy. I made him crazy. What I needed was someone who brought out the best in me.

I needed Adrian.

I wasn't yet ready to date him—or anyone else—and I definitely didn't expect him to take me back after everything I'd put him through. Not right away, and likely not ever. But I still needed him to know I was sorry. I owed him an apology, not just for being a shitty girlfriend, but also for being a terrible friend. I was such an awful friend that I didn't even know whether he was staying in town for summer. I'd been so absorbed in my own drama with Matteo and Luca and graduation that I hadn't even asked about Adrian's summer job prospects. Or his mom's health.

God. If I were Adrian, I'd never agree to give me another chance at friendship.

It was hard to show up at Adrian's unannounced when my dad required that I go everywhere with a bodyguard, but I owed him an apology in person, and I needed to do it before he left town for summer.

~

Adrian

The knock on my door was so unexpected that I almost didn't even bother to see who it was. When I peered through the peephole at Giada and Enzo, my stomach tightened. I opened the door despite the pit in my stomach. Obviously, she'd come to say goodbye. Now that graduation was over, I'd already begun to distance myself mentally from her. She was moving to New York City with her fiancé. I hadn't realized she'd even come to see me again before leaving for good.

"I owe you an apology," she said, seemingly oblivious to my discomfort. "A couple, actually."

I sighed and turned back towards the kitchen where my chicken was cooking. "Does your, um, security detail want to come in?" I asked, only partially kidding.

"Enzo will wait by the door," she replied. She followed me into the kitchen and watched me season the meat before flipping each breast with tongs. "Adrian, I know you're pissed at me, so I'll get out of your hair if you just let me explain."

I exhaled firmly then turned to face her. "I'm not mad. You told me before we even got back together how important it was to you that I was honest with you about everything, and I wasn't. I could've said no to your father, or I could've told you what I was doing, and I didn't. That's on me." I stopped myself before I repeated the entire speech she'd given me when expressing her disappointment in my behavior and declaring I was no better than Luca.

"Matteo told me you needed the money to help your mother."

"That doesn't change anything."

"Yes, it does, Adrian. I wish you'd been honest with me, but you had a good reason for doing what you did. You're not a bad person. I was wrong to compare you to Luca."

"Well, it's water under the bridge now. You made your choice."

She took her time answering. "But you were right. I chose wrong."

My jaw dropped at her words. I turned slowly. "What do you mean?"

She frowned. "I broke up with Luca. Things are over between us for good," she said, wiggling her fingers to show me that the stupid diamond was gone. "I thought you were aware."

I swallowed the lump in my throat and turned back to the stove. "I had no idea," I said, my voice cracking.

"Oh. Well, I don't expect you to take me back now. That's not why I'm here. But I did want to explain." She waited until I flipped the chicken again and turned back to face her.

"When he saved me that day by my apartment, I mistook gratitude for love. And when my family thought we might get back together again, they were all so happy and proud of me." She paused and shook her head. "I just so rarely feel like I have their approval. It's hard to question my actions when initially it feels right, and they're telling me I'm making the right choice."

I focused on my cooking more than I needed to. Giada's face was pained as she spoke, and as much as I didn't want to hear the rest of her explanation, I realized she wouldn't stop until she'd finished.

"I imagine from where you're standing, I look like a total moron, going anywhere with Luca or believing anything he says after everything he's done. And I do feel like an idiot, for what it's worth. I just…" This time she paused to sniffle, and as I turned, her damp eyes turned into full-blown tears.

"Gia, I understand. You don't have to do this."

"I thought it was different this time. I thought he was different. God, the things he said to me… I was so sure he was trying. And all along I think I knew deep down it wasn't right. I was so desperate to prove my family right, to prove to myself that I could be happy with the guy they always wanted me with that I was willing to believe anything."

I didn't want to give her the wrong idea, but I couldn't stand seeing her cry all alone like that. I switched off the burner and pulled her into my arms. "Giada, stop. It's fine. I understand."

She sniffled again and wiped her nose on a tissue from her pocket. "You don't, though. I think it's been you all along that I loved, and I was just so determined to ignore it because my family had me convinced I was supposed to be with him. And now I should be focused starting a career and celebrating my graduation, but instead I can't stop thinking about how I hurt you."

I hugged her tighter, then paused. "Wait, that's what you're upset about?"

Giada pulled back and eyed me warily. "Yes."

"I thought you were upset over Luca."

She practically laughed between her tears. "No. I'm disappointed he isn't the person I made him out to be in my head, but… I am so grateful that he showed his true colors before I did something really stupid like married him."

"Me too," I said.

"I've been a terrible friend to you lately, and I don't know how to make it up to you. You were there for me whenever I was scared and every time my feelings were hurt. You were there for my whole family when Matteo was shot." She paused and shook her head. "Even when I'm awful to you, you still show up for me. You are literally the best person I know, and I can't believe I've taken you for granted."

"Giada—"

"I haven't even asked about your mom lately," she continued, ignoring my attempts to sneak a word in. "Is she okay?"

I couldn't help but smile as I answered that question, "Yeah. She's great. She just finished her last round of radiation, and she's feeling good. All her scans are coming back great."

Giada cast her eyes up to the ceiling in a way that made me think she was literally thanking God for answering her prayers. I nearly laughed out loud at the realization that a woman who prayed multiple times a day came so close to marrying the devil incarnate.

"I'm so glad to hear that. There's so much I've neglected to ask you about, so much catching up we have to do, but I needed you to know I'm sorry, before you head off to wherever you're going this summer."

"Thank you?" I said, confused enough that it came out as a question.

"I should be sad about breaking up my engagement, not

relieved. I mean, I am sad, but mostly just that Luca didn't turn out to be the person I wanted him to be, you know?"

I nodded, even though she'd completely lost me.

"I wanted him to be the kind of guy who wouldn't lie to me, the kind of man who wouldn't hurt someone else no matter what they did, the kind of fiancé who would never cheat on me." She paused and swallowed, the sound filling the small room. "I wanted him to be more like you."

My breath hitched as I realized where she was headed. I shook my head. "Giada, stop. I can't do this with you again. I just can't. I'm not mad, and I understand why you did what you did, but I can't go back to square one with you."

She sucked in a breath. "I don't expect you to. I just wanted to tell you how sorry I am for everything. I've been such a fool, and now it's too late. But if you ever can forgive me, I'd love to be friends with you again." She turned towards the door, but didn't actually walk away.

I couldn't tear my eyes off of her, but I also couldn't bring myself to speak. No part of me wanted her to leave, but I was sure I'd never survive another round with her. Every time I opened my heart up to Giada Conti, she brought even more happiness and light into my world than before. And each time when she broke my heart, it hurt more. It took longer to feel normal again. It changed me.

"I just..." she began, then stopped.

I saw her shoulders trembling, heard her sniffling.

"I hate knowing you'll never forgive me. I don't deserve another chance, but I wish I could go back in time and not screw everything up so badly."

I squeezed my eyes shut. The room was spinning, and I couldn't breathe. It was all so unexpected. It was too much. *She* was too much.

I waited for her to leave, then quickly came to my senses.

What the fuck was wrong with me? I'd been pining for Giada

since the day I met her and mourning her absence since the day she chose Luca. Now she was back, saying everything I needed to hear, and I was going to let her just walk out?

No.

I couldn't.

The thought of opening myself up to her again was terrifying, but the thought of going on with my life without even giving her the chance she sought—well, that was unbearable.

"Giada, wait," I said.

She turned to face me, her eyes red and her cheeks damp.

"I'm scared," I admitted. "You broke my heart. I just don't know if I can survive another pain like that."

"I don't blame you. If I were you, I wouldn't give me another chance either."

I took a step closer to her. "Giada, you and I belong together. We've both made mistakes, but as long as you love me, I can forgive anything."

She gazed up at me with those big brown eyes. "You know I love you, Adrian. I always have. I just…" she shook her head.

"I know, Gia. You were confused, and the pressure from your family, and all the stress you've been under lately, I understand. You have history with him. But I want to be your future."

"I want that too," she said, rising to her toes to kiss me lightly.

Her lips barely brushed across mine, but it was enough to wake up every part of my body.

"I can't… just go back to where we were, though. I need time. And you need time. You were just engaged to another man. We can't just—"

"Let's be friends, Adrian. We'll take our time getting reacquainted, and we'll both take some time to heal. But this time, I won't be a shitty friend. I'll be there when you need me. It won't be so one-sided."

I nodded. Time was exactly what we needed. We both had the same vision for the future, but we couldn't just jump ahead to get there. We'd tried that before and failed miserably. Friendship was good. We could build from that.

"Stay for dinner," I asked, my voice hardly more than a whisper.

She hesitated. "Enzo is…" she gestured to the door.

I turned to the stove, plucked out one of the chicken breasts and dropped it into a plastic container. I spooned some of the sauce over it and topped that with a heap of cooked spaghetti. I pressed the lid over it all then handed it to Giada along with a fork. "Give him this and send him away. I'll take you back to your apartment later."

She stared at me for another moment, uncertainty filling her face, then went to the door. I couldn't hear their hushed discussion but didn't care, because she returned to me, alone.

"He said to text him later and he'll pick me up," she explained, settling onto a barstool. "Unless you've recently learned how to shoot."

I rolled my eyes. The danger was over. We all knew Luca had ended this battle when he murdered the man who came after Matteo. In a matter of weeks, the men in Giada's life had effectively ended a cartel that had thwarted the DEA and Homeland Security for years. With results like that, it was hard to be completely opposed to their methods.

"You are safe now. When is your father going to relax?"

She smiled softly. "The man sent me away to boarding school after his father was shot. I'm pretty sure someone shooting at me and my brother justifies at least fifteen years of paranoia in his mind."

"Great," I said, retrieving plates for our food. When I'd begun cooking, I'd planned to save most of the food to last me several nights this week, but I had no complaints about sharing it with Giada, even if it meant I'd have no leftovers to get me through the week. "Maybe I should start carrying."

I was completely kidding, of course. Having grown up in a

staunchly anti-gun home, I'd never even held a gun, let alone shot one.

"That's not a bad idea," Giada said.

"It was a joke. It's a terrible idea."

"Enzo could give you lessons."

I turned to face her, flummoxed by the line of discussion. "Less than three months ago, you broke up with me because I was doing a job for your father. A job with absolutely no threat of danger. Now you want me to arm up and what—become one of your fake uncles that follows him around?"

She rolled her eyes. "I think if you had a gun and knew how to use it, my dad would back off a little with my security detail. That's all."

"Well, why don't you have a gun then? You could protect yourself."

I had been kidding, to prove a point, but hadn't expected her to laugh quite as hard as she did.

"Could you imagine my dad's face then?" she said, her eyes bright.

I realized she hadn't touched the food I'd placed in front of her. A half-hour ago, I'd been starving, but now...

"Something wrong with the chicken?" I asked.

Gia smiled. "It smells amazing."

"Not hungry?"

"Not for food," she said, offering a hesitant half smile.

I blew out a sigh and turned to the wall, plying my pulse to slow down. "Friends, Giada. We're just friends. Friends eat food together. They don't make out." I repeated it as much for my benefit as hers, but when I'd finally collected myself enough to turn back to her, she was biting back a smile.

"What?"

"Nothing. You're absolutely right. I'm just going to eat this delicious pork chop."

"It's chicken."

"Right. Yep. Eating my chicken with my old buddy."

Giada placed the tiniest bite of chicken in her mouth and made a pathetic effort to chew. She offered me an overly enthusiastic grin as she swallowed. "That's what it was. I missed your cooking," she teased.

I lifted her off the barstool so abruptly that it toppled over to the floor with a resounding thud. She shrieked playfully, then wrapped her thighs around my waist. I paused by the bedroom door, focused more on kissing her than arriving at our ultimate destination across the room.

I wanted to pinch myself to prove this was real, that it wasn't just another mid-shower fantasy to get me through the lonely days while Giada was still with *him*. But I didn't have to. Her touch was all over me, her warm thighs cocooning me with their embrace. Her hot breath fell onto my cheeks and neck in rapid spurts as her soft lips tickled across every inch of my bare skin. Her catlike purrs were like music to my ears, and the familiar taste of her berry lip gloss drove me to devour her mouth.

She squirmed against me and loosened her grip, so I slowly lowered her to the ground. Grinning mischievously, she slipped off her shirt, then unfastened her jeans. "Your move, Adrian," she taunted.

God, how I'd missed her playful side. As much as it had pained me to see her happy with Luca, it was even harder seeing her unhappy with him. Being with that monster had sucked all the life right out of her, but now, after just a few minutes with me, it was back. My Giada was back.

I tugged my own shirt over my head and then lunged at her, wrapping my arms around her as I kissed her chest, then abdomen, tugging her jeans down as I lowered myself to my knees. She picked up one foot, then the other, assisting me with the undressing. By the time I gazed back up at her, she'd removed her bra as well. I licked her roughly through her lacy panties, eliciting a surprised giggle, then hoisted her back into my arms and deposited her on the bed.

I slipped her panties down her legs then stood back to admire her. Giada, completely nude, was a sight to behold. She was the sort of beauty that men of ancient times went to war over, and finally, she was all mine. I climbed over her, blanketing her eager body with my own.

CHAPTER 20

Giada

drian and I agreed to take things slowly.

Well, first we spent an entire night making love and feeding each other cold chicken and pasta in bed. But after that, we decided not to jump right back to where we'd been. We needed to date, to gradually rebuild what we'd once shared before, even as both of us felt like everything between us was finally right again.

Unfortunately, my dad was too terrified to leave me alone at my apartment, so Enzo was stuck sleeping on my couch until I moved back home. Adrian had secured a paid internship near campus, though, so he wouldn't have time to come visit me back in Bridgeport. It just made sense for me to move back home, but spend a few nights each week with Adrian. Then I still saw plenty of him, but Enzo was free, aside from driving me back and forth to campus each week.

So, after a whopping two dates, that was what Adrian and I

decided to do. I moved most of my stuff back home at the end of the week. It was hard to believe that only a week had passed since I graduated and already my life was so different. I returned to Adrian's apartment after dumping my belongings back home. The next day was my twenty-second birthday, and I wanted to spend as much of my day as possible with Adrian.

I hadn't seen or heard from Luca since the break-up, so I wasn't sure if he'd gone to Italy without me, or even if he knew I was back with Adrian. My dad had agreed to stop meddling in Adrian's life and promised not to ask him for any more favors that he couldn't disclose to me. Adrian agreed—after copious nudging from me—to keep the car. Adrian wouldn't budge on the whole gun ownership thing, so we still had Enzo following us almost everywhere, but I didn't mind. Eventually, my father would relax and let me live my life in peace, and until then, I would just accept his overprotectiveness as a misguided yet well-intended sign of love.

Adrian baked me a delicious cake—insisting we eat it for breakfast—and then we were headed back to my home for a dinner with my extended family. It meant so much to me that Adrian was even willing to deal with my whole crazy family again so soon after welcoming me back into his life.

We had planned to lounge around his apartment for a while longer, but Matteo had texted that morning saying he had a surprise for me. It was typical Matteo to cook up his own birthday surprise ahead of the family party, plus it perked me up knowing he must be fully recovered and back to his usual self to pull off a surprise.

I was in such a good mood, that the subsequent text from Luca hadn't pissed me off nearly as much as it should have. It was a simple, "Happy birthday, Princess."

Had I been smart, I would've just deleted it and moved on with my happy day. Instead, I replied "thanks." I figured that my response would let him know I was mature enough to answer and that nothing he could say or do would bother me. Instead, it prompted him to ask what my plans were.

I could've ignored him. But stupidly, I told him where Adrian and I were headed and that it was for some big surprise from Matteo. Luckily, he'd shot back a quick "have fun," and left it at that. Enzo picked up Adrian and me to drive us home a little later, and even though he pretended not to know anything about Matteo's big secret, he agreed to the detour.

My phone buzzed again in my purse, for the third time since we'd left my apartment. I loved all the birthday calls and texts, but at the moment, I wanted to focus all my attention on Adrian.

"You could silence it if you're not going to answer," he said, brushing a kiss along my hair.

I reached into my purse, chiding myself for not having done that earlier. I switched the phone to vibrate then frowned, realizing I actually had three missed calls—and all were from Luca. I grimaced, but I couldn't ignore the voice mail. Ever since missing news of Matteo's shooting, I made sure to listen to every message right away, just in case it was important.

Luca sounded frantic in the call, and he rambled on about how I couldn't go with Adrian, how Matteo wasn't there or never planned to be.

"Don't go," he kept saying. "It's not Matteo."

I groaned aloud, and Adrian quirked an eyebrow. I replayed the message for him, shaking my head disapprovingly.

"He's not making any sense," Adrian agreed. "Is he drunk?"

I shrugged and deleted the voice mail. Maybe Luca missed me and regretted screwing things up. He'd always made a big deal about my birthday, so I supposed it made sense that he'd think of me on my birthday. But trying to ruin my brother's plans or whatever he was doing—that was too much.

Adrian and I snuggled together while we drove. The address Matteo said to meet him at was much closer to my hometown than to campus, so it wasn't a short drive. When we finally stopped, my legs were stiff from the lack of movement, but I was still excited to see my brother. I wasn't sure if he had planned a full surprise party or something smaller, but knowing Matteo, it would be perfect, whatever it was. The fact that he hadn't even let Enzo in on the secret was even more impressive.

The sun was shining so brightly that even with my royal purple, wide-rimmed sunglasses, I still had to squint to appreciate the tranquil blue sky as Enzo opened the car door.

There weren't any other cars there yet, but that didn't mean Matteo couldn't have been dropped off. He still walked with the cane, so I completely understood him wanting a driver. Of course, if other people had arrived, I would've expected to see their cars.

Enzo's phone rang, and he turned to answer it. "Why don't you guys wait in the car?" he suggested.

"I'm sick of sitting," I said. I didn't want to be completely disobedient since he was only trying to appease my dad by playing the bodyguard role, but it was my birthday. I'd walk around if I wanted to.

Adrian and I had only made it a few dozen yards away when Enzo called back to me. Reluctantly, I started closer.

"It's Luca. He wants to talk to you," he said.

I rolled my eyes and walked quicker. Glancing over my shoulder, I noticed that another car had pulled up on the other side of the building.

I stepped closer, then spotted a man. I didn't recognize him, and he appeared too casually dressed to be an associate of my brothers.

Enzo called my name again, but I kept walking towards the other guy, trying to guess if there'd be a singing telegram or what craziness Matteo had planned.

"Giada Conti?" the man asked in a thick Hispanic accent.

I nodded.

"I have a message for your father," he said.

I started to question that, assuming he meant to say my brother, but then that didn't make sense either. The message should be from my brother, not for him. And certainly not *for* my father.

Before I could reply, another car flew into the alley beside the warehouse and screeched to a stop. Confused, I turned back to the man just as two more men stepped out from behind shipping crates to stand beside him.

There was a flurry of motion near the newly arriving car, and I noticed the men in front of me all startled.

In an instant, everything became a blur.

As I watched the suspicious car, I instantly recognized the man climbing out of it. It was Luca, and for some reason, he started sprinting towards me. He said something, but his voice was muffled by the hurried Spanish shouts of the men in front of me.

Suddenly, Enzo sprung closer, pulling out a gun. I braced myself, half expecting him to shoot Luca, when Adrian shouted.

Time skidded to a standstill.

In the seconds that followed, I finally pieced it all together in my brain. I realized how stupid I'd been, and how arrogant—assuming Luca was stalking me and not just calling to warn me about the trap I was naively walking into.

Luca—always the hero—had yet again come to my rescue. Whatever was about to happen, everything would be okay now. Luca was here and he was going to save me.

With time still moving in slow motion, I turned back just as the man directly ahead of me pulled out a gun. I heard the all-too-familiar sound of gunshots, saw a flurry of movement, then felt the concrete as it slammed into my cheek.

My hands raised to my head, then I sensed Adrian huddling over me. He was saying something, wanting an answer, but my ears were ringing. I remembered thinking about that saying, how bad things happened in threes, and that hopefully this was the last of it.

When I sensed the activity around me had dulled, I lifted my head.

The ringing in my ears dulled to a sharp buzz, then instantly all the voices became clear and painfully loud again. Enzo and Adrian were both shouting.

"I'm fine," I said in response to Adrian's repeated question, even though I felt anything but. I peered closely at his face and barely recognized him with how distraught he seemed.

And then I turned, and everything changed.

Immediately in front of me, slumped at an inhuman angle, was Luca. His eyes were open but empty.

Suddenly, I heard an ear-piercing scream.

It went on and on, until Adrian started shaking me, and I realized the screams were my own.

I yanked free of his arms and dove down to Luca. Alessio was already huddled over him, his fingers pressed firmly at Luca's neck.

I leaned close to Luca, nudging his warm frame with my hands. He didn't move, didn't speak, and then Adrian pulled me away.

"We have to go now!" he said.

My legs refused to move. "Luca!"

"He's gone, Giada," Enzo said, his voice eerily calm.

I screamed again, and then everything went dark.

By the time I came to, I was safely inside the car, Adrian's arms wrapped tightly around me. I wanted to feel safe and secure, but even in my disheveled state, I knew my nightmare was only just beginning.

The End